Cover by Ana Grigoriu-Voicu, books-design.com.
Edited by Stephanie Parent
www.oliviahayle.com

OLIVIA HAYLE

PROLOGUE
ISAAC

I walk down the same flight of stairs my father once strode every day, and my grandfather before him. The marble with the gold pattern inlay is softly sloped from a century of heavy use, taking guests from the restaurant to the lobby.

It's old. It's used. And it's still beautiful. The aged aspects of the Winter Hotel, historic and unique, are what allows us to charge thousands of dollars per night.

I let my hand slide down the bannister and take the steps in quick succession. It's been another late night at work, going over our international expansion. Our almost-finished resort in the Caribbean has shown enough promise that we're scouting locations in Greece for a second one, with the same resort feel and Winter luxury, surrounded by turquoise ocean rather than New York's concrete jungle.

I walk across the smooth checkered floor of the lobby. Outside the front doors, the daylight is gone. It's late, and there'll only be a few good places left open on the block to get takeout.

My staff could bring something up, but I need the walk, and the air. I roll my shoulders back and feel the telltale protest of stiff muscles.

"Sir," Andrej says from behind the front desk, with a nod

of greeting. He's in his mid-forties, originally from Croatia, and has an eye for impeccable detail. He's in charge of everything in reception.

One of the finest men I've hired during my tenure as the president of the Winter Corporation.

"Evening," I say. "Is everything running smoothly?"

He nods. "Sure is. We're almost at capacity."

"Great," I say, and lengthen my stride. Flake's down the street has good enough food. I can be in and out in under half an hour and still have enough time left over tonight to hit the gym.

The sound of high heels on marble echoes behind me. The pace is furious, the speed unrelenting.

A woman is racing from the emergency staircase with the wings of her camel coat open and flowing behind her. The half-run alone is unusual, but it's her face that stops me in my tracks.

Tears stream down her cheeks, and she reaches up to wipe at her face, her steps quickening.

She looks destroyed.

A pair of Winter security guards appear behind her. They must have followed her down the staircase. They're hard on her heel and I see Larry hold a finger up to his earpiece, talking to someone.

Are they calling in reinforcements for a crying woman?

I'm moving before I make the conscious decision.

"Here," I say and draw her behind one of the old stone pillars in the lobby and out of sight of the guards. "Ma'am, are you all right?"

She shakes her head and struggles to catch her breath. Mascara has smudged beneath her eyes and tears streak down cheeks rosy with exertion.

"You're okay," I say. I put a hand against the pillar to block her from view. "Just breathe. Take a deep breath... Yes, that's it."

The woman nods and takes a shaky breath. Small

diamond studs in her ears glitter beneath the hotel lights and her brown hair hangs blow-dried and smooth around her face.

She's younger than me, but not by much, I'd guess. Finely dressed. A guest?

She reaches up to wipe her eyes. Two rings flash on her left hand. A wedding band and a diamond-studded engagement ring. "Oh my God," she whispers. "I can't... I just... *oh my God.*"

"What's wrong?" I reach inside my suit jacket and pull out a packet of tissues. She takes one with a breathless laugh that sounds anything but amused.

"Thanks," she murmurs and wipes her face. Her breathing is starting to come fast again. "I just caught him red-handed. In the act, even... Oh my God."

"Caught who?"

"My husband," she says, but her voice breaks on the word. Her eyes well up again and something inside my chest twists. I can't stand the sight of people crying. Never fucking could. "I suspected for *so* long. And I knew he was using the Winter Hotel because he loves this place, and I found those tiny shampoo bottles in his bag last weekend, and he always, *always,* steals the hotel shampoo. I don't know why. But he does. And he said he had a business meeting tonight but I came here instead, because I suspected..."—another another broken sob—"and I was right. I was *right.*"

The picture is clearing up by the second. I hand her another tissue. "You were?"

She nods and wipes at her face. She has freckles, I see. A smattering of them across the bridge of her nose. "I told the woman at reception that I was here to surprise my husband for our anniversary. Showed them my ID and they could see... could see that we're married. Oh my God, I'm going to have to leave him." She closes her eyes, voice dropping. "I have to move out of my home."

"I'm sorry," I say, and I mean it. I glance around the pillar and see the two security guards, watching us from a safe distance. I give them a nod. *Got this.*

"So I went up to his room, and I had the second keycard…"

Part of me registers what a mistake this was on the receptionist's part. This should never have happened. But we've added new staff over the month, and some are greener than others.

Andrej is going to have to let someone go.

"I opened the door to his suite." She buries her head in her hands and sobs again. It's a desperate sound and my hand tightens into a fist against the pillar.

"Don't cry," I say. *Please don't.*

She shakes her head, but tears keep streaming. "They were together, in bed. They were… I saw it. All of it."

Something grim tightens around my mouth. "I'm sorry."

She sniffles. "I raced out of there and he chased me, in… in only a bedsheet. We passed some guards by the elevators and he yelled that I'd been trying to… to… *break in.*"

And my security guards had chased a fully clothed woman down the stairwell instead of the half-naked man who raced down the hallways of my hotel?

Another necessary conversation.

"I've lost everything," she whispers, eyes turning up to meet mine. They're peculiarly clear, like the tears have deepened them, left them free of any artifice. They're light blue, a contrast to her dark hair and pale skin. "I'm so sorry for bothering you. God, I've just… sorry. I just told you…"

"You haven't done anything wrong," I say, and slowly, unwillingly, lower my arm from where it shielded her against the pillar. "You're in shock."

"Shock. Yes. Even if I suspected it." She reaches for the ties of her camel coat, knotting them tight around her waist. She's probably around thirty, I think. "I'm sorry. Um, I didn't mean… that is to say… hello? Nice to meet you?" Her face softens with an embarrassed little laugh.

"My name is Isaac," I say. "It's a pleasure to meet you."

"Oh."

"I work here."

Her brilliant eyes clear up, back into a liquid pool of light. "Oh! I'm sorry for doing what I did with the receptionist. It was all me, I can be very convincing when I… they won't get in trouble, will they?"

"Don't worry about that." I lean around the pillar, but the lobby looks empty apart from a few couples sitting in the lounge couches. "Do you think your husband might come down to follow you?"

Her eyes widen. "Oh. No. I mean, he might. Unless he went right back to…" She grimaces. "I should leave."

"That might be for the best," I say. "Tell me, what's his name?"

"Percy Browne," she says. "Why?"

I know that name, know the family. But it doesn't change the conviction in my voice. "Because I'll make sure he's given hell at check-out. We'll charge him for the entire minibar."

She laughs. The sound is over as soon as it begins, and yet it draws a lift to my own lips. Smiles feel much more natural than tears on this woman. "Thank you. Don't give him a late check-out either."

"Never." I gesture toward the front doors and she falls in step beside me. "Did you arrive in a car?"

"I took a taxi."

"Then I'll flag one down for you," I say. "Mrs…?"

"Sophia," she says, and then adds shakily, "I suppose I'm just Sophia, now. I guess I'm getting divorced."

There's aching sadness in her voice and it's painful to hear. Suddenly, and with a ferocity that takes me by surprise, I feel hatred for Percy Browne.

"Better that," I say, "then being with a man who doesn't appreciate you."

Sophia looks down at her hands. *Sophia,* I think. The name fits her. Soft and strong and classic, somehow. Steady.

She doesn't respond to my words and I raise an arm to hail for a taxi. Lord knows I don't know what to say to crying women. Or crying men, for that matter, not to mention crying babies. My younger brother has one on the way now, and no doubt the little kid's favorite activity will be screaming his lungs out whenever I hold him.

A taxi rolls to a slow stop in the designated waiting spot outside the Winter Hotel. Sophia looks up at me. "I'm embarrassed," she says softly.

I shake my head. "Don't be. You reacted exactly like a person in your position would."

She blinks away a new set of tears. They glitter like diamonds along her lashes. "Thank you. Truly."

"Anytime," I say, and open the car door for her. Sophia Browne, soon to be something else, the woman with the heaven-blue eyes and balls of steel, steps into the car. Dark hair, camel coat, nude loafers. The picture of elegant put-togetherness, marred only by the devastated expression on her fine features.

I can't let her go just yet. I pause with my hand on the door. "Just promise you'll do one thing for me?"

"Yes?" she says.

"Don't let this ruin your image of the Winter Hotel."

Her mouth curls into a small smile. "It won't. It's thanks to your shampoo bottles that I even found out!"

I watch as the taxi drives off down the avenue, hugging the edges of Central Park in the direction of the Upper East Side.

Then, I shove my hands in my pockets and walk down the street toward Flake's, my original plan intact, even as my mind dwells on the diamond-like eyes that shone brighter than the one on her finger.

1

SOPHIA

Ten months later

Divorce has taught me a lot of lessons.

One is that the cushions, towels, and cutlery adorned with the couple monogram is a spectacularly bad idea. It hadn't been mine, of course, but my former mother-in-law's, but that doesn't change the fact I now have a set of beautiful towels I don't want to use. A couple monogram is only useful as long as the couple exists.

And Percy's and mine no longer does.

But the lesson that hurts the most has little to do with cutlery or the artful intertwining of our initials. No, it's all about our mutual friends.

I've now learned the hard way that there's no such thing. In the trenches of divorce warfare, everyone takes a side.

It had started as soon as I filed, the slow decline in texts, phone calls, invitations, brunch invites and hellos from the people we'd surrounded ourselves with during our seven years as a couple, four of those married.

Our mutual friends chose a side, and it was very rarely mine. Oh, our female friends were very understanding when I met them, of course. *I was so sorry to hear about it all,* Maud had told me at a dinner, two months post filing for divorce. *Was there no way to... repair it? To look past his little indiscretion? Here, let me give you the name of the couple's therapist Mark and I used when we were going through something similar. Just think about it, Sophia. You two have so much together.*

Yes, I'd thought. We have a shit ton of monogrammed junk.

So maybe they weren't so very understanding, after all.

Most of the people Percy and I knew were more his friends than they were ever mine. His old camaraderie of buddies from school, be it the semester he did at boarding school or from his Ivy League college. His squash friends and his golf buddies, and his parents' friends and their children, and the entire vast, ivy-covered network we'd built together in New York—except it wasn't *our* network, and I didn't build it. He and his parents did, and I had naively thought I'd become a part of it.

That I'd made it my own and that I had a life here.

But one divorce later and I'm as much of an outsider as I'd been when I arrived in New York a decade earlier. Percy's part of *them.* I'm not, and what was once a hairline fracture is now a yawning gulf between us.

I'm Sophia Bishop from Marhill, an outsider, no longer invited to bottomless brunches and couples' golf sessions.

So, I've done the one thing I can... and that's work.

Distraction, my therapist likes to say in a lecturing tone, *isn't the healthiest way to deal with your problems, Sophia.*

Maybe not, but it sure is the most comfortable, not to mention profitable. My nonstop work hours began immediately after the divorce, when the Exciteur office became a homier place than the three-bedroom apartment I was emptying with Percy.

And they bore fruit. I'm now a senior project manager in the Strategy department, a step up from project assistant, and all it took was my personal life imploding.

The promotion came just in time for me to switch from

avoiding the apartment I lived in with Percy, to avoiding the new apartment I'd found for myself. It's a one bedroom in Midtown, modest by New York standards, and still expensive as hell for a single-payer household.

It's also painfully empty.

The one begrudging silver lining is the kitten my sister had foisted on me. One of the cats that patrol her husband's barns had a litter, and when I holed up in Marhill after I'd seen Percy *in flagrante,* the little ones had kept me company with energetic pounces and naps. Rose insisted I take one home.

So now I have a cat I never wanted, a too expensive apartment, and a job that requires an ungodly number of hours per week.

And that's the third lesson I learned from my divorce. You don't just lose your husband, or your marriage. You lose the entire life you'd built for yourself.

Sophia Browne no longer exists. And I'm not sure who Sophia Bishop is anymore.

She desperately wanted to become a New Yorker, that I know. I'd once had a poster of the skyline in my childhood bedroom and used to watch *Sex and the City* like it was an instruction manual. Moving here had been a dream. Percy had helped me fit in, showed me the ropes... I'd married a New York man and into a New York family. *This was my home.*

But now I'm not sure who I am anymore.

The first task on my to-do-list is to work. I've always loved it. Percy often complained, in his characteristic voice that turned just a little petulant when he didn't get his way, that I worked more than I should. That he'd offered to take care of me, time and time again, if I chose to stay at home.

I'd remind him that he'd always said he liked my ambition. He would then relent and nod and say that, of course, he did.

But I wonder how much of that had been true.

I take my usual walking route to work. Exciteur has its

offices in a tall skyscraper a comfortable distance from my new apartment. I stop at my usual bench in the little greenery nearby, where most junior Exciteur employees eat their lunch during the warmer months, and switch from my ergonomic sneakers to a pair of low-heeled slingbacks. Then I undo the protective braid I keep my hair in during my walks. Nothing ruins blow-dried hair like the wind, and that's a lesson I learned long before my divorce.

I've got my morning routine down to a science.

I grab a coffee from the cart outside of work and head up to my floor.

Exciteur is a huge consulting firm.

Actually, *huge* might be too mild of a word. Colossal. Global. I have more coworkers across the globe than the small town I grew up in has inhabitants.

Let's just say the *reply all* button in emails has been permanently disabled.

Jenna is already at her desk. Her sleek, black hair is pulled back in a severe ponytail. It's her killer look, one she often wears to meetings with important clients.

"You made it in before me," I say.

She shoots me a look over her shoulder, eyes sparkling. "There's an almond croissant on your desk."

"You didn't."

"I did," she says.

"I'll get in here before you next week. Do you want your muffin with blueberry or chocolate?"

"Sure you will," she says. Jenna lives across the city but has, for some reason, decided to start biking to work. She arrives earlier than anyone so she can use the Exciteur gym showers. "But just in case you actually do… chocolate all the way."

I head into my office to grab the croissant waiting for me. It's a big day for my team. She knows it, ponytail and all, and so do I.

Then I head back out to her desk. "Are you going over our notes?"

"Sure am." For all our teasing, Jenna has the sharpest mind. She's my right hand and the third-in-command in my business development team at Exciteur Consulting.

And she's doing all of it while studying part-time for her MBA. For someone who started just six months ago, she's doing incredibly well.

I take a sip of my coffee. "This project hit us fast."

"It did," she says. "Do you know if we're going up against another consulting firm for it?"

I shake my head. "Not that I've heard. Apparently there's a family connection, or some sort of friendship, with Victor St. Clair."

"Ah," Jenna says. Our CEO at Exciteur prefers to be heard and not seen, hands-off but omnipresent. But he sure is well-connected, and he expects the best. Always, and with no exceptions. His response has been... severe, in the past, when teams failed to deliver.

"Yes," I say. "That means we need to nail this meeting."

She nods, face settling deep into thought. Jenna is second-generation Vietnamese, positive to a fault, and loves dressing in lemon-yellow blouses. I've never worked better with anyone than I have with her. "Toby is coming with us today?" she asks.

I nod. "I want you two to be my support on this project. We'll see what the client says today, but... this could be major."

"Major," she repeats, and turns back to her computer. With a few quick clicks she's pulled up the hotel's website.

Our potential new client.

The Winter Corporation.

It's the single biggest client I've ever been assigned to run point for on a project, and yet I can't quite look at the name without remembering.

The Winter Hotel, my own private salvation and my own

private hell, all in one. The place I learned the truth after months of suspecting, of questioning Percy's unusually late nights and wandering eyes.

"Is the attendee list up to date?" she asks, and pulls up our internal briefing for this meeting.

We have names and pictures of everyone attending from Winter. Background research is expected from consultants like us.

I need to make sure we walk into that meeting today and kill it... And I need it for so many different reasons.

"Yes," I say, and narrow my eyes at the list of names... including the one at the very top. "They'll all be there."

A few hours later Toby, Jenna and I file into the taxi ready to take us to the imposing stone structure that is the Winter Hotel. It's an institution in the city, one of the first great hotels, filled with history that dates back to the Gilded Age.

As old and storied as the family itself. Although Percy's parents consider themselves firmly enmeshed in the world of the Upper East Side, the Brownes' place is nothing compared to the Winters. They're woven into the fabric of society itself. Hell, they probably wove it themselves.

I knot my hands tightly together and look out the taxi window, away from Jenna and Toby's pre-game warm up. Nerves rise up like hummingbirds inside my chest.

It had taken me a while to figure out *who,* exactly, had helped me that fateful evening at the Winter Hotel.

He wasn't a receptionist or a cleaner or a security guard. Not that he'd looked like any of those. He'd had eyes too sharp, a bearing too straight, and a suit far too expensive. There'd been something faintly familiar about him, too, with a face I could have sworn I'd seen before in a crowd.

But I'd just had my world destroyed, and the details had faded, mixed with the emotional whirlpool of that night and all the screaming conversations that followed with Percy.

So I'd almost forgotten about the man who lent me a

tissue until the Winter project landed in my newly promoted lap at Exciteur two weeks ago.

The client is a special friend of the CEO. Give it everything you have, and make it fast.

So I'd done that, and it had involved a fair amount of research about the Winters, both the institution and the family that still owns and manages the century-old hotel chain.

It's one of the few companies that has gotten stronger, and not weaker, under the stewardship of the third and fourth generations.

It took me three minutes into my research to find the name and picture of the current owner and manager of the Winter Corporation. His face had stared back at me from a professional photograph, taken at the foot of the stairs in the Winter Hotel lobby, his dark hair brushed back and eyes looking into the camera like he's telling the photographer to hurry up.

It was the man from the lobby who I'd so embarrassingly overshared to, who had gotten me a cab and given me a tissue.

I'd been a hairsbreadth away from passing on the project. But I'd just been promoted, and my apartment still felt too big and too lonely to return to in the evenings. So I'd taken the Winter job and decided I'll just swallow my pride when the time came.

Only that time is now, and my pride doesn't taste so good going down.

The taxi pulls into a smooth stop outside the Winter Hotel. The main operations remain in the building itself, on a floor dedicated to office space. It speaks to the type of business this is. Old, family-oriented, and a little in love with its own legacy.

Stone columns flank the gilded entrance. Doormen wear a uniform, familiar to me after visits to this hotel with Percy and his parents. They loved to dine at one of its restaurants… and their son loved to meet his mistress here. It was a one-stop-shop for all Browne appetites.

"We got this," Jenna murmurs between me and Toby. "Break a leg, Soph."

"Lunch is on me after this."

"Thai?" Toby says.

"Yes please," Jenna chimes in.

We walk toward the main staircase, past the spot where I'd accidentally blabbed my heart out to Isaac Winter, CEO and one of the most influential people in New York.

"Sure," I say. "Let's have a glass of wine with it, too."

I don't look at the spot where I'd made a fool of myself. I don't look toward the emergency staircase either.

You're in control, Sophia.

"Just through here," an associate in a formal uniform says, and uses her keycard to access the staff door. We're escorted down a hallway. Into a conference room. And there, waiting for us, are the five people who make up the Winter Corporation's executive team. I know all of them by name and position.

And at its helm sits the man himself. Isaac Winter.

Staring right at me.

2

SOPHIA

There's a slight lift to one of his eyebrows.

That's it, the only hint of recognition he gives. It soothes the jagged edge of my nerves and sets off my professional script.

I've done this many times before.

I extend a hand to the man closest to us. One after one, they all rise.

"Sophia Bishop," I say. "It's a pleasure to meet all of you. Thanks for considering Exciteur for this project."

They introduce themselves. I don't hesitate when I reach Mr. Winter.

His hand closes around mine. The skin of his palm is warm and dry, the grip firm. "Isaac Winter," he says. "A pleasure, Miss Sophia... Bishop, was it?"

"Yes, that's right," I say. "Bishop."

"Lovely last name," he says.

Yeah. He remembers, all right.

"Thank you," I say, and release the hand I've been shaking for a tad too long. "This is my team, Jenna Nguyen and Toby Sutton. They're both invaluable to Exciteur's business development department."

Jenna and Toby have snapped into professional mode.

Their voices are clear and comfortable, and standing side by side, they radiate competence.

We all sit down again.

I end up opposite Isaac Winter. Him, the head of the entire corporation. Me, head of my development team.

I've met with plenty of companies where the CEO doesn't take the time to attend these meetings.

This one has.

I lay out the information they gave us in brief, sweeping sentences, and reaffirm our commitment to excellence. "Whatever you need," I say, "Exciteur can provide."

There's silence on the other side of the table. Isaac runs a hand along his jaw, eyes moving from me to Toby and Jenna. Like he's evaluating us.

"I'm considering expanding into a new chain of hotels," he says.

I nod. This had been part of the brief overview that had landed on my desk. "You want a spin-off brand," I say. "Targeted at a different clientele, with franchise possibilities? I'm guessing it needs long-term capacity to spawn a chain across the country, not just in big cities."

"Potentially," he agrees. "I loathe to use the word *budget*, but…"

I hide my smile. "More economical, perhaps?"

"Let's use that word, yes. Economical in all but quality."

"Naturally," I say. "What elements do you want to keep from the main Winter Hotels?"

Isaac lays out their vision. His chief acting officer does too, filling in on technical specifications and details. Beside me, Toby and Jenna take note of all of it.

This is the info we'll need to deliver a pitch in just a few weeks' time, complete with sketches, budget options, names and logos, and the contact details of potential architects.

They want a new hotel chain? We'll design an entire one from scratch for them.

I look at Isaac during their presentation. His face doesn't

give anything away, but I can't stop looking for clues. He looks just like he did in the picture included in my research. Thick, dark hair cut fairly short and swept back. Eyes that pierce. A flawless suit and just the hint of a stubble across his cheeks, at odds with the polished conference room.

There are faint lines around his eyes and across his forehead, but if anything, they make him look more distinguished. His age had been a part of my research. Thirty-eight, turning thirty-nine in a few months.

And never married.

Unusual, I think, for a man of his station in life.

"Sophia," Jenna says. She's using her professional voice, sharp and intelligent. "Care to wrap this up?"

I ask them to trust us with this project and promise a six-week turnaround on the pitch. "We'd love to be allowed inside your flagship hotel here in New York. A tour by one of the staff, perhaps, through the different parts of the hotel?"

"We can arrange that," Andrew says. I know from my internal brief that he's fifty-two and Isaac's right-hand man in running the company. He also has twin daughters who attend a fancy prep school three blocks from here and likes to golf on the weekends.

It's scary how thorough Exciteur is at research sometimes.

And then we're done, sitting across from this executive team, one woman and three men, all led by the man who'd seen me sob so hard my mascara ran down my cheeks. Jenna makes sure everyone has a copy of our contact details and Toby gathers up our notebooks.

Show time, Sophia. I let people file out of the conference room before I direct my words to the man-in-charge.

"Mr. Winter?"

Isaac stops by the door. His second-in-command sends me a curious look, and so does Jenna, but I ignore them both.

"Yes, Miss Bishop?"

"Might I have a brief word?"

His eyes remain unreadable. "Certainly. Andrew, please

escort Miss Bishop's team to the lobby and make sure they get a cup of coffee."

He pulls the door half-shut behind the others. The room feels smaller with just the two of us in it, and without the designer table separating us. Less formal.

More nerve-racking.

"Well," he says. "I'd be lying if I said I wasn't intrigued."

I lean against the table. "I just wanted to thank you for trusting Exciteur with this project," I say. The next words are rehearsed. "I'm not sure if you remember what happened in the lobby of your hotel, almost a year ago, but if you do, I can assure you that you'll get nothing but professionalism from me going forward."

One of Isaac's eyebrows rises. "You planned this speech ahead of time?"

The question *almost* throws me off my game. I give him my most corporate of smiles. "I did. This project is important to me, as is doing a good job. Is there a chance we could forget about what happened?"

"There is." He looks down at the papers I'm carrying, the folder with the Exciteur logo on it. And then he says the next few sentences matter-of-factly, like we're still discussing his company. "We delayed your husband's check-out process by forty-five minutes. From the curses he aimed at my staff, I believe we ensured he missed an important business meeting."

I blink at him. "Oh."

"We threatened to sue him for civil indecency too, for leaving his hotel room naked," Isaac says. Face still serious, eyes unreadable on mine, but with the same quirk to his eyebrow. "He's not welcome back as a guest. Ever."

It takes me a moment to find the words. My hand tightens around the hem of my blazer. "Thank you. He'd have seen that as a pretty heavy blow."

"Well, I don't take kindly to people exposing themselves in my hotel hallways."

I feel like I'm having an out-of-body experience. "No, of course not. That makes sense."

"So you divorced him."

Isaac's words aren't a question, but I nod anyway. My left hand curves into a fist. The absence of my rings has finally started to feel normal. Freeing, even. "Yes."

Isaac uncrosses his arms. His face looks settled, as if something that previously bothered him had been resolved. "This can be our first meeting, if you'd like. What happened in the lobby won't affect our working relationship."

Working relationship. Familiar words. They lead me back to safe ground and my professional smile stretches back into place. "Thank you, Mr. Winter. I appreciate that a great deal."

He extends a hand, and this time, the shake lasts longer. Dark brown eyes lock on mine.

"I'm looking forward to working with you... Miss Bishop."

3

ISAAC

The Exciteur team comes back three days later.

Judging by the emails my own team is getting, and the few ones that get filtered through to me, they're on top of things. Asking for preferred color palettes and budgeting guidelines and endless lists of follow-ups.

She's thorough, I think. And then I have to correct myself. *They're thorough.*

Sophia is head of a team. A team my brother helped me hire through Victor St. Clair, and a team I have significant expectations from.

I get into the elevator from my apartment on the twentieth floor. Not that *mine* is the right word, exactly. It's the Winter apartment, built into the hotel itself, and each generation has used it. My brother and I spent a lot of time there as kids.

Not that my parents ever actually lived there. They'd preferred the townhouse, with my father coming in to the hotel every day. And then every other day.

And then every third…

The lack of oversight had made its mark on the place when I finally took the reins.

The elevator moves too slowly. I look in the gilded mirror and see the familiar face staring back at me. Gray suit, dark hair, the same set jaw as my father. My brother had inherited it too, and damn if it didn't make all of us look like surly bastards.

What came first, the look or the attitude?

I run a hand down my face. I'd shaved, and perhaps that makes me look somewhat younger, but there's no denying the man staring back at me isn't twenty-five anymore, and he's not thirty, either. It's not something I've thought about in a long time. Hadn't cared.

I shake off the thought and step out of the elevator.

She's right there, standing in the lobby, only a few steps away from where I'd first met her. She's talking to her two trusty lieutenants. The brown hair is swept back in a low ponytail and she's in a navy blue dress that hugs her body.

Competence and beauty combined.

Sophia's eyes land on mine. "Mr. Winter," she says in a warm, corporate voice and extends a hand. She's good at that, making fake enthusiasm seem real. She could've had a career in hospitality.

"Miss Bishop," I say. "Allow me to escort you and your colleagues up to the conference room."

Andrew had planned to do this. His face had been priceless when I told him I'd take over the task.

Sophia and her colleagues set up shop in the conference room right away. I stand sentry at the door and watch as they unpack laptops and notebooks. They'll spend the entire day at the hotel, talking to my employees and getting the ball rolling on their concept.

Inputting, I believe, was the business term they used. Consulting is an industry I've never understood, but I can respect its results.

"Have you had a tour of the hotel?" I ask. My question is for the entire team, but I can't stop myself from looking at Sophia when I say the words.

She looks up. "Are you offering, Mr. Winter?"

"Yes."

She looks at Jenna, busy firing up their computers, and then nods. "I'd love to join you, yes. My team has a tour scheduled with your head of reception later. We'll divide and conquer."

It's hard to stop the unprofessional pleasure I feel at that. Sophia joins me and we head out to the elevators. Her shoes make sharp, clicking noises on the marble floor. She's a tall woman, and with heels on, we're nearly the same height.

I lead us down the double stairs. We'll start in the lobby and The Ivy. Styled as an Old World orangery with vaulted ceilings and olive trees, the restaurant is where we serve breakfast to the hotel guests, and in the evening, dinner to everyone else.

"I've been to the hotel a few times before," she says, "but there's no way I could resist a tour from a Winter himself."

"You should take notes."

She's quiet for a moment, and then she chuckles softly. "You know what, I probably will."

"Oh?"

"Yes." She pulls out a notepad from her bag. "Give me as much history as you think I need."

"Be careful what you ask for," I say. "My mother wrote a book about the hotel's history. There are three hundred pages worth of facts about this place, each one as painstakingly detailed as the last."

"A biography?"

"Yes," I say. "The book was never published, though. It's kept in the family."

"I'm sure it could be successful," she says. "If you chose to publish it wide."

I look over at her. "She included a tad too many… revealing details about the family."

Sophia nods, and the glint in her eyes tells me she understands perfectly. "I see. But you might be able to turn it into a coffee table book. You could use images from the hotel over the past century, including some of the most prominent guests, with stories about each of them. From the Roaring Twenties to the crazy rock bands of the eighties. The Winter Hotel is legendary. You could mythologize that. Why not capitalize on your own legacy?" she asks. "You could involve your mother, too."

I pause on the first marble step up to The Ivy. "Did you just think of that?"

"Yes," Sophia says. "Want us to draw up a quick proto-type and include it in our pitch? We have in-house graphic artists. I'd be happy to include it."

I look at her for a long moment. "Are you well compensated at Exciteur?"

Her eyes widen. "That's an unexpected question."

"I hope the answer is yes," I say, "or I'll strongly suggest to St. Clair that he increase whatever he's paying you."

A flush rises on her cheeks. "Thank you, Mr. Winter. But I assure you, I'm paid well. I was recently promoted to this position."

"Ah," I say. "Do you enjoy it?"

"I do, yes."

"Good. Because if the answer was no, and if I was entirely lacking in morals, I might just be interested in poaching you."

She smiles. "That's a compliment, Mr. Winter. Thank you."

We walk into The Ivy. It's in the last hour of breakfast service, and the majority of guests have left.

"I've been here before," she says. "For dinner."

"What did you think?"

"I love the seasonal menu. Very classically European."

I nod. "Etienne is a master."

She pauses at a round table with seating for twelve. "My former parents-in-law threw us our engagement dinner here."

I feel a pang of irritation at that, irrational as it is. Of course the Brownes had chosen The Ivy for such an occasion.

"Oh," I say. My hotel already holds a lot of memories for her.

She shakes her head. "Sorry, that's not relevant."

"It is. You have memories here." I gesture toward the back of the restaurant. "Let's see if Etienne has a moment. Now, what does the Winter brand mean to you?"

She tells me about her impressions, and asks me about mine. Her questions are engaging. Tough, occasionally, and I watch as she writes down key words and phrases in her notebook.

I show her the newly installed winter garden next to the pool and gym area, the latter renovated just last year. We stop on the balcony overlooking the oval-shaped indoor pool. The room retains all of its old-world art deco charm, with gilded wall art and lavish lounge chairs.

"Wow," she murmurs, running her hand along the bannister. I watch her reaction instead of the familiar rooms. The widening of her eyes, the easy appreciation. And the clever remarks—*so that's how you seat all the guests?* And, *Your restaurants must be a significant source of income on the weekends. Can guests pay extra to reserve this space?*

"Have you been to the pool and spa area before?" I ask.

"Never," she says. "I've never stayed the night here as a guest."

I nod at the grand room. "What the Winter Hotel has is old-world charm. Its history, understated glamour, and impeccable service. Those things need to be a core part of the... more economical hotel chain."

She hums and turns away from my view. "Mr. Winter," she says, and there's something almost gentle in her voice, like she's preparing me for bad news. It makes me want to smile. "Impeccable service is a good principle to carry on. Old-World charm probably isn't. Imagine how that'll translate to a newly built property."

"It won't be a Winter Hotel if it doesn't have that."

"Precisely," she says. "You want to create a spin-off hotel chain, not copy-paste what works so well here and in your other main locations."

I narrow my eyes at her. She narrows hers right back. "You feel strongly about this," I say.

"I've done my research, Mr. Winter."

"I have no doubt," I say. "But I know this hotel brand better than I know myself."

I've dedicated my entire life to it.

My younger brother had always pursued other avenues, and made it clear that while he might lend a hand from time to time, he wasn't interested in working for the family business. And my father? He had retired as soon as he felt comfortable that I could run it on my own.

He'd been a steward of the legacy, and not a visionary.

But this company is our lifeblood, and I'll be damned if it does anything but flourish under my leadership.

Sophia's eyes are still on mine, unflinching. Reminding me that this woman had lied her way to a keycard just to confirm her husband's infidelity. There's steel beneath her impeccably tailored dress.

"Sometimes, Mr. Winter," she says, "people closest to an issue are the last people to see it clearly. Forest for all the trees, and all that."

I have to grind my teeth together to keep from smiling. "Interesting saying, that one."

She nods, lips softening in a half-smile. "Trust me to take your words seriously. But I also hope you'll trust us to give you a pitch we are confident can work."

"Mhm," I say. "Come on, let me show you the newly renovated gym."

By the time we return to the conference room, Sophia is brimming with increasingly ambitious ideas, and I have a meeting I can't push back any further. I leave her to her team and my associates, and she sits down at her notes without a second glance in my direction.

Stupid, I think as I walk away, tugging at the collar of my pressed shirt. I never get involved. I never cross lines, and I'm never bothered by inconvenient attractions. *Stupid and unnecessary.*

The woman has nothing but negative associations with the Winter Hotel. I'm not going to give her another.

———

It's much later that night when I walk through the staff corridor. The executive offices are all closed for the day, and my office is the only one with the lights still on. Construction is halfway through on our new Caribbean location and I've been going over images and notes from our contractor.

Taki's for Thai, or Flake's again for a steak and potato gratin. Those are the options. I'm halfway through dialing the number to Taki's when I pass the conference room.

The lights are still on.

I pause. "Sophia?"

She looks up at me. She's wearing a pair of glasses, a new addition, and her ponytail has given way to a messy bun. A few strands frame her face.

"Oh, hello." She pulls off her glasses with a chagrined smile. "I had to take out my contacts."

"You're still working?"

She nods. "We got so much great information today. We're technically not in the brainstorming phase yet, but I couldn't resist staying a bit longer to gather my thoughts."

I frown. "Have you eaten anything?"

"Yes," she says. "Your team got us food from The Ivy."

"That was hours ago, for lunch." I glance over at the door to the main staircase. "Do you like Asian fusion?"

"Yes."

"Consider this research too, then." I grab my phone and call up to the top floor.

Jake answers on the second signal. "Boss?"

I can hear the sound of the busy restaurant in the background. "I need a tasting menu for two delivered to the staff corridor. We're in the conference room."

"Got it. Wine?"

I look at Sophia and consider the question. She's scribbling something on her notepad, and then she digs her teeth into her full lower lip, and I know I'm going to hell. "Yes."

"It'll be there in ten."

"Thanks." I hang up and meet the incredulous look of the woman across the table. "Everything all right?"

"Yes," she says, and then she shakes her head. "Was that Room?"

"Yes."

"Your rooftop restaurant is booked for *weeks* in advance."

"It's popular, yes."

"Your chef has a Michelin star!"

"He does." I pull out a chair and sit down opposite her. "Want to meet him later, too?"

She snorts. "Now you're just showing off."

"Maybe a little," I say, and find that it's true. I want to paint over all her memories of this place with new ones. Better ones. "Tell me about the ideas you've been brainstorming."

"They're not quite ready yet," she says, but excitement flashes in her eyes. "But maybe I can tease a few…"

"I promise I'll act surprised at the pitch."

Her lips tug into a genuine smile. "Thanks. Well… I've really loved seeing the Art Deco details here today. And I'm thinking maybe we could use that as the inspiration for the logo."

I nod. "Go on."

She does just that, throwing out ideas faster than I can follow. This is her forte, I realize, watching her in action. Ideation. Creativity. If she can successfully pair that with a sense of business, well… she's in the exact right job.

The food arrives from Room, and Andrew Chiu is as talented as always. The ceviche melts on the tongue, the spice burns, and all of it is made considerably better by the company.

It takes me fifteen seconds to see how much Sophia loves the food. She tastes every single dish like she's reviewing the restaurant.

I look from her to the dish she's sampling and can't help but smile at the third *aaah* she lets out.

She sees it and stops, fork in midair. "What?"

"You're enjoying the dinner."

"Well, yes." She dabs at her mouth with a napkin. "I've wanted to go to Room for ages but never managed to get a table."

"Percy never took you?" I ask.

The room falls quiet, but I hear the echo of my question. Fuck. I've broken the one request she asked of me. "Never mind. You asked me to forget how we first met."

A crooked smile curves her lips. "Perhaps that was a lot to ask for. It was pretty memorable, wasn't it?"

"Yes," I say. "Beautiful women don't cry in my lobby every night."

She looks down at her food. "Probably a good thing, or your Tripadvisor score would tank."

"Yes, or we'd start attracting a very peculiar clientele."

She shakes her head, laughing. "The indignity! You'd never get the WASPs back."

I take a long sip of my wine. "The WASPs," I repeat.

She looks over at me, a brief flash of regret in her eyes. "Sorry. I shouldn't have said that."

"Why not? It's not untrue."

"Perhaps not," she says, and leans back in her chair. I get the feeling she's weighing her next words carefully. "It wasn't meant to be disparaging, but it is a core feature of your clientele. At least for the New York location."

"You're concerned," I say, "because you consider me a member of that group, and I might have been offended."

She sighs. "Yes."

"I think you'll find that I'm very difficult to offend, especially with the truth."

"Really?"

"Yes. I spent the first two years of my career in the reception."

Her eyes widen. "You did?"

"Yes. All Winter kids have to work summers in reception. My great-grandfather instituted the policy with his kids, and it's been a thing since. I haven't checked in a guest myself in… well, it's almost been twenty years. But I know how it's done."

"That," Sophia says, "is a factoid I bet your mother included in the book."

I chuckle. "Yes, including which of her children were the best at it."

"You?"

"Naturally," I say. "It's why I'm here and my brother isn't."

She looks at me for a long beat, like she doesn't know if I'm serious or not. But then she smiles. "He treated the guests poorly?"

"Terribly," I say. "He never told anyone the check-out time, and when a member of the Rolling Stones checked in, he asked them for an autograph."

"Yikes."

"He got away with it when the head receptionist explained who he was, but Dad wasn't happy." I shake my head. "Honestly though, he was good at the job. But he never wanted to have it, and it showed."

"You did?" she asks.

I focus on cutting through the coriander-crusted sirloin. "Someone had to do it."

She makes a humming sound, and I can hear what she's thinking. *That's not quite the same thing.* But if I say one thing I fear I'll say another, because my tongue is already looser than it should be around her.

"So that's why you're unoffendable," she says. "You've worked in hospitality."

"Handled every type of guest," I say, "including the ones who throw a few well-chosen curses your way as they check out."

"Somehow I thought there would be less of that in a place like this. You know, so upscale?"

I shrug. "Few people are as quick to anger as the rich."

Sophia breaks into a half-laugh. "Well, that's definitely true."

"Enjoying the food?"

"Yes," she says, "and the unexpected company. I'm grateful to get so much of your time, Mr. Winter. I wasn't expecting it."

I take a bite of my food to delay answering. "Well, I care a great deal about this project, and I have every incentive to make sure your pitch is as good as possible."

She nods. "You want a more accessible, scaleable hotel chain."

"Yes. The Winter Hotels are our core brand, but they're..." I pause, because I hate this word. "Exclusive."

"Of course. You can't build a place like this in every state."

"No," I say. She puts her glasses back on, and in front of my eyes, transforms into yet another version of herself. I've seen her professional, I've now seen her relaxed, and I once saw her heartbroken.

Curiosity gets the better of me. "Where are you from?"

"A little town called Marhill. It's five hours north of here." She puts down her fork, the dish clean. "It's not big enough to warrant one of your new hotels, let's put it that way."

More questions rise to my tongue. About how she met Percy. What she studied. How her life led her here, to my conference room past nine at night, eating takeout.

But that would be crossing the line, and I've spent my entire career avoiding that.

"Interesting," I say, and finish the last of my wine.

She clears her throat. "I'm sorry for staying so late. I'll work mostly out of Exciteur's offices going forward, now that we've had the full tour."

"You're welcome here whenever," I say. "After all, you need to learn the ins and outs of the Winter brand, to do your job well. Don't you?"

Her eyes sparkle. "Yes, I suppose I do."

4

SOPHIA

All the walls in my apartment are beige. It's the off-white that's too off to be called white, and the brown that's too light to be called brown.

It's also a color too plain to be called a color.

I lean back against my couch and look at the absence of art on my living room wall. Six months of living here, and I haven't made any of the changes I'd planned to.

There'd been a frenzied week of attempts. Hanging my favorite paintings in my bedroom—check. Asking the landlord if I could repaint the kitchen—check. Receiving no for an answer—check.

The place is too new to have any character yet. I'd loved that when I desperately needed out of the apartment I'd shared for years with Percy.

That place had enough character to choke me. Two generations of Brownes had lived in it before us. And I'd loved it. The windows overlooking the park, the wainscoting on the walls, the wallpaper in the guest bathroom. *Mine.* Expect it hadn't been.

My name might have been added on the door for a few years, but it was sure as hell not on the deed.

But this beige place is *mine*, plain as it might be. Milo

jumps up on the couch beside me. He walks carefully around my tray, paw over paw, ignoring the leftovers of my pasta.

"Hey," I murmur and stretch out a hand. He rubs his head against it, soft and insistent. "How many mice did you catch today?"

Milo starts to purr.

"Not a single one today either, huh. I'm sorry." I scratch under his chin. "My sister says your mom is an excellent mouser. You should be living with them, you know, and not here in this apartment with me. You must think you're the unluckiest cat in the world."

He presses his front paws against my thigh and stretches big and long, his gray-striped body going fluid, the picture of feline contentment.

"I'll bring you with me when I go back upstate next time," I tell him. "Our little experiment will be over by then."

But I lift him onto my lap regardless. He's a soft, warm weight, the damn cat, and not for the first time, I thank my sister's stubbornness in giving him to me.

I'd told Rose I was barely looking after myself, and she'd looked at me as if to say *yes, exactly. That's why.* She had added triumphantly, as if it would win the argument, that "you always loved cats as a little girl!"

Yes, I'd told her. *But I also loved pink ribbons and lollipops and ponies.*

"Just take him," she'd said, in the tone my little sister used when she didn't want you to argue.

And that had been that.

Milo burrows his head against my fluffy sweater and his purring vibrates from his body into mine. At least there's someone who wants to spend their evenings with me.

My friends from college are nonexistent. With all my focus on my career, and then my marriage, we've grown apart. And the friends I made through my marriage? Gone.

I try to focus on the TV. I've put on an old romantic comedy, a classic, but it's not holding my attention. It's like beautifully, occasionally outdated, background music to my overthinking.

I lean my head back against the couch. The Winter pitch has occupied more of my time this week than any of my other projects. There's something about it that demands excellence.

Perhaps it's the bonus I'll receive if I pull it off, I think, but that's not it. Not completely. Being a part of an expanding business is thrilling.

And so is the owner himself. Involved, expectant, and available. He'll want perfection. Hell, he'll expect it, and he won't hold back from giving us critique if it's not.

My fingers itch to dive back into the brainstorming document I share with Jenna and Toby.

I grab my laptop and prop it up beside me on a pillow. Milo burrows harder into my lap, like he's reminding me that he's here, and he won't be moved for anything. I stroke his soft ears and open my emails.

Toby sent over a few links to hotel chains of a similar scale to what our budget allows. Jenna replied, commenting on ones that might work as comps.

And there's an email waiting for me, from an unexpected source. It's not from andrew.hall@winterhotels.com, and it's not from amanda.jenkins@winterhotels.com.

It's from isaac.winter@winterhotels.com

Subject: Access to the archives

Miss Bishop,

Our discussion by the pool got me thinking about the history of the hotel. I've attached a number of files from the archives that show all of our logos, typefaces, and promotional material going back for a century. Perhaps it might be useful in brainstorming the name and logo for the new hotel.

The past is valued at the Winter.

Isaac.

I dive into the files he's sent, my eyes widening at the images. It's like a time machine. The eighties, the sixties, the forties. And monograms. There are monograms everywhere. *I can never escape them,* I think, smiling.

It's a treasure trove, and there are definitely things to work with here. I forward it to Jenna and Toby with the note to keep it strictly within the team, before I pen a thank-you to Isaac.

Subject: Re: Access to the archives

This is incredible. Thank you! I'm sure there are elements there to draw from for the design process.

Don't worry. I promise to respect the past in the pitch, in one way or another. Thank you for the personal tour the other day, and for dinner in the evening. I truly appreciate the access you've granted us.

Best,
Sophia

I send it off before I can second-guess my words. He's intense, and his demeanor is carefully controlled, but I always feel like there's a lot he's thinking that he's not saying.

I don't expect a reply. Trying to focus on the couple arguing on my TV screen, I almost forget to check my email. Almost. Because when I check half-an-hour later, he's replied.

Subject: RE: Access to the archives

Glad you find them useful. There's more where that came from.

The Winter executive team is going down to our DC hotel next week, Tuesday to Thursday. Come with us and bring your team. Touring another of our locations would be useful.

Isaac

I look at the screen. He really is giving us an incredible breadth of access, and not just to the New York hotel.

My fingers type in measured strokes across the keyboard of my laptop. I picture the columns of the lobby, strong and straight, housing one of the most prestigious adresses in the country.

Subject: RE: Access to the archives

Thank you! That's a very generous offer, and I'd be glad to accept it on behalf of myself and my team. I'll contact Andrew tomorrow to make arrangements for Jenna, Toby and me.

Sorry for answering your email so late. Seems we're both burning the midnight oil. Hotel empires don't run themselves!

Thanks,
Sophia

I regret the final line as soon as I've hit send. It wasn't pithy. It wasn't clever, and it wasn't professional, either. But here I am, the email sent, never to be undone.

I focus on the heroine in the movie. She's standing, sad and beautiful, in line to board an airplane. Then the movie cuts to the hero racing across the terminal building to get to her.

She's sad because they can't be together for some banal reason that barely made sense to me the first time I saw this movie.

I want to shake her.

You have a man who's good and true and you're not willing to put in a little work?

I want to shake him, too. It had taken him long enough to realize his feelings, and now he's running through a damn airport, cutting it too close.

It's *almost* like the filmmakers timed his great realization for maximum dramatic effect. I sigh. They're probably going to get married and then divorced a few years later when one or both of them cheat. Or when they realize they actually have nothing in common and wake up as strangers one day.

I look down at my laptop. There's a new email. Mr. Winter has responded to my stupid message.

Subject: RE: Access to the archives

Don't apologize. I'm the one who chose to check my emails. As for hotel empires, they don't design themselves, either, it seems. I take it my project is so challenging that you need to work nights?

Emperor

A shaky breath escapes me. So I hadn't messed this up. The words *special friend of the CEO* ring out in my head. And then I see him, ordering food from one of the most exclusive restaurants in New York with a quick phone call. He'd written "Emperor" facetiously, picking up on the lame joke I put down in my own email, but it's not untrue. He rules the Winter Corporation.

Subject: RE: Access to the archives.

The best projects are challenging, but that's what makes them exciting. Yours more than most. It's distracting me from the movie I'm watching, as opposed to the other way around. That's a good sign.

Enjoy the rest of your evening,
Sophia

I send it off, and then wait with bated breath for another email from him. A response of any kind. But I hadn't asked a question, and what would he even respond to? *What movie are you watching?*

I shut the laptop and shove it under the pillows in the corner of my couch, refusing to look at it again. Instead I bury my hands in Milo's soft fur and try to enjoy watching the couple make up on the screen, confessing feelings that have been obvious to anyone with eyes for the last hour of the film.

It isn't until the next morning that I read his response. Because he had responded.

Subject: RE: Access to the archives

That probably says more about your choice of movie than the project we're working on. Enjoy your night off, Sophia. The hotel will still be there tomorrow.

I'd still give you a raise, if it was up to me.

Isaac

5

SOPHIA

The Winter Hotel in DC isn't as old as the original New York location, but it's larger, built in a place where square footage isn't a species on the endangered list. It has most of the same grand features, with a gym twice the size of the one in New York, but it's clear it's built more for utility than glamour.

"You can tell it's designed for visiting dignitaries," Jenna comments that morning, as we eat breakfast. "I saw them adding signs on the breakfast buffet in Mandarin."

"Are they hosting a summit?"

She shrugs and reaches for her orange juice. "They sure might be. And with locations like this, I understand why they're reluctant to give up some of the older decor. It's served them well in the past."

"Mhm. But their new hotel chain will cater to different customers, to normal families, to friends road tripping, to hip, young—you're smiling," I say. "Why are you smiling?"

Jenna laughs. "Because I'm on your team. I'm already convinced. The person you need to convince is coming later today, and he might not be so easy to impress."

I look down at my plate of toast, fresh fruit, and an omelet that's been cooked to my exact specifications. Yes, Isaac

Winter is joining us this afternoon. Here on business just like us, after he'd graciously extended an invite to my team and me. Toby couldn't make it, but Jenna and I? We packed our bags immediately. It's not every day you're staying at a Winter Hotel for free.

"You stayed late last week," Jenna says. "Did you get everything sorted?"

"Um, yes," I say. "I sent over a new brief to our graphics department."

"A new direction for the logo?"

"Yes. I want us to have options."

I hadn't told Jenna about the dinner I'd shared with Isaac in the conference room. The moment belonged in that space, and spoken out loud, I feared it would lose its magic.

Jenna digs into the miniature acai bowl she'd grabbed from the buffet. "Well," she says, "if we're going to make a budget version of *this*, it will still be miles above the competition."

I laugh and cut into my omelet. "I think that's what they're aiming for."

We spend the rest of the day discussing strategies and touring the Washington DC hotel. A kind receptionist shows us all the different suite options. Jenna takes notes and I twist and turn ideas over in my head. How to incorporate a sense of luxury without the luxury price tag it takes to build it.

How do you sell a budget idea to a man with an eye for perfection?

By late afternoon, he still hasn't joined us.

"Mr. Winter sends his apologies," the kind receptionist says. "He's been delayed and will be unlikely to make it tonight. Feel free to grab an early dinner and he'll see you both tomorrow."

"Tomorrow? We have the midday flight scheduled," I say.

The receptionist's eyes widen. "Oh. Well, I'm sure he'll be in touch, one way or the other. If you'll excuse me…"

When we're alone, Jenna sighs. "Well, nothing we're not used to. We work in the shadows, and they talk to us when they have time. We still got great input."

"Yes, we definitely did," I say, ignoring the pang of disappointment.

And that's how I end up at the hotel bar later that evening, alone. Jenna is taking advantage of the early evening to meet with an old college friend in the city.

I twist my glass of Chardonnay by the stem. A few years ago I'd discovered my love for the grape, and the grape's love for me, and so far that's one relationship that's never failed me. I've finished half of it, and I'm debating whether I should order another one or go to my hotel room.

At least the walls will be a different shade of beige than the ones at home.

But then a deep voice cuts through the silence. "Miss Bishop. You're still here."

I turn to see him, familiar but unknowable, standing beside my chair. "Yes," I say. "I take my job seriously."

His lips tug. "So do I, although you'd be forgiven for thinking I don't, with the delay today."

"Where were you?"

Isaac pulls out the chair next to me at the bar. He undoes the suit button as he sits. "I had meetings with developers across town," he says. "They ran late. I'm sorry I couldn't meet you and your associate here."

The wine and the wait have left me off-kilter, and with more courage than sense. "Jenna Nguyen."

He nods. "That's right. I apologize for forgetting. There are a... lot of people in my organization."

"How many?"

"Too many for me to know the exact number," he says, and raises an eyebrow. "What do you think about this hotel?"

I look away from the intensity in his eyes. "Stunning. It has a mellower feel than your main location in New York, lighter in color. It feels more... business and less vacation. People come here to recharge after a day of work, not after a day of boozy sightseeing. But it's still built to impress, just in a way that's less glamorous and more stately."

"You have a good eye, Miss Bishop."

"Sophia," I say. It slips out. "Please call me Sophia, when we're... well. I prefer it."

"Sophia," he murmurs. "All right."

Nerves make my next words quick. "Thank you for dinner the other night, and the cab home. The tasting menu was incredible."

He shakes his head and signals for the bartender. "Brandy, neat. Sophia will have...?"

"Another glass of Chardonnay, thank you."

He drums his knuckles against the bar. "Also, two glasses of water—still."

"Of course, sir," the bartender says, already reaching for my now-empty glass.

Isaac clears his throat. "There's no need to thank me for the food. It was research. So, which suites did you and your colleagues get?"

"The standard," I say. "It looked lovely at check-in."

His mouth tightens. "They're decent."

"Decent? There's a pillow menu next to my queen-sized bed and a fully stocked minibar." I smile at him. "I don't know if you've heard, but this is a five-star hotel."

He snorts. "I hadn't, actually. Did you do a lot of research before you booked it?"

"Oh yes. I spent a solid hour reading reviews and compared this place to every hotel on Pennsylvania Ave."

"And what made you choose us?" He leans back in the chair. "You know, customer satisfaction is our main priority."

My hand curls around the stem of my new wineglass. "Well, the reviews mentioned excellent personal service. It convinced me."

His lips curve. "You want a personal touch?"

"Yes, I do."

There's a long beat of silence between us, and Isaac looks down at the brandy that's appeared in front of him. His long fingers curve around the tumbler and I catch the hint of stubble along his jaw.

"You know," he says, "I've never seen you before."

"Before? Do you mean before we met in your lobby?"

He nods. "You were married to Percival Browne. Surely I would have run into you both together somewhere. Manhattan is small, and Percy went to school a few years behind me."

"Oh." I run a hand over my neck, finding my ponytail. I ease out the tie and let the hair spread around my shoulders, considering my answer.

Manhattan isn't small. It's enormous.

But just like my ex-husband, Isaac uses *Manhattan* as the name for their social circle. The small, insulated group of people that never live further than a few blocks from Central Park.

"Well, we didn't go to a lot of parties together after our first couple of years. Percy preferred meeting his friends at the golf course or the club."

"Ah," Isaac says, and there's a world of meaning in the word.

I sigh. "Yeah. It didn't exactly help me make friends in the city."

"Which club is the Brownes members of?"

"Grandview," I say. It's a famous country club with a location on the Upper East Side and one in the Hamptons. It has a waiting list that I'd only been able to bypass because of Percy, who'd had membership since birth.

Isaac takes a sip of his brandy. "You moved to New York a few years ago," he says.

It's a statement, but I nod regardless. "Yes. Marhill is a

tiny place, and I always wanted to leave. New York was the dream. After college, I moved to the city, and despite all the things that are frustrating about it, I love it." I shrug. "I met Percy at a bar during my first year in the city. I guess I was... never mind. Let's talk about you instead of my ex-husband."

Isaac's eyebrows rise, and I want to take the words back. I'm talking to him like he's a friend.

"Me?" he asks.

"Yes. Do you have an ex-wife we can talk about, to make things more even? Or was that a terribly inappropriate question?"

The hint of a smile curves his lips. When you get past the first impression, which is intimidating and distinguished, he's handsome. Never approachable, I think. But handsome.

"I'm sure it was," he says, "but I don't mind."

"Phew."

"I don't have an ex-wife," he says, "and I'm not dating anyone at the moment."

"That was fast. I figured you'd deflect on that one."

"It was an easy question." He raises an eyebrow. "I know the first answer for you, but what about the second?"

"If I'm dating anyone? No, I'm not. I mean, my divorce went through only a few months ago, even if we've been separated for almost a year."

I've turned toward him, almost without realizing it, and my knee brushes his.

"I see," he says, his eyes dark on mine. "Let me guess. You work too much. You mainly eat takeout in your apartment... your new apartment, right? You moved out of Percy's but you haven't fully decorated your new place yet."

My mouth opens softly. "I haven't had the time."

"Right." He nods, and twist the glass of brandy around. "No, you threw yourself into work instead, and it's become your life. Dating again scares you, because it means trying at something again. Something that you might fail at, as opposed to work, where you know you can always perform."

I stare at him.

His lips curve again, into that half-smile. "I shouldn't have said any of that."

"It's all true. But how... Oh," I say. "That's you too. Isn't it?"

His eyes sharpen, and the moment stretches into an eternity-long silence. But then he gives a single nod. "Yes."

"That makes sense," I breathe. "Who hurt you?"

Isaac takes a long sip of his brandy. I watch his throat shift and in the silence I realize what I've just asked him.

"God, I shouldn't have asked that. I'm sorry."

"Perhaps not," he says. But then something softens around his mouth. "But after our meeting in the lobby, maybe we're past things like shallow niceties."

"I've never liked them much anyway," I say.

"You don't? You surprise me, Sophia."

"I do? In what way?"

He lifts a shoulder in a half-shrug. "You're not who I expected you to be, after the first evening."

"Not constantly weeping, you mean?"

"No, not that, for sure." His eyes hold a challenge. Like he's expecting me to be offended and he's considering whether or not to say it.

"Go on," I say.

"You were married to one of the Browne kids. I didn't expect you to work, for one. And I didn't expect you to be this... well. This is where I'll insult you."

"Please don't censor yourself on my account, Mr. Winter. I think you're the one who said you'll never be offended by the truth? I won't, either."

He smiles. "Fine. The word I'm looking for is sharp, Sophia. I didn't expect you to be this sharp."

"Because I married Percy Browne?" That makes me chuckle, and I lift my glass. "You know what, I understand that. It wasn't the smartest decision I've ever made."

A smile spreads across his features. If his good looks were

45

austere before, this makes them come alive, and I catch my breath.

"I'll toast to that," he says, and our glasses touch.

Warmth spreads through my chest, and I can't resist teasing him. "Do you often think women are less intelligent?"

He gives a surprised chuckle. "I've never been asked that before."

"Because the women you surround yourself with are usually too dumb to ask it?"

"Oh, I'd love to hear you say that around my mother or my sister-in-law."

I laugh. "So that's a no, then."

"Definite no. And for the record, I don't think women are unintelligent. I didn't think you were." His eyes glitter with teasing. "I made a snap judgement about your character based off what I knew of Percy's. That's all."

I should let it go, but I can't. "And what did you think of Percy's character?"

"Let's just say," Isaac says, "that my opinion of him has increased a lot since getting to know you."

I take a long sip of my wine and let the words float through me, like a rock settling into a lake. The compliment makes me warm. "So you went to school together."

"Yes. But he was a few years behind me."

"Not that many."

"Enough," he says. "Still, his parents and mine occasionally meet."

"They're friends?" I say, frowning. My former father-in-law, in particular, would have name-dropped the Winters every moment he could.

Isaac chuckles. "Not exactly. You know how Manhattan is. Many acquaintances, very few friends."

I nod. That's never been clearer to me than now, after my divorce. But I didn't think Isaac would see it that way.

He's married to his work, I think, looking at the way he takes up space so naturally in the hotel that bears his name. He'll never work with anything else. Won't dedicate himself to networking and social climbing the way so many other Upper East Side families do... because he'll never need to.

He's already a permanent fixture in that world.

"Sophia?" he asks.

"I must have seen you," I say. "These past years."

"We both must have."

"In the lobby, I thought you looked familiar, but I had... other things on my mind."

"That's one way to put it."

I shake my head. "Sorry. I never really fit into the world of Manhattan as well as my ex-husband had hoped. And by Manhattan I mean, very specifically, his social circle."

Isaac nods. "It can be a hard one to crack."

"Yes," I say, and force my voice to lighten. "Do you know why they're so obsessed with monograms?"

"Monograms?"

"Yes," I say. I need to steer this conversation away from me and my divorce again. We end up there more often than I'd like, and I have the suspicion I'm the one who leads us there. The thought makes me feel pathetic. "They're everywhere here. It feels like every home we went to for dinner would have a couple monogram proudly embroidered on the guest towels."

He runs a hand along his jaw. "I think all the Winter towels are monogrammed. In the hotels, I mean. With the W."

I laugh. "Of course they are."

"It's a personal touch."

"Yes, very personal," I say, and take a long sip of my wine. "That's the personal service for you."

"Exactly. Some customers say that's important when choosing which hotel to stay at."

"So I've heard," I say. "Personally, I only look at the minibar."

He chuckles. "Does it need to be stocked with Chardonnay?"

"Five bottles, minimum," I say.

"Speaking of," he murmurs, and nods to my glass. "Time for a refill?"

My second glass of wine turns into a third, and his glass of brandy turns into two. And as we talk, he angles his body toward mine, and I realize a number of things about this man.

He's loyal to the company down to his very bones. His father is still on the board and he fully expects his brother's children to run it one day, if, as he puts it, they're not complete idiots.

A family legacy.

I also realize he truly does nothing but work. No wife and no girlfriend. And I wonder why that is, and if he's ever tried, and if so with whom. The man in front of me doesn't seem like he was made to live alone. No one is.

He's a good conversationalist. A great listener, and when he comments on my stories, it's tinged with a dry wit that surprises me.

I learn that his younger brother is part of the venture capitalist firm Acture, who owns and controls Exciteur.

That little factoid briefly blows my mind. I try very hard to keep my face professional, and years of training helps me succeed. The people who bought Exciteur had always been nameless and faceless in my mind. A vague and insanely wealthy conglomerate that likely had presidents on speed dial and four personal assistants each.

"Is that why you hired Exciteur?" I ask. My voice comes out casual, but my insides are anything but. That's why he's a special friend of the CEO.

Getting this project right isn't just a matter of professional pride. It'll end my career if I get it wrong.

"Yes," he says. "It's closer to mixing business with pleasure than I'd prefer, though. The two don't mesh well."

"That seems like a paradox, coming from the man who runs a family company."

He chuckles. "Oh, I'm aware of the irony. Trust me, managing the family is often far more difficult than managing the hotel."

I run a finger along the rim of my wineglass. "You must have... *insistent* family members."

"I do," he says.

I should end this, should excuse myself and call it a night, but I don't want to stop talking to him. Tonight his handsomeness is approachable, the CEO facade down somewhat, and an intimacy has settled over our corner of the hotel bar.

Next week he'll be a professional stranger again.

"I do too," I say. "Not to mention insistent acquaintances. There's a benefit in a few weeks that I've been badgered into attending by my tennis coach."

"Benefits," Isaac says, his mouth curling around the word like it tastes bad.

"Yes, exactly. But guess who'll be there?"

He pauses with his brandy halfway to his lips. "He will?"

"Yes. I haven't seen him since we signed the divorce papers."

"Oh," he says. "This wouldn't be the benefit for the Museum of Contemporary Art?"

"It is, yes. Did you get an invite too?" I shake my head. "Sorry, of course you did."

A slow smile stretches across his face. "I did, yes. I hadn't planned on going, but you've given me an idea."

"I have?"

"Yes. Let me take you."

My mouth falls open. "That would look like..."

"Yes. I know your ex-husband, Sophia. Not well, but I know what he was like in school, and I've heard about him since. Seeing me by your side will be a blow to his ego."

"You'd do that?" I ask. *For me?*

"He disgraced my hotel," Isaac says, voice as calm as if

49

we're discussing a business project. "So yes, I'm in the mood for a little payback."

The word flips over in my mind. Once, twice. *Payback.* To see his eyes widen in surprise when I walk in next to Isaac Winter. To make him feel just a smidge of something, be that jealousy or irritation or anger. To be the one in control.

So I touch my glass to Isaac's. "To payback."

6

ISAAC

I've seen marital bliss happen to friends, sure, but I've never been as up close and personal with it as in the last couple of years. It's cloying to anyone not involved in the happy twosome.

My sister-in-law is resting her hand in my brother's hair, right at the nape of his neck. It's a casual gesture.

Like we're not in the middle of a conversation about the holidays.

"We could do it in Montauk," Anthony says. Little Theo is asleep in his arms, a bundle of gray fabric and a tightly screwed-up face like he's concentrating very hard on sleeping. "The house is big enough for Mom and Dad, not to mention your family, Summer. All the dogs would fit, too."

Christmas is four months away, and the August air is still sweltering in New York City.

Welcome to my family, I think. My mother has been harassing everyone in the family text thread about our plans. Despite her having caterers on retainer and several houses to choose from, it's apparently, of the utmost importance that planning starts *now.*

"Oh, imagine the ocean at that time of year..." Summer

says, her voice dreamy. "It could be lovely. We could heat the pool, couldn't we, honey?"

Anthony nods. "Sure."

"We could use it like a jacuzzi on Christmas Eve. I could go out the week prior to set up decorations. I like this idea."

I run a hand along my jaw. "Sounds good. I'm flexible with whatever you guys want. I just can't be away from the city for too long."

Summer's eyes turn disapproving. "Isaac, you need to take more breaks. You haven't been out to Montauk more than a few weekends this summer."

"The company needs me," I say. "But I'd love to come out more often if I could."

My sister-in-law isn't satisfied. She sits down next to Anthony and places a tiny kiss on her son's forehead. "Isaac," she says, "please, please, just consider letting me give it a try. Just once. If you don't like it, I promise I'll never mention it again."

I groan. "That's what this is? An ambush? You feed me delicious food and wine, and then you attack."

"Consider it an intervention," she says.

I look at my brother. "Help."

Anthony laughs darkly. For all my occasional annoyance with my bubbly sister-in-law, that laugh, right there, is worth every pestering question she asks about my love life.

Anthony had been in a dark place after his diagnosis. His gradually deteriorating eyesight robbed him of joy long before it started robbing him of sight.

But Summer had restored that. She's helped him work through his hurt and fears until the future, while still painful, is once again something to look forward to. And the small son in his arms, the first baby in the family, has shown me a new side to my brother I never thought I'd see.

He's happy.

And I'll never stop being in Summer's debt for that.

"I'm sorry," Anthony says. "But I think I'm on my wife's side on this one."

I narrow my eyes at him. "You would never have accepted this yourself, you traitor."

"I did," he says. "Didn't exactly work out the way she predicted, but it gave results. Just unexpected ones."

Summer nods. "That's right. Isaac, there are a ton of women I think you'd match really well with. I have a shortlist prepared."

This again.

She'd tried twice before, and each time was more insistent than the last. Together with her aunt, she runs an elite match-making company for New York's high society.

That's their tagline and not my words.

Their hands-on approach and careful curation of partners leads to a very high percentage of successful matches. Or, at least, that's what I've been told several times by Summer herself.

I look at my sleeping nephew. He's clearly not being fussy enough of a baby if Summer still has the energy to think about my love life.

"Isaac?" she says. "There's a beautiful, newly divorced woman who just signed up for the service. She has a good job, a stellar social life, and I think you two would really hit it off."

My eyebrows rise. "Really? What's her name?"

"Valerie Simmons. Do you want to know more? I could pull up her profile."

I feel myself deflate at the unfamiliar name. "No."

"Oh." Summer sighs and then shakes her head. "It can be something super casual. Dinner here at our house, just the four of us."

Anthony snorts. "Well, that's not casual at all."

I look at him with gratitude. "Exactly," I say. "Look, I appreciate it, but I can handle my own love life. Thank you, but no thanks."

She raises an eyebrow. "And are you? Handling your own love life?"

"Anthony," I say.

But my brother doesn't come to my defence again. He looks at me with the same dark eyes I see in a mirror. "Isaac," he says. "Honestly, man. You gotta get out there. You're living the life of a workaholic monk or a princess locked into a tower."

"A princess," I repeat slowly, "locked in a tower?"

He reaches for his glass of brandy. "Yeah, that was a metaphor. The point is, you're living half of a life."

"Half of a life," I murmur. The words feel like a slap. The life I live is one dedicated to them. To the company. To the *family*.

To the little son he's holding in his lap right now. If he wants to have a piece of his heritage, one of us needs to ensure there's a heritage left, and Anthony made it clear he doesn't want to be a part of the day-to-day.

Doesn't stop any of them from benefiting, though. It doesn't stop my parents from booking out The Ivy free of charge for events, or my brother from drawing a monthly salary from a nominal position on the board.

But God forbid I spend my life ensuring any of that's even possible.

"Yes," Anthony says. I doubt he notices my sharp silence. I've become good at keeping my occasional resentments hidden. "The hotel is doing great. The business can take care of itself far more than you'd let it. It's time you took care of you, too."

"Right," I say, my hand curving over the armrest of my chair. "And both of you are convinced that means finding a life partner?"

"Yes," my brother says, "because you just said the words *finding a life partner*. I just want you to get laid consistently, man, and have fun doing things that aren't spreadsheets."

I chuckle. "The offer is appreciated, Summer. But I don't need any help."

She gives me a wide, serviceable smile. I've seen it work well for her before. "When was the last time you went on a date?" she asks like she's already interviewing me for her matchmaking service.

"I'm actually seeing someone right now," I say.

"You are?" Anthony asks. "Define seeing someone. Because if it's just—"

"Anthony," Summer murmurs.

He gives us both a half grin. "You know I'm right. Both of you. Because there's a difference."

As if I didn't know. As if the woman I used to see briefly, casually, wasn't *different* than actually dating someone. Beverly and I had a very clear understanding. Always cordial, never dramatic, and never any expectations.

"I know there is," I say. "But this is more than that, even if it's early."

Summer's blue eyes are narrowed on mine like she's a detective interrogating a suspect. "What's her name?"

"Sophia," I say.

"What's her hair color?"

"Brown."

"How long has it been going on?"

"Just a few weeks." I reach for my brandy. It burns going down my throat, along with the last of my good sense. *Fuck.* I shouldn't have said her name. There was no reason to, and it isn't right to her.

My brother looks from my grim expression to my newly drained glass. "And it's not going well," he says. "Is it?"

"It's complicated."

"But you like her," he says and leans back on the couch like he's cracked the case.

"Yes," I say and wonder how the hell I ended up in this situation. The indignity. Not that I wouldn't...

Jesus. This is why it's become hard to spend time around my family lately. I'm aware they have these conversations behind my back, and the knowledge grates like a thorn beneath my skin.

Summer doesn't look convinced. "All right. If you think this could be serious, I'll lay off. But my offer stands. One of these days, I'm going to organize a date and just text you the time and place."

"You wouldn't dare," I say.

"I would," she says, and I know she means it. My sister-in-law is many things, but timid is usually not one of them. "I can even set the date at The Ivy so you don't have to go anywhere, and I'll make sure it doesn't run longer than half an hour."

I rise from my armchair. "This has been a lovely evening. Thank you both."

Anthony grins. "Yeah, I'd leave now, too, if I was you."

"You would have left an hour ago," I say.

He chuckles. "Yeah, and I wouldn't have been as nice about it as you are."

"Mhm."

He stands, shifting the sleeping baby to his other arm. "The women she set me up with weren't for me," he says, nodding toward Summer. "I had my sights set elsewhere. But they might be for you."

I put my hand on his shoulder and give him the most aggressively polite of smiles. "You're so lucky you're holding my nephew right now."

He smiles crookedly. "You haven't punched me since we were kids."

"Clearly an oversight on my end."

I leave their townhouse, the heavy door falling shut behind me. Summer and Anthony are living in one of the family's houses. It had been our grandparents' once, and under Anthony and Summer's stewardship it's been lovingly restored.

Not that they spend a lot of time there during the warmer

months, anyway. My brother had bought a Montauk house a few years back, not far from our parents' summer house, in an area where we'd spent most of our holidays as kids.

I roll my head and start walking back to the hotel.

Seeing my brother happy has lifted a burden off my shoulders I didn't know I'd been carrying. He's now once again the person I remember from my childhood.

I rub a hand over my chest. His damn eyesight, though. It's a problem without a solution, an issue I can't fix, and not a day goes by when it doesn't bother me, even if he has come to terms with it.

My mind lingers on Summer's hand on my brother's neck, casually possessive. And then I see Sophia's eyes, bright and teasing, as she says something she suspects I'll disagree with.

I shouldn't have said her name. Shouldn't have implicated her in my white lie.

Shouldn't have lied at all.

I pull up my phone and scroll through my emails as I walk. None from her or her team.

It's been a week since DC, and the Exciteur team hasn't been back at the hotel. Why would they? They've gotten the full tour. They've spoken to all my employees. They're working on the pitch now, just as instructed. I have no reason to talk to her or contact her.

Around me, New York is abuzz.

It's early in the evening still, the weather oppressively hot, and the city's inhabitants who haven't left it for greener pastures are all outside. Sitting on stoops and drinking in the park. A teenage boy skates past me, upbeat pop music pounding from a speaker in his backpack.

I shove my hands in my pockets. Walking had been the right choice. *Sophia,* I think. *Sorry, but you saved me tonight.*

When I finally make it to the hotel, I find it every bit as busy as the city streets I've just left behind. I walk through a group of newly arrived tourists in the lobby. I listen to them talk to one another in a language I don't understand. One of the youngsters lies in one of our chaise lounges, half-asleep, a teddy bear tucked beneath her. Must have been a long international flight.

I stop by the offices. Andrej is there, looking through the systems.

"Everything all right?"

"Yes, sir. We're almost at capacity."

"Things running smoothly?"

"Yes," he says. "For the restaurants, too. They're all fully booked."

I nod. There are few day-to-day issues that require my oversight. The machine has always been designed to run that way. "Good. Make sure you get something to eat if you're working the late shift," I say. "Get Flake's and put it on the company."

"Thank you, sir," he says. "There is one other thing…"

"Yes?"

Andrej frowns like he's not sure about his next words. "A woman checked in earlier today."

"Oh?"

"She's from the Exciteur team, sir. The ones you're working with for the potential expansion." He shrugs. "Sorry, I heard Andrew talk about it."

"That's okay. What's her name?"

"Sophia, sir. Sophia Bishop."

My hand tightens around the doorframe. "Miss Bishop checked into the Winter Hotel?"

"Yes."

"What room?"

Andrej doesn't look fazed by my question. It's one of the many things he's great at. He juggles the curveballs of hospitality like he was born to it. The hotel could be on fire, and I know he would call the fire department in a calm, orderly fashion before beginning the evacuation protocols.

"1402," he says. "Standard double, ensuite, courtyard view."

She's in one of our cheapest rooms. It's still good. Solid standard. But...

"Is the penthouse suite booked tonight?"

Andrej doesn't need to check his systems for that. The entire hotel staff knows whether or not the penthouse suite is occupied because if it is, it's usually a guest of worldwide renown.

"No," he says, "and not tomorrow night, either."

"Upgrade her to the penthouse."

His eyes widen. There's a pause before he answers. "Yes, sir. Right away. I'll send someone to her room to—"

"I'm on it." I reach for a key card and code it to the penthouse suite. "It's cleaned?"

"Of course, sir."

I take the elevator to the fourteenth floor. It's intrusive, what I'm doing. I know that. And yet, the idea has taken too firm of a hold in my mind to be shaken off.

I'll atone for it in the morning. I walk down the corridor in search of 1402. It's been a long time since I've been in this corridor; since I've been in any corridor apart from my own and the admin floor.

I give the door two sharp knocks. "Miss Bishop?"

There's a shuffle inside, silence, and then her voice. "Yes? Is everything all right?"

"It's Isaac Winter," I say.

There's absolute silence on the other side.

Then her voice comes, just a tad frantic. "Just one minute!"

"There's no rush," I add. "I know I'm bothering you. Just wanted to offer a complimentary—"

The door opens and there she is, standing in the hotel's fluffy robe. Her hair is damp around her shoulders, and she's wearing those glasses again.

Her skin looks clean and soft. "Hello," she says.

"Hi."

"I'm sorry about this."

I frown. "About what?"

"Staying here without letting you or your team know." She shrugs, an elegant motion. "I feel like I just invited myself."

"It's a hotel, not my apartment."

Her lips curve into a half smile. "Yes, I suppose. But it's hard not to think of it like that. Your name is on the building, after all."

A part of my brain is occupied with very unhelpful thoughts. The awareness of her robe and what might be beneath it is like a hammer beating against my skull.

"An upgrade," I say. "We'd like to offer you a complimentary upgrade."

"Oh." She looks back into her room. I glimpse the corner of a queen-size bed. "This room is plenty good for me."

"To the penthouse suite."

Her eyes widen. "Oh."

"Consider it research, Miss Bishop. That suite has a lot of history, you know. And you could take pictures for your team."

She looks from her bag on the floor to me, and then the decision is made, her face settling into professionalism. "You're right, I'd love that. Let me pack?"

"Whenever you're ready," I say and pull the door closed to give her privacy.

The business excuse was a good one. It's not untrue, either. The penthouse suite is one of the things we're most famous for, at least within a certain circle. Seeing it would be helpful. I just hadn't thought of it until I stood here.

Five minutes later, the door opens again. She's in a pair of black pants and a tank top, leaving her tanned arms bare.

"All right, lead the way," she says brightly. She motions to her wet hair, braided down her back. "Sorry for this, by the way. I enjoyed the spa area earlier."

"You used the pool?"

"Yes."

I reach for her weekend bag, and she lets me take it. "Thanks," she says.

It's a gesture I've done a thousand times. But tonight, it's hers, and not Summer's or my mother's or a date's.

We walk toward the elevators. "Did you choose to stay here for research?" I ask. "If so, I wish you would have spoken to the team. We would never have charged you for the night."

She shakes her head. "Oh, I couldn't."

"Of course, you could."

"I already enjoyed your hospitality in DC."

I call for the elevator. The penthouse suite has its own, but it's located half a building away. "So, you didn't check in for research, then?"

"Partly," she says. "I've wanted to swim in the art deco pool since you showed it to me. The vaulted ceiling is even more stunning when you're floating on your back."

"I can imagine," I say, my hand tightening around the handle of her bag.

"I just want to make sure we get this right," she says. "This pitch."

"Your dedication is admirable." I hit the code in the elevator. It overrides the standard operations and will take us up to the top floor without interruption. Not directly into the suite, though. That exclusive elevator is only available behind the desk in the lobby.

"Thank you for the upgrade," she says beside me.

"You haven't seen the room yet."

"Oh, I don't have to," she says. "I already know it's going to be incredible."

"It sure is something," I say.

The elevator falls silent, and in the quiet, I can hear her soft breathing. She smells like clean shampoo and jasmine.

"Thank you," she murmurs.

"For what?"

"The drinks, down in DC. I had a nice time."

"Thanks for the company," I say. And I mean it.

"Did you just get back from work?" she asks.

I shake my head. "No, but part of it sure felt like work."

She chuckles. "A family thing?"

"Yes." The elevator stops, and I press the button to keep the doors open, gesturing for her to get out first. "I meant what I said. My family can be… very persistent."

"Somehow," she says, "I don't think you have any problem fending them off."

That makes me smile. "It's harder when I know they mean well."

"Oh, yes. Makes you feel terrible when you have to say no. That's how my sister guilted me into taking care of one of her kittens."

"A kitten?"

"Yes." She smiles over her shoulder. "I'm still trying to figure out how I ended up saying yes."

"So you have a roommate?"

She chuckles. "Yes. I upgraded from Percy."

I bite my tongue to keep from smiling. If there's one thing I'm always willing to listen to, it's her putting down her asshole ex.

I hadn't been there when he checked out after the first time I met Sophia. But I had watched a recording of him cursing out my staff—very thoroughly—as they threatened to press charges for public indecency.

I stop outside the door to the suite. There's only one on this floor, and it doesn't have a number on it. "It's a bit big for one person," I warn her. "If you decide you want to switch to a smaller suite, you tell me. Any free suite is yours tonight."

"Oh, I'm sure this will be fine."

I push the door open for her. "Take a look and see."

7

SOPHIA

My goal for today had been a simple one. Swim a few lovely laps, use the spa, and sit in the sauna. Then I'd order room service from The Ivy, most likely the truffle burger. And then I planned on passing out dead in the most comfortable bed I can imagine to the sound of an old sitcom playing on the TV.

I had hoped, too, that I wouldn't think about my ex-husband too much, either. It would have been our fourth wedding anniversary today.

And I'd gone to the very hotel I'd caught him cheating in. But not in my room, at least. I know exactly where he was. 1714.

It felt full circle. It felt better than sitting at home.

But the night hadn't gone as planned.

Isaac is quiet beside me, as if he's taking in my reaction to the suite he's upgraded me to. Only I'm not sure suite is the right word.

Mansion, is my first thought.

The foyer is tastefully decorated, sparingly furnished, and leads into the living room.

And the living room is tremendous.

The penthouse must be a duplex, because the living room's ceiling is three times the height of a normal one. The entire wall is covered in beautifully trimmed windows that look out over the glittering city. Tasteful white sofas are arranged around a giant marble coffee table. On it is a vase of fresh flowers, their scent spreading throughout the room.

"Oh my God," I whisper.

"It's big," Isaac says. I hear him set down my bag and move around behind me. Opening doors, perhaps. I don't know. I can't look away from the wide expanse of oriental carpet and the open doorway leading into a study.

A study. In a hotel room.

"I can't imagine who's stayed here," I say. "Presidents? Superstars?"

"Yes, and yes." His voice comes from somewhere far away. "The security protocol it takes to host heads of state is a bitch, honestly, but we have it down to a science now."

"Wow." I run my hand over the back of one of the couches. "This place is old."

"Yes. We've renovated the penthouse suite three times, but it still has some of its original features." He's on the steps to the stairway. "Sophia, I want to show you something."

I follow him up the stairs. "You must have had old movie stars staying here, right? During the black-and-white film era?"

"All of them," he says. "Diana Dunne took that famous photo here. You know the shot of her with the martini glass and pearl necklace?"

"Yes," I say. "It's only one of the most iconic images ever taken."

He pushes open the door to the upstairs bathroom. "It was taken in this tub."

The room is familiar. The lip of the giant standing tub, its gold wrought legs, and the skyline of New York behind it. The entire bathroom is clad in subtle marble and lightened with inlaid sconces.

"Oh my God," I whisper.

Isaac's watching me. "The view from the tub is one of this suite's best features."

"How much is the penthouse per night?" I ask. Then, I shake my head. "Please don't tell me. I can't possibly accept spending the night here."

He closes the door to the bathroom and heads to the stairs again. I follow him, catching a glimpse of the master bedroom on the way. The bed is enormous.

Gigantic.

"You can," he says, "and you will. The suite is empty tonight regardless. And maybe it'll change your mind about the pitch. This is the old-world glamour we're famous for, after all. Give the new chain some of this elegance."

I chuckle. "You're trying to win our argument?"

"Of course, I am, Miss Bishop."

"Sophia," I say. "We said… Sophia, when we're like this."

What exactly *like this* means is unclear, and yet it makes perfect sense. When we're alone.

When we're talking like equals.

He smiles. "Okay. Sophia."

"Thank you for this. I don't know how I'll ever repay you."

"Blow my mind with the pitch."

"I will, I promise."

His eyes are dark with intensity. "Oh, I have no doubt about that."

I sink down on one of the couches. "I appreciate the vote of confidence."

Isaac takes a few steps back toward the door. The suit he's in looks near-black in the dimmed lighting. "Enjoy your stay."

"Thanks," I say. "Oh… wait a second."

"Yes?"

"Do you want a nightcap?"

The presumptuous words hang in the air between us,

filling the giant suite with tension. My hand curls around the plush fabric of a pillow.

But then he nods. "Yes."

I walk to the well-stocked minibar, but in this place, absolutely nothing deserves the prefix *mini*. The bottles are full-sized.

Isaac joins me, opening the built-in wine cooler with the ease of someone who's been in this suite a lot. He pulls out a bottle of white, and I catch the label. It's a Chardonnay.

"You remembered," I murmur.

"Of course." He pours me a glass and himself one of brandy before we settle on the oversized couches. I want to draw my legs up beneath me and resist the impulse. The suite is too pristine and filled with too much history. It feels like I'm on a movie set or at a museum.

Look, but don't touch.

"Will you tell me more about this suite?"

He takes a sip from his glass and clears his throat. "What do you want to know?"

"Who's stayed here?"

"You want names?" he asks, an eyebrow rising.

"A few," I say. "Maybe not too many, or I'll never be able to fall asleep in that bed."

He chuckles and stretches his legs out. "We change mattresses pretty frequently, especially in this suite."

My mouth drops open. "Because it gets so…"

"To make sure the springs are fresh," he says. "Get your mind out of the gutter."

I laugh. "God, the things I was picturing."

"I can only imagine." He taps a finger against the tumbler, and it makes a soft clicking sound. "All right, so you want some names. How about these…" he says and goes on to recite a long list.

My eyes grow wider with every single one. "Oh," I say, "my *God*."

His lips curve. "Yeah. It sounds a bit unreal all laid out like that."

"The last two you mentioned... did you have to sanitize the suite after they were done?"

Isaac snorts. "My dad had the whole suite reupholstered and scrubbed down with bleach. This is confidential, but every glass surface had traces of cocaine on it."

"Oh my God."

"It was the nineties," he says, "and they were the biggest stars in the world at the time."

"Do you interact with them? The guests who stay here, I mean?"

"Not often." He looks down at the glass in his hands. "That sort of thing loses its appeal pretty fast. Besides, guests of that caliber aren't here to talk to the staff."

"You're not exactly staff."

"Oh," he says, and there's humor in his voice, "to a foreign president visiting for a UN summit, or to a young pop star with an entourage, I am very much the staff."

"I guess I've never thought of it like that." Isaac and his family are giants on the New York stage, and he's a giant in the world of hospitality, but his name might not be one every household knows.

I look away from his dark eyes. The coffee table sports a few huge books, along with the vase of flowers.

"Look," I say. "The Winter coffee-table book would look stunning on here."

He chuckles. "Always working, Sophia?"

"It's hard to turn it off sometimes."

"I know all about that," he says, and I know he means it. "Although, you might just have me beat here. You came to the hotel to spend a night off just for research."

I run a hand along my neck. My hair is drying, and without a blow drier, it's quickly becoming a frizzy mess, braid or no braid.

"Well, I wasn't just here to do research."

"You weren't?"

I shrug. "Well, today is technically my wedding anniversary."

His eyebrows rise. "It is?"

"Yes, and it's the first since the divorce, and I didn't want to sit at home. I figured that using the lovely spa you'd shown me and ordering room service would make the day... better."

It had also been something to placate my mother and my sister. Both had called today, and I love them for their thoughtfulness. But there's only so many questions about how I'm feeling that I can handle. *You could come back home,* had been said by both.

I'd sent them a picture of the spa area and told them I was treating myself. My mom had responded with six thumbs up and a heart emoji.

"I would have thought this particular hotel would be a difficult place to be," Isaac says, "especially on an anniversary."

I look down at my wine. "I've already been here for work, and that's taken the edge off the memory. Besides, I can't let him ruin the best hotel in New York for me, can I?"

"You know, I agree with that," Isaac says. But there's a frown marring his face, making the lines around his eyes deeper.

Maybe I've overstepped. Here I am, talking about myself and my divorce. Again.

I'm like a broken record.

I take a long sip of my wine, the *sorry* hovering on my tongue.

"Look," Isaac says, and his voice is rougher around the edges. "About the thing we spoke about last week. In DC."

"Oh?"

His eyes are steady on mine. "I suggested we go together to the benefit in a few weeks, where your ex-husband will be a guest, too."

Heat rushes to my cheeks. He must think I'm pathetically

hung up on Percy, a man he's made clear he doesn't particularly respect.

"I remember," I say.

The benefit is one of the few social things over the past months I haven't been able to get out of. And now, I don't want to, either. I want to show up and prove... well. What, I don't even know.

That I'm still here. That I'm doing great. That Percy made the biggest mistake of his goddamn life.

"I just want to say," Isaac continues, "that the offer still stands."

"I couldn't possibly ask you to do that."

"It would be helpful for us," he says, and his jaw works. "I guess, I have somewhat of an... unconventional proposal."

"You do?"

"Being seen with you would benefit me as well."

My mind goes perfectly blank. I can't think of a single reason why that might be. My social capital in these circles is a pebble to his mountain, and lesser still after the divorce.

"It would? Why?"

"I mentioned my family," he says. "The insistent ones."

"I remember."

"Well, they're under the misapprehension that I don't date. Ever."

"But you do?" I ask. It's not meant to sound incredulous, but the conversation is taking a turn I can't quite follow.

His mouth thins. "Yes, I do. Just not very publicly."

"Right," I say. "Okay."

"Let me bring you as my date," he says, "and we'll make a statement. To your ex-husband, and to my family and friends."

The idea is outrageous. Inappropriate on as many levels as this hotel has floors. I can't. I know I can't. And yet the part of me I'm not proud of—the petty, revengeful part that still replays the image of Percy on top of his mistress in that hotel room—sees this for the opportunity it is.

I swallow. "Are you absolutely sure it would serve your purposes, as well?"

He chuckles. "Yes. Trust me, you'd be doing me a favor."

"What about our work?"

"It won't be affected," he says. "I can keep the two separate."

"Well, you said you prefer to keep business and pleasure separate."

He lifts an eyebrow. "Pleasure?"

"Oh, never mind. I guess this will technically also be business. Just of a different sort?"

"Yes," he says, and his voice sounds gruffer. "Just business."

"People at my company might find out."

"I don't think it would be a problem," he says. "You're not doing anything wrong by dating a project client. If anything, we can say that we used the events to talk more about the pitch. It's networking. I know it's big in the consulting industry."

"It is," I admit. "Meetings are often held... anywhere. I have a colleague who likes to have them on the golf course."

He nods. "Right."

"Gosh, can we do this? Really? I would love to. Just to see the look on Percy's face..."

"I promise you this, too. If it ever becomes a problem, I'll call St. Clair and set the record straight. He'll accept that the lapse in judgement was on my side."

I look at the man opposite me. There's not a hair out of place on his head, and the intensity in his eyes tells the tale of a man who lives and breathes control.

Lapse in judgement and *Isaac Winter* don't belong in the same sentence.

"Okay," I say and make what might be the second biggest mistake of my life. But I've already made the biggest, and that was saying "I do" on this very day four years ago.

There's something freeing about having had your life fall apart. After that, there's very little else to worry about losing.

"What do you think?" he asks.

I take a deep breath. "I'd love to go with you to the benefit. If you need to sell the image of us as... dates to your family, I promise to uphold my side."

"As do I," he says, and there's a dark promise in his words. "I know how to make Percy jealous."

I have to stand to reach him, and he rises too, accepting my outstretched hand. It's the first time we've touched since we shook hands weeks ago, surrounded by our teams.

His hand is strong and warm around mine. "Just business," he says and shakes my hand.

A shiver races up my spine. "Yes. Just business... and revenge."

He releases my hand. It's a slow slide of his palm against mine, and then he steps away, voice curved around the edges with a smile. "Always a pleasure working with you, Sophia."

8

SOPHIA

I turn, looking at myself in the floor-to-ceiling mirror in the lobby of my apartment building. The dress is good. It's floor-length and dusty blue, setting off my faint summer tan and fitting for the benefit's dress code.

I'd had a salon blow-out earlier today, and my hair looks glossy beneath the lights. It's grown longer this summer, and I haven't kept up with the trims. Gone is my sleek shoulder-length hairdo, consigned to history, along with the person I was when I sported it.

Makeup, clean and minimal.

I look... appropriate.

I take a deep breath. And then, I take another. All week, I'd been so sure I wouldn't really be anxious when the time came. It's been almost a year, and I no longer carry his name or his ring. I don't bear the weight of his expectations or my own suspicions. They'd been so heavy of a burden that I didn't realize I'd suffered under it until it disappeared.

But here I am, and anxiety is a pounding beat in my chest, making my stomach turn. It seems there are parts of myself that remain foreign, even to me.

I look at my watch. Isaac will be here soon.

He'd insisted on picking me up. Our emails over the past week have been quick and focused on the practicalities.

The intimacy we'd shared over drinks didn't carry over into logistical texts between meetings. And now? I need to pretend I'm dating him.

But the real problem is that, somehow, I think that might just be the easiest part of the entire evening.

A black town car pulls up outside my building, and Isaac steps out. He's wearing a snug dinner jacket that looks tailored to his form. "Sophia," he says, and then his eyes drop down to my dress, doing a slow sweep of the tight bodice and flowing skirt. "You look… stunning."

"Thank you," I say, "but we don't have an audience yet."

He pushes the car door open for me. "I'm not pretending."

I slide into the car and watch as he follows suit. A warm, spicy scent reaches me. His cologne. I tighten my hands around my clutch. "This will be a networking event for you," I say. "Right?"

He nods to the driver to set off, and the car glides smoothly out into the New York traffic. "Yes. It's hard for them not to be, honestly."

"You must go to a ton of them. How do you stand it?"

"Practice," he says. But then he looks over, and there's a teasing glint in his eyes. "I've had a few approaches over the years."

"Tell me about them."

"Well, I'll admit that when I was young and green, I abused the open bar."

"You did?"

"I'll take your surprise as a compliment," he says. "But yes. I was young and asked to go to dinners and parties that were… well. Not very engaging."

"They bored you to death."

"Yes," he says. "The open bar was the only thing that made them tolerable."

"I imagine your parents weren't too happy about that?"

He snorts. "They didn't mind, but my grandfather did. He put a stop to it."

"So, you had to move on to tactic number two."

"Yes, which was to network as aggressively as possible."

"You threw yourself into the game?"

"No," he says, eyes teasing. "I mastered it."

"Wow. The confidence!"

He chuckles. "I did that for almost a decade. It opened a lot of doors."

"Oh, because so many of them were closed before?"

He raises an eyebrow. "Are you implying that I was born with privilege?"

"No," I say. "I would never."

"Good." But then he leans his head back against the seat and sighs. "I was, though, and I'm aware of how fortunate I've been. But I still needed to… make *me* memorable. Many of the people I spoke to in my early twenties knew my grandfather, my aunt, or my dad. Not me."

"You needed to establish yourself," I say.

He nods. "But networking that aggressively is… tedious."

"Oh, I know. I did the same thing when I first arrived in New York, and then when I got married."

"Did your ex help?"

"A bit," I say, and my stomach gives a nervous lurch at the reminder. I'd almost forgotten we're heading somewhere he'll be, too. "I take it you moved on from that tactic? What do you do now?"

"Now, I wait for people to come to me," he says. It's not said with arrogance. It's just a matter-of-fact statement made by a man who knows his worth. "And I never stay past midnight."

"Like Cinderella," I murmur.

"Exactly like her," he says. "Except I make it a point to keep my shoes on."

The seriousness in his voice makes me laugh. His humor and sarcasm is surprising, so at odds with the man he presents as. "Does that make me the pumpkin?" I ask. "In this analogy?"

"I think the car is," he says. "But considering the other options are mice and barnyard animals, I think it's best we end the analogy here."

I dig my teeth into my lower lip to keep from laughing. "Thank you for not calling me a horse."

"You're welcome," he says in a tone of deep seriousness, and my laughter bursts free.

We arrive at the museum. The city is dark around us but alight with life and music. The benefit has attracted a lot of people, both guests and passersby, who occupy the steps.

Isaac offers me his arm. It's unfamiliar, touching him like this for longer than a brief handshake.

"Ready?" he murmurs.

I know what awaits us. Who's waiting inside those giant double-doors, beckoning in the warm light of the chandeliers. My former in-laws will be there. Former acquaintances and friends who chose Percy's side. Everyone from my old life... before it imploded.

"Yes," I say. "I am."

Isaac's eyes linger on mine for a moment. "All right. Let's do this, then, Miss Bishop."

"Sophia," I say quietly.

"That's right," he murmurs. "Sophia."

We walk up the worn stone steps and into the golden light of the chandelier-filled lobby. On a normal New York day, this hall would be filled with elementary school classes and tourists speaking languages I couldn't understand, the commotion all echoing up the vaulted ceiling.

And tonight, it's only for the invited guests.

Guests who, the organizers hoped, would be wealthy and generous enough to dip their hands into overflowing pockets and support the museum.

Somewhere in the distance, I catch the mellifluous tones of

a string quartet. It's interrupted by the clicking of expensive shoes against the marble floor.

"What's your step one?" I whisper to Isaac.

He leans his head my way. "My step one?"

"Yes. Of your current networking plan."

"Ah," he says, and his voice warms. "Letting people come to me doesn't require a lot of work on my part. That's the beauty of it."

"Do you stand in a corner and look intimidating?"

He chuckles. "That would make my life a lot easier. Unfortunately, I do have to look approachable for the method to work."

I make my voice teasing. "Do you think you'll find your prince here, Cinderella?"

"I haven't spotted him yet," Isaac says. "Will he be the tall, dark, and handsome one?"

"Most likely," I say and can't resist the rest. "But make sure you avoid mirrors, or you might get confused."

There's silence from the man beside me. But then he chuckles, the sound a bit hoarse. "Well, well," he says finally.

We head toward the bar. I walk beside him and glance around. Lizzie and Tate Winthrop are here. So is Maud Astor. Her eyes widen when she sees me, and then she finds her composure and gives me a quick smile hello.

She's best friends with Percy's sister, and I've spent a lot of summer weekends with her and her husband. I've hugged her when she's cried, and took care of her dog one weekend, and played a lot of charades on opposite teams.

She'd dropped me like a bad habit after the divorce.

But then she clocks who I'm walking beside. Her eyes linger on Isaac before returning to me and then darting quickly away.

Petty satisfaction wells up inside me. It's not a noble emotion, but it sure is human, and I'm going to revel in all of it tonight.

"Chardonnay," Isaac asks, "or champagne?"

"Champagne, please."

He hands me a tall flute and takes one for himself. Flutes. Not coupes. My mother-in-law would have commented on that. She had gifted Percy and me a set of twenty-five Cristal Champagne coupes for our wedding and insisted I never use flutes.

The hag.

"Sophia?" he asks.

"Yes? Sorry."

"Are you all right?"

"Yes," I say and force a smile. "You know, it surprised me when I first came to New York how important events like these are for one's job."

"Oh?"

"Yes. I'd thought, naively perhaps, that business was done during office hours. A handshake in a conference room, a phone call or an email sent. But it's not."

"No," Isaac says, "not always."

"It's a shame it's tacky to bring business cards to benefits," I say, looking out over the crowd. "It would make remembering people's names the next day a hell of a lot easier."

Isaac breaks out into surprised laughter, the arm beneath mine trembling with it. And when he speaks, his voice is warm. "It's a wonder how alike we think sometimes."

I feel warm. "You know, great minds often do."

"I can't tell you," he says, "how often I've struggled to remember the name of someone on Monday morning after a weekend of these things."

"Might be a bit awkward when you verbally agreed to build a hotel together with someone you can't call?"

He nods. "Exactly," he says, "although I save things that big for when I have lawyers present."

I look around the room at the gentlemen in tuxes and women in floor-length gowns. Isaac and I blend in perfectly. "I think there are a fair amount of lawyers present," I say.

"Probably, but I bet there's not a single practicing one."

"You don't think at least one of the couples invited their divorce lawyer along?"

"I don't know," he says, and looks down at me. "Did you?"

I take a sip of champagne. It feels bubbly on my tongue, adding to the symphony inside of me. "No. She was excellent, expensive as hell, and I never want to see her again."

"I think that's the mark of a job well done for a lawyer."

"Yes. Quite the opposite of you, the emperor of hospitality."

He chuckles. "Yes. If my customers never returned, I'd have a serious problem."

Isaac's eyes are light on mine, lighter than I've seen them before. There's gold mingled with the dark brown, flecks of them forming a ring around his pupils.

He smiles. "Although, you— ah. We have incoming."

My stomach tightens. "Who is it?"

"The vultures are circling," he says, but his tone is amused. "My aunt and uncle."

"Oh." *Showtime.* I smile, at the ready, and realize that we never decided how long we've been dating for or how we met.

But they don't ask, even if they're curious. It's there in their eyes, flicking between Isaac and me. And they're not alone.

Isaac's strategy works. It's not long until we're weaving through the throngs of people who come up to talk to him.

He knows nearly everyone by name.

I mention it to him, and he gives me a wry smile. "I've been in this game a long time."

We stop by the blind auction. Items are listed one by one, and each has a box beside it. Guests are expected to bid on them blindly, dropping their offers into the box, with the highest bid announced as the winner later in the evening.

Isaac and I walk side by side down the line. I watch in amusement as he bids on half of the items.

"A vintage bottle of champagne," I say. "Are you a collector?"

He shakes his head. "No."

"Hmm. And a private cooking class by a world-renowned sushi chef... are you trying to up your skill set?"

He sends an exasperated glance my way. "No. When would I have the time to do any of these things?"

"And yet," I say, sweeping my hand at the ludicrous sum he's currently writing on a scrap of paper.

"It's expected of me," he says. "The committee will read through all of the names. I have to be on at least some of them."

"Are you trying to win?"

"It would look good if I did," he admits and then smiles wryly. "But I'd rather win the champagne than... a couple's spa retreat."

I laugh. "I can't imagine you taking a weekend off to lie in a Jacuzzi, but I'm sure you'd enjoy it if you ever let yourself."

He leans in closer, voice warm by my ear. "I think," he says, "that I might, too, but it depends entirely on the company."

Somewhere between my second glass of champagne and the hors d'oeuvres, I make the cardinal sin of relaxing. I'm so busy pretending to be a couple with Isaac, standing close by his side and sliding smoothly in and out of the conversation with strangers, that I forgot who might be here.

Who I'm here for.

And when you let down your guard, the wolves descend. It's the second law of New York, and I learned it quickly after I arrived. The first is to never, ever walk as anything but at a brisk pace.

I spot my former mother-in-law first.

Celine Browne is holding court by an old fresco, her diamond earrings catching the light beneath her tasteful perm.

My breathing comes faster.

This is the woman who'd begged me to come to my senses right after I'd found her son in bed with another woman. When I said leaving him *was* me finally coming to my senses, she'd said she was disappointed I valued my wedding vows so little.

Oh, because your son lives by them? I'd asked, and she'd turned pink with anger.

This was two days before she unlocked the door to Percy's and my apartment without telling me first and started packing up our wedding china, the champagne coupes, and the set of silver spoons Percy had been gifted at birth. Celine's pointed looks had made it very clear that this was an Insult, capital I, planned and orchestrated. And I was to bear this Insult humbly, as the failure she now made it clear she thought I was, while she not-so-subtly reminded me of the prenup.

These are heirlooms, she'd said, packing up the spoons. *I'd hate for them to end up outside of the family.*

I was a failure *and* a potential thief.

Isaac's voice is quiet. "Sophia, are you okay?"

"Yes," I say. "Absolutely. Yes."

He looks down at my empty glass. "Would you like another?"

"Please."

And keep them coming.

He takes the glass gingerly from my fingers, which are cramped around the thin stem. "I'll be back," he says. "Then, we'll do another round at the blind auction."

"Yippie," I whisper. He rewards me with a smile, just the slighest curve to his lips. It feels like a victory. All of his expressions do.

I watch his retreating back through the crowd and wonder why I don't remember seeing him at events like this before. I can't imagine laying eyes on Isaac Winter and not having the memory burned into my mind.

I catch Maud standing next to Celine, one of the many

rapt listeners to one of my former mother-in-law's embroidered tales. Probably about the one time she dined in the same restaurant as JFK.

I look away. And that's when I see him.

Standing right next to *her*.

Together.

9

SOPHIA

Percy is wearing his wedding tux.

I recognize it immediately because I was the one who picked it out and suggested alterations to the tailor. His reddish-blond hair is cut shorter than it was the last time I saw him. His skin is deeply tanned from the summer. I imagine he's spent most of it at his parents' house in the Hamptons.

My stomach feels like it's at sea, with a storm whipping up mile-high waves. The winds pick up when I focus on the woman beside him.

Shorter than him by a solid head, dainty in frame and face. Her strawberry-blonde hair is in a classic updo.

He's here with Scarlett.

The last time I'd seen her, she'd been naked and wrapped around my husband.

I can't tear my eyes away. I'm locked in place, an animal torn between fight and flight.

Percy nods at something Scarlett says, his mouth in a wide smile. Enjoying himself and enjoying her. And then, he looks up.

Our eyes meet across the room.

The floor sinks beneath my feet. It's like the century-old

marble has suddenly become unstable, fractured at the seams, and sent me into the deep.

He says something to Scarlett and leaves her with their friends. I watch from somewhere out of my body as he walks through the crowd to me.

At our wedding, he'd worn a white pocket square. It's not there now. I stare at the pocket on his breast and avoid the familiar eyes coming closer.

"Sophia," he says. "I didn't think I'd see you here."

I've always been half an inch taller than him in heels. It had bothered him, I know, even if he pretended it didn't. Now, I revel in it.

I'd hate to ever look up at him again. "How could I miss it?" I say. "You know how passionate I am about protecting the arts."

He looks over his shoulder. Not at Scarlett, but at his mother, still with her court of followers. "Right. It's been a long time, Soph. I've been trying to call you."

"Well, I think we said everything we needed with our lawyers present."

He shakes his head. "I didn't want it to end like that."

No, of course not. He'd wanted to keep his marriage and his unblemished reputation intact.

Only I suspected he wanted to keep his mistress, too.

I clear my throat. "You're here with Scarlett?"

"It's a benefit," he says and smiles like I've caught him with his hand in the cookie jar. "You need to go with a date, or it's unbearable. You're here with someone. Isaac Winter, Soph?"

"Yes."

His smile doesn't falter, but there's something tense around his eyes. "I didn't know you two knew one another."

"We met recently," I say, and then I look over in the direction of the bar. Like I can't *wait* for Isaac to return. I make my eyes doe-y, forcing them to sparkle so damn hard I should win an Oscar. "He's... quite the man."

The smile slips from Percy's face. "He's too old for you."

I chuckle. "Don't be ridiculous. What's five years?"

"How'd you two meet?"

My mind casts about. *Work.* But that wouldn't sound believable. He knows how much I care about my career, and that I wouldn't do anything to risk it.

God knows we'd fought about it enough.

"At the club," I say, "playing tennis."

Percy's eyebrows rise. "At Grandview?"

"Yes."

"I thought the Winters preferred the Whitebridge. They've never had memberships at Grand."

I chuckle. It sounds shrill, even to me. "Oh, I don't know about that. We haven't been dating for long, but it's... oh. Welcome back."

Isaac wraps an arm around my waist. I lean into it, into him—the man I've never shared more than a handshake with before. His body is a firm wall beside mine. "For you," he says and hands me a glass of champagne.

I give him a warm smile. "Thank you."

The hand at my waist tightens in response, and then he looks over at Percy. "Hello, Browne."

"Winter," Percy says. "It's been years."

"Yes it has, hasn't it?" Isaac takes a long sip of champagne. "How have you been?"

"Good, good. Just the usual." Percy's eyes drift to mine. "Soph was just telling me how you two met at the club, playing tennis. I didn't know you went to Grandview."

Isaac shrugs. "My usual courts were being refurbished, and the Grandview's are passable."

"Yes," Percy says. His jaw looks tight. "Passable indeed. The hardcourts were just refinished, and the squash courts were repainted last winter."

"Is that so?"

"Yes. I'm sure you've already seen it, Soph, but there's a doubles tournament for members next weekend." There's a challenge in Percy's eyes, one I recognize well. "If you two already play, you should join in."

"Next weekend?" Isaac asks. There's polite disdain in his tone; one like he's making conversation because it's expected of him, but he has no interest in the topic.

It's glorious.

"Yes," Percy says. "I'm playing with Scarlett. It'd be fun if you two joined in. You always liked a good contest, Soph."

The edges of my vision turn hazy with anger. "Why not?" I say. "Isaac and I love to play. We'll see if we can make it."

"Great," Percy says.

"Terrific," I say.

"I'll see you there."

"Can't wait."

Isaac extends a hand. "Well, always a pleasure, Browne."

His voice drips with the opposite meaning.

Percy shakes the offered hand. "Likewise, Winter... Soph."

"Bye," I say and lean into Isaac's side. He supports me away from my ex-husband. Away from the situation, and through the crowd.

Perhaps people are looking. Perhaps they all are, but I can't see anything, can't focus on the goings-on around us.

"Oh my God. I'm sorry, Isaac, I shouldn't have said yes. Of course, I won't force you to do that. I'll get us out of playing doubles, I just had to... wow."

"You're okay," Isaac says quietly and pulls open a door that says *Staff Only*. "In here."

We walk up a flight of old stone steps and emerge onto a small balcony, complete with lounge chairs, that overlooks the vaulted hall beneath us. It's replete with guests, servers, and music.

I sink down onto one of the chairs. "I'm sorry," I say again. "Don't know what came over me, truly."

He takes a seat opposite me and reaches for my empty champagne flute. I watch as he sets it down gingerly on the stone floor. "It's all good."

"It is?"

"Yes."

I lean back in the chair and close my eyes. "He didn't seem unbothered. Did he?"

"No," Isaac says, "he definitely didn't."

"Good." I take a deep breath, then another. "He's here with her."

"With who?"

"The woman I caught him with in your hotel. Scarlett."

There's a quiet curse from the man opposite me, so unexpected it makes me smile.

"Yes," I say. "Exactly."

"That's who he's partnering with in the tournament, too?"

"Yes."

There's complete silence from Isaac. And then, in sepulchral tones: "No offence to you, Bishop, but your ex-husband is a son of a bitch."

A laugh slips out of me. "Yes. Quite literally."

"He taunted you by saying it would be a contest. Between her and you." Disgust drips from Isaac's voice. "The motherfucker."

I look up at the vaulted ceiling and the intricate designs and laugh. It's a fight against the constriction of my tight dress. "Yes," I say. "That, too, although not literally. Not that I know of, anyway.

"We're beating them at tennis."

"We are?"

"Yes." Isaac leans forward and brushes a hand against my thigh. Getting my attention. I look over and catch the dark eyes, now trained on me. "You play. Don't you?"

I nod. "Yes. It's become... well, my obsession since the divorce, after work."

"Good. We'll win, then."

"You're confident."

"Just being a realist," he says. "And I rarely lose."

I smile. But then it dies, and I sigh. "I'm sorry. For implicating you in all of this, for taking up even more of your time. I know you don't have a lot to spare."

He looks out over the crowd. "Don't worry about it. We'll sell the illusion even better like this. What couple wouldn't play together?"

"Yes, I guess we will."

"My aunt and uncle bought it," he says. "Seems like Percy did, too."

"Do you think they'll tell your parents? Or your brother?" I know what his family tree looks like. More than I should, probably, all courtesy of the well-packaged brief on the Winters I'd received from the background team at Exciteur.

"They will," Isaac says. "I suspect my aunt is calling my mother as we speak."

"Will that get them off your back for a bit?"

"I hope so." He leans forward. "It's almost midnight."

"Oh. The carriage is about to become a pumpkin."

"Yes." He looks out from the balcony again, down to the patrons below. "They'll announce the winners of the blind auction. Nothing we have to stay for."

"You're right." The dress is becoming uncomfortable, restrictive. I can't wait to take it off and sit down on the couch with a cup of tea and Milo in my lap. The damn cat who proves my sister right every time I see him because he's far too cute for me to ever resent.

Isaac extends a hand and helps me out of the chair. "How are you feeling?"

"I feel okay," I murmur. His hand is still around mine, and we're close enough that the tip of his leather shoe brushes against mine. "I can't wait to take off this dress, though. It looks great, but it feels awful."

He doesn't answer. No wonder, either. I'm saying too much, and none of it's good. Tonight had been a lot. Too much champagne, and too many close calls.

I slip my hand from his. "Should we?"

"Yes," he says and clears his throat. His voice is hoarser. "Lead the way."

We walk down the stairs and back out into the main hall. The low, murmuring chatter and the music blend together, and where it had before been imperceptible, I now long for silence.

Isaac walks by my side. He offers me his arm, a silent gesture, and I take it. It's steady and unfamiliar in the most exciting of ways.

The sound of friction against a mic rings out through the hall. "Sorry about that, folks. It's finally time to announce the winners of tonight's blind auction!" I look over to see Maurizio Madden on stage. He's the eccentric head of the charity and organizer of this benefit, year after year. "You've all been most charitable indeed, let me tell you. It's been a wonder to go through all the blind bids. Let me start off with the 1998 bottle of Château Margille, one of only twenty bottles produced in that vintage. And the winner is... Celine Browne!"

Isaac's steps don't falter. Neither do mine, despite the ringing in my ears. This time I notice the people looking at us as we pass.

Seeing him, and then me.

Recognizing him, and not me.

"The second item received an astonishing number of bids, which isn't surprising because this is a special one. It's a weekend stay for two at the legendary Marmont Manor Hotel in Connecticut this fall, complete with the executive suite and access to the spa. The winning bid is from none other than Isaac Winter!"

Applause erupts around us, and beneath my hand, Isaac's arm tightens. But he doesn't slow down.

"You have to accept the gift card," I murmur.

He shakes his head. "It's not important."

"It wouldn't look right not to," I say. "You know that."

"That's okay."

"I don't mind," I say. "Truly."

He changes direction, a smooth shift that's nearly imperceptible, and steers us in a circle back toward the stage. "I shouldn't have bid at all," he says.

"You had to," I murmur. He knows it, and I know it. There are social expectations around these things, and with his place in this crowd, he was obligated to.

He accepts the ornately decorated envelope from Maurizio, containing one very expensive gift card. Then, he raises a practiced hand and gives a wave and a smile to the audience. I notice Celine standing nearby, her son to her right. I don't meet Percy's heavy gaze.

But I feel it.

"All right," Isaac mutters beneath his breath. His free hand lands on my lower back again. "Let's go. Finally."

Everyone's still watching us. Their eyes feel like a weighted blanket on my skin, and I feel reckless, a little drunk, and too emotional.

So I lean against Isaac and look up at him, my eyes sparkling again. And I let a slow smile spread across my face. "Yes, please," I whisper. "I'd like that."

His eyes dip briefly to my lips before he raises an eyebrow. "Well played, Bishop."

"Thanks. I'm one of the most useful pieces on the chessboard, after all."

"Are you?" He bends to rest his lips against my ear, playing the part I've cast him in. "And do you think you've checkmated your king?"

I close my eyes, shutting out the too-curious gazes of the crowd. "Not yet," I whisper, "but I have him in check."

He chuckles, a warm exhale of breath against my skin. I shiver. "Yes, and I bet he knows it very well." His cheek brushes against mine as he pulls back, stubble pleasantly rough, and then he's straight again. "Let's go."

We walk out of the hall and emerge back into the warm, late summer air of the city, his hand staying on my lower back the entire time. Caught between longing for the safety of my own apartment, and the desire to stay close to this man for as long as I can, I don't realize the full meaning of his words until much later that night.

Who was the king in that analogy, really?

Which man do I have in check?

10

SOPHIA

I frown down at the design sketches we've received from the Exciteur graphics department. Jenna and Toby are sitting opposite me at the table in my office, the glass surface covered in graphic profiles, color schemes, and logo designs.

"It's not right," I say. "It's way too traditional."

"It's what they say they want," Toby says with a shrug. "Every single part of the brief has the word 'traditional' in it. I think I counted it sixteen times."

"Yes, but I don't think they've fully thought that through," I say. "Look at this color scheme. It's stunning and elegant in the New York location where you have a century-old building and legacy power. But can you picture a gold brocade sofa in the hotel lobby of a newly built hotel in Santa Barbara?"

"No," Jenna says. "Or rather, I can, and it's not looking good."

"This needs to be fresh and exciting, and modern." I drum my fingers against the table. "We have four weeks left until the pitch."

"And a lot of work to do," Toby says. "Did you see the shortlist of architecture firms I sent over?"

"Yes, and they're excellent… for the traditional vision. How about this? We create two pitches."

Toby's eyes widen. "Two separate pitches? In four weeks?"

"Yes," I say and shuffle the papers in front of me. The color schemes aren't bad, but they aren't excellent, and we're paid for excellence. "One pitch based on their specifications. But the second pitch? That's for us. I want it to be modern, innovative, and elegant. It should reflect the Winter spirit—not the actual color scheme of its New York location."

"I'm all for it," Jenna says. "The only way to convince them that their way is wrong is to show them the opposite and have these side by side."

Toby laughs and takes off his designer glasses. He cleans them against the sleeve of his cashmere sweater. "Sometimes, I think you're crazy, Sophia. Correction—I think you're crazy most of the time."

"Thank you," I say and grin at him.

"That's why I like working with you. We've never, not once, taken the easy road."

"No," I say. "But clients don't hire Exciteur for easy. You both know Isaac Winter is an important friend of the CEO."

Both Jenna and Toby nod. Exciteur is strongly performance-based and performance-review driven, and that's reflected in promotions... not to mention bonuses. "So, we pull out all the stops," I say. "They're hiring us to do the thinking for them. So, let's think big and blow them away at the pitch."

"I can get to work on the modern pitch right away," Jenna says and starts to scoop up the papers. Her love of yellow is reflected in a thin belt today, wrapped around a black dress. "I'll separate what we already have into folders and get the graphic department on board. I'll commission second options for all of this."

"Perfect. Toby? Can you continue working on the traditional pitch?"

"Right," he says and looks between us. "Because I'm such a boring traditionalist and a beacon of conventionality?"

Jenna and I laugh. "Yes," she says and leans her shoulder against his. "We didn't want to tell you, but that's the exact reason."

He shakes his head in mock sadness. "If only I'd known," he says. "It would have made my high school years so much easier."

The work day runs away from us after that, like it so often does. The opportunity to be creative and business-driven is one I love, and as I work on the Winter project, I can see the lobby in my mind's eye. I picture the spa, and The Ivy, and Isaac's deep voice telling me about every aspect.

After work, I have a headache from the hours spent in front of a screen. I pop an Advil and grab the tennis bag I keep in my office. It always has a fresh change of clothes and the keys to my locker at the Grandview club. My membership lasts until the end of the year, and I'm determined to make the most of it, uncomfortably familiar faces or not. It's a wonder I've managed to avoid Percy for so long.

Which isn't, strictly speaking, true. It's just very good planning on my part. I know how that man operates, and I know his schedule. I spent years living my life by it.

Marisol is an excellent tennis trainer. She cuts me no slack, standing on the other side of the net and hitting shots my way. "Forehand!" she screams. "Keep your side angled toward the net! Connect with the ball earlier! Don't forget the speed!"

We drill, and we drill, and we drill, and at the end, we play a set like we always do.

And it ends the way it always does.

I collapse on the bench and reach for my water bottle. "I almost had you on the last one," I say.

Marisol grins at me. She's forty-seven to my thirty-three, but she's also a former Olympian, and her skills are unmatched. "Sure," she says. "Let's say you were close."

I roll my eyes, and we both chuckle. Mine's significantly more tired than hers, age difference or no.

"Same time on Thursday?" she asks.

I nod. After the divorce, this sport had become my lifeline. I need the distraction and the constant, steady improvement of skill. Something to throw myself into that's mine and mine alone.

"Hypothetically," I say, "would it be okay if I brought someone?"

"Sure," she says. "Your sister coming to town?"

"No. God, Rose would hate this. No, I'm playing in the doubles tournament in a few weeks."

Her eyebrows rise. "You are? I'll be judging it."

"Really? That's great!"

"Doesn't mean I'll judge every point in your favor, Bishop."

"Oh, I'm not hoping for an overt display of favoritism," I say. "Just a small discrete one."

She laughs. "I'll see what I can do. So, who's your partner?"

It's funny. Marisol knows almost everything about my life, and I know a lot about hers, all due to talking on and off the court in between serves and chatting with our water bottles in hand.

She knows about Percy. That, though, isn't entirely from me. Gossip travels quicker than light at this club, and he's a staple here.

"It's a new guy," I say. "We're friends, and now we're sort of dating, too."

"Sort of?"

"Yes. It's early days still."

"Right," she says. "So, you thought you'd introduce him to all of New York society by throwing him into the vipers pit that is Grandview?"

I laugh. "Can you imagine? No, he's already a part of... well. This group of people."

"Oh," she says. "He's one of *them*."

I nod. Marisol and I had bonded early on about our small-town upbringings.

"You could say that," I say.

"Well, sure. Bring him along sometime and we can work on your game as a double."

"Thanks," I say. "See you Thursday?"

"You bet. I'll send you some videos about kick serves, by the way. I want you to study them."

"Got it." I throw my bag over my shoulder and wave at her. She's staying on the court, a new client already waiting in the wings.

I walk home. It's a long way, but I need the air and the energy that's always present on the streets of New York. There's a complete lack of it in my apartment, so I'll take it where I can get it.

My phone rings about halfway, and I have to dig through my bag to find it.

It's Isaac.

We've never called each other before.

"Hello?" I answer.

"Bishop," a familiar voice says. "Free to talk?"

"Yes, absolutely. Is everything all right?"

"Yes," Isaac says. We haven't spoken since the benefit last weekend. I've been working at Exciteur, him at Winter, and there hasn't been a reason to. Professionally or privately. "Thank you for the other night."

"No, thank you," I say. "I had fun."

There's a pause on the other end, and I can hear the disbelief in it. "Did you?"

"Yes. Well, before and after the... *incident*. Watching you win the prize you've always dreamed of helped."

The teasing breaks the formality between us. I can hear it crack. "Thanks for reminding me about that," he says dryly.

"No problem."

"What date is the doubles tournament?"

"It's not this Saturday, but the one after that," I say. "But,

Isaac, it's completely fine if you can't do it, or if you don't want to. I'm not expecting—"

"I'll be there," he says. "Text me the address and time."

"All right. I will." A pulse of mortification sends heat to my face. Here I am, forcing him to play tennis with me all because I want to shove my ex's face in it. And he's a client. It's so beyond anything proper that the embarrassment sinks down to my very toes.

"It's actually a good thing," he says, "because I have another favor to ask of you."

"You do?"

"Yes. There's a party in the Hamptons this weekend."

"It's late August," I say. "There are parties in the Hamptons every weekend."

He snorts. "Very funny."

"One tries."

"There are, indeed, but there's one in particular that I need to be at. More members of my family will be there."

"Oh."

"If you're able and interested, it's this Saturday." There's a brief pause. "Food, drinks, and transport will be included."

"It's an all-inclusive offer?"

"Yes. I'll up the personal service, too. I know how you enjoy it."

"I do." Being his date to another party would lessen the debt I'll owe him for the tennis. We'd be even. "Of course, I'll be there. Text me the details."

"Good," he says. "Thank you."

"Is it something I should be thanked for? Will your extended family pounce on me?"

"They might ask you how we met," he says, "but we already have that story settled."

I chuckle. "Yes, on a tennis court at a club you don't go to. I didn't think that one through."

"It works as well as any other story might." There's a

sudden increase in music playing on his end. It sounds classical.

"Where are you?" I ask.

"The opera," he says. "In Chicago. It's the intermission."

"Oh. Enjoy the performance," I say. A business trip? Or a personal one? He'd said he wasn't dating anyone, but it's hard not to picture him standing in a tailored tux, phone to his ear, a beautiful woman waiting beside him to finish his call.

"Until Saturday, then."

"Until Saturday," I murmur. "Don't stay past midnight."

"I never do," he says. "And Sophia?"

"Yes?"

"We'll win the game."

11

SOPHIA

That Saturday, Isaac stops outside my building to pick me up for the drive to the Hamptons. It's not a town car this time. It's a large SUV, and he's in the driver seat.

I get in and tuck my summer dress around my knees. "Hi."

"Hello," he says. "You look lovely."

I smile. It's likely ingrained in him, this. The manners that lead a man to opening doors and complimenting dates. "Thank you," I say, enjoying it regardless. "So do you."

He chuckles and turns the wheel, taking us back into the traffic. "Well, thank you."

I mean it, too. The beige suit is a sharp contrast against the darkness of his hair. And he's newly shaven, the cut of his jaw sharp in profile.

Isaac drives smoothly. Skilled and silent, he's the same behind the wheel as he is away from it. I look at him from the corner of my eye.

He notices. "You're thinking about something."

I stretch out my legs. The car has ample legroom. "Doesn't everyone, all the time?"

"No," he says. "They don't. Tell me what you're thinking."

"About you, actually, and the Winter Hotel."

"Ah, yes. Famously one and the same," he says so dryly that I know there's a hint of truth in the joke. For all intents and purposes, he *is* the hotel.

"Almost," I say. "Except one stands just a bit taller than the other."

"Well, one of them is also a bit more open to strangers spending the night than the other."

"Just a bit?" I say, my smile widening. "Good thing only one accepts payment, too."

He gives a surprised laugh. "That's one thing I've yet to do."

"Good thing, that."

He taps his fingers along the leathered wheel. "Now, what were you really thinking about?"

"The dichotomy between traditional and modern," I say, "and where you and your company land on that scale."

"Are you turning this drive into a business meeting?"

"I've never been able to resist multitasking."

"I'm impressed by your work ethic, Bishop."

"Are you?" I ask. "I'd have thought you expected it from the people you work with."

He's quiet for a beat. "I do. But not everyone lives up to it."

"Not everyone can."

"No," he says. Then, he clears his throat like he hears how unyielding that sounds. "So, traditional versus modern?"

"Yes."

"You're too smart not to know the answer to that. We're a traditional hotel chain," he says. "Why don't you ask me what you really want to know?"

A thrill runs down my spine at his words. "All right. What makes you think a traditional look for your budget hotel chain would make it unique? Stand out? Impress?"

He runs a hand along his jaw. "Well, now I know where you stand on the matter."

"You do. But I'm not asking to start an argument here. I

genuinely want to know why you and your team see that as the best option."

"Tradition conveys strength," he says. "And it would tie in beautifully with the rest of the Winter brand."

"Mm-hmm." I bite my lip, fighting the urge to argue. It's not time yet, not until the pitch.

"You don't agree," he says.

"I think those are key aspects of the Winter brand," I say. "But I don't think those are the only ones, or maybe even the most important ones."

"Interesting." He taps his fingers against the wheel again and looks over at me. The landscape behind him has changed, Manhattan receding in the distance. We're leaving one jungle for another entirely.

"I want to do a good job on this pitch," I say. "But I also want to deliver what you've asked for."

"You think they're mutually exclusive?"

"I think they're at odds, yes," I say carefully. "But you can trust us to deliver on your vision. I promise there will be a traditional option at the pitch."

"I wouldn't expect anything less from you."

"Now you're just being polite."

He shakes his head. "That's not what I sound like when I'm polite."

The words sink into my mind and I turn them over, examine them. There's truth there.

And a compliment.

I look out the window and take in the greenery passing by. We don't speak again until I start to recognize the familiar landscape of Long Island. It's a place I've been to before with Percy, many times, driving up on the weekends to his parents' house. The trip is long but comfortable.

It's funny how the people in the city and the Hamptons just switch places. The same people, different locations. It's insular and familiar, a social circle so small, it's almost incestuous.

"We're not stopping?" I ask. We're halfway through Southampton, and Isaac shows no sign of slowing down.

He shakes his head. "The party's in Montauk."

"Oh, that's a lovely place."

"Been before?"

"Yes, we'd go up sometimes from the house in Southampton." There's no need to explain who the *we* is. "But that was a few summers ago. Montauk's nice. Less crowded."

Isaac nods. "That's why we like it. It's the furthest from the city."

"You have a family house there?"

"Yes. My parents do, and my brother bought a place for him and his wife a few years ago, too." There's a brief pause, and then something tightens in his voice. "They're considering moving here permanently one day."

"Wow. Are they tired of the city?"

"In a way," he says. "They're hosting the party we're heading to."

"Your brother and your sister-in-law are?"

"Yes."

I blink at him. "Wow. Didn't think to mention that?"

"I am now," he says and looks over at me with a smile.

"It isn't distant relatives today, then," I say. My stomach does a little flip. We'll really be playing a couple.

"No, but they'll be pretty busy with the guests. Don't worry, Bishop. This isn't a meet-the-parents kind of thing."

"But they'll be there," I say. "Right? Your parents will be there?"

"Yes."

I lean back in my seat. "Oh."

"Too much?"

"No, I can do it." I think of my former parents-in-law and of judgmental looks and tests phrased as get-to-know-you questions. "What have you told them about me?"

"Nothing," he says. "We can use the tennis-meet story, if they ask. I don't think they will." He looks over at me, and there are frown lines between his dark eyebrows. "Don't worry, Sophia. I'd never bring you into a situation where I thought you'd be uncomfortable."

Somehow, I believe that. "Thank you."

"I should probably tell you what the event is, too."

"I'd appreciate that," I say and aim for a teasing note in my voice. "If you're bringing me to an impromptu wedding, I'll be very upset."

"No one's getting married that I know of."

"No ritual sacrifice? I left my goat at home."

"Not that, either." His voice is smooth, but there's a tension about him that wasn't there a few minutes ago. "It's a summer party for a charity."

"Another benefit?"

"Of a kind," he says. "There's a door fee, and every penny will go to a foundation for the blind and vision-impaired."

"That's beautiful," I say.

"I'll cover our door fees," he says.

"I'd be happy to—"

"I invited you. Besides, it's already been paid." He takes a breath. "My younger brother is losing his eyesight."

"Oh my God, Isaac. I'm so sorry to hear that."

"Yeah. It's... yeah. It is what it is."

"I didn't know that," I say.

He shakes his head. "It's not something he discusses with people outside of the family."

"I see."

"Not that it's a secret, exactly, but..."

"I understand," I say, because I do. "It's not something I'll talk about."

"Thanks."

"Your brother doesn't usually go to events, right? Like the benefit, or any of the country clubs?"

Isaac chuckles. "Hell no. He stopped going to them at the same time we both grew out of the open bar fascination."

"So, no Winter wingman for you?"

"No, he chose his own path... And now he's doing it again."

There's more here than he's saying. More pain, perhaps, or struggles than he's willing to share. I try to imagine losing my eyesight—losing the sense I use every moment of every day—and feel a shudder of fear.

"Is there nothing to be done?"

"No," Isaac says. His voice is tight. "Mitigation, adaptation, research, yes. There might be exercises to delay the degeneration. He could live for thirty years without losing it entirely, and from what I've understood, it's rare that you lose all light perception."

Anthony Winter, I think. That's his name. Married to Summer Davis, father to a new baby boy. They must have kept this under wraps for it to have been left out of my briefing on the Winter family.

"Anyway," Isaac says, "we don't have to stay long."

"I'm happy to stay for as long as you want." The words come out with more force than I'd anticipated. His brother's losing his eyesight and raising money for charity. "I'll stay way past midnight if you'd like, and I promise I'll act like the perfect date. Won't be able to take my eyes off you."

Isaac glances my way. "Thank you," he says, and there's warmth in his voice.

We reach the small town of Montauk. He drives the car down Main Street and then turns onto an adjoining road, heading toward the ocean. The street is lined with cars. One after the other, all parked along the street.

"It's already started?" I ask.

"It's a day party. My brother made it very clear to his wife that everyone had to be out by nine p.m."

I laugh. "He's not fond of parties?"

"That's an understatement."

We drive past the cars and turn onto the property. Two cars are parked side by side on the driveway, and beside them is space for one more. They'd kept a family spot open for Isaac.

The house is gorgeous. White and huge, blending into the surroundings seamlessly in a way that's so common with the rich. Giant hydrangeas erupt from white pots on either side of the porch steps.

From the back comes the sound of a live band.

Isaac gestures to a path between the house and the garage. He looks right at home, tall and well-dressed, standing on a stone path half-overgrown with well-cut grass. "Ready?"

"Yes," I say. "Your family must be really intense about your dating habits for you to want them to meet me."

"You have no idea," he mutters. "My sister-in-law co-owns an elite dating service."

"Wow. Really?"

"Really," he says.

"And you've never been the least bit curious to try it?" I ask.

He raises an eyebrow. "Would you be?"

I shake my head. "Gosh, that sounds like the complete opposite of what I'd want."

"Right. You're done with men like Percy Browne, right?"

"Yes," I say and chuckle. "My sister is actually trying to set me up with my old high school boyfriend back in Marhill."

"Is she?" He pauses just before the gate. Behind it, I can hear the sound of laughter and conversation. "And are you interested in your high school ex?"

"God, no. Robbie is a great guy, and he was exactly what I needed at seventeen. But we live completely different lives. No, I think I need someone in between."

"In between?" Isaac asks. "Not a client of an elite dating service, and not your hometown sweetheart?"

"Exactly," I say, smiling up at him. "Like a nice, respectable math teacher who lives in Brooklyn."

Isaac chuckles. "A math teacher. And are you especially interested in math?"

"Not particularly," I say. "But people like to say that opposites attract."

"Yes," he says. "They do say that, don't they?"

We look at each for a long beat, standing there, hidden behind the white picket gate. The late August air is warm, and yet, I feel goose bumps rise on the back of my neck.

Isaac reaches for the door handle. "Well," he murmurs. "I think we're doing pretty well despite it."

Right. Because we're not opposites. Not at all.

I'm starting to think we're exactly alike.

12

SOPHIA

Beautifully dressed guests mill about on a wooden deck overlooking the beach below. There's a pool house with wide-open glass doors, and inside is a bar, complete with a bartender busy mixing drinks.

And there's an infinity pool.

It curves along the edge of the deck, and I suspect that if I were to lie down on a sun lounger, the edge of the pool would blend seamlessly into the ocean.

"This place is stunning," I say to Isaac.

He nods. "It cost my brother an arm and a leg, but it's worth it."

"Should we— Oh." I catch sight of a golden retriever with a wagging tail racing through the throng of people, a stolen shawl hanging from its jaw. "Look at that dog go."

"Yeah, my brother and his wife have two of them. One's an actual guide dog, and the other was supposed to be but failed his exam."

That makes me smile. "Let me guess, the one we just saw is the school dropout?"

"Definitely."

We head to the bar and get drinks, and then it's on—the networking. Just like we'd done at the benefit.

But it's even more apparent here how little Isaac Winter needs to do to work a room. Everyone wants to say hello. Everyone wants to talk to him. And he's warmer here, different somehow, asking people about their families, their children, and their parents.

These are people the Winters have known most of their lives, I suspect. Friends of family and members of the same circle.

"This is Sophia," he says, introducing me to everyone we talk to. The eyes that turn to me, each and every time, are curious.

I give them all a wide smile and lean into Isaac just a little. *Yes, we're together.* "It's a pleasure to meet you."

Isaac handles the conversations well, includes me easily in topics, and it flows with the practiced ease of people who've mastered the art of small talk. We talk about the rising interest rates, the best place to summer, and how to master kite surfing—something Isaac's apparently tried more than once. Topics flow from the latest production put on by the New York Opera to the unusual heat wave and back around—as if it's inevitable—to the rising interest rates.

We're halfway through the group by the pool when Isaac puts a hand on my lower back, pulling me aside. "Let me introduce you to my brother."

"I'd like that."

The man we approach is not someone I've ever met before, and yet I instantly recognize him. The family resemblance is there in the dark hair and the even darker eyes. Anthony is rougher around the edges, somehow, his face equally striking but less classically handsome. And while he's broader across the shoulders, he's not quite as tall as Isaac.

"Anthony," Isaac says.

His brother turns to us. "You made it."

"Didn't I promise I would?"

Anthony's eyes drift to me. "Hello," he says. "You must be Sophia."

"Yes. It's a pleasure to meet you," I say and extend a hand. If he knows my name, they must have spoken about me beforehand. "You and your wife have a beautiful house."

"Thank you," he says and looks at Isaac. "Well played, man."

"Think Summer will back off?"

"Most likely," Anthony says. He looks at me, and his smile turns rueful. "I don't know if my dear brother has told you, but my wife works as a matchmaker."

"I've heard about that, yes."

"My brother has been her primary target for a solid year now."

"Poor Isaac," I say, and Anthony laughs. "Good thing I'm here, then."

"Yes, and don't leave his side," Anthony says. He gives me an appraising look. "You're from New York?"

"No, I'm from Marhill. It's a small town upstate."

"Oh," he says. "That's great."

I don't get a chance to ask why that is because a beautiful blonde woman comes up beside him. Her blue eyes dance between me and Isaac.

"Why, hello!" she says. "I'm sorry I haven't had a chance to say hi yet. How are you, Isaac?"

"I'm good." He leans in to kiss his sister-in-law on the cheek. "This is Sophia, the woman I've told you about. Sophia, this is Summer."

"Welcome," Summer says. An entirely genuine smile takes up most of her face. "It's so lovely to meet you."

"Likewise. You have a beautiful—"

"Where did you two meet?"

"Oh." I look at Isaac. "It's a funny story, actually. We were playing tennis at the same time, and he had the court next to mine."

"She kept hitting the ball over to my side," Isaac says. His face is neutral, but there's a tick to his jaw that hints at a suppressed smile. "Great icebreaking technique, I must say."

I elbow him. "That's slander. I might not have a slice down, but I can keep the ball on my own court."

"You're right," he says, eyes on mine. "The truth is, I saw her play and couldn't resist saying hello."

I nod. "Our trainers got a bit annoyed. I think we spoke more than we played that hour."

Summer sighs. "Oh, that's the perfect way to meet."

I look away from Isaac's dark eyes and the amused glint hidden within. "Yes, it worked out well for us so far."

Isaac's hand returns to my lower back. I like it there, a warm and comforting weight. "Are the others from Acture here?"

Anthony nods and gestures to the far end of the pool. "Tristan and Carter are over there, and St. Clair said he'd show up, but I haven't seen him yet."

An icy tendril snakes down my spine. St. Clair, as in *Victor St. Clair*. The CEO and boss of my company, and the person who had requested that Isaac's project be prioritized and given the utmost attention.

I suppose being Isaac's date qualifies for both... but not the way it had been intended.

"We'll go say hello," Isaac says, and Anthony nods. "Is Theo inside?"

Summer nods. "He's in his room with the nanny, happy as a clam."

"I'll go in and see him later," Isaac says. "That okay?"

"Of course," Anthony says. "Enjoy the party, Sophia."

"Your nephew?" I ask Isaac as we're walking away.

"Yes," he says. The idea of him sneaking away from a party to see a baby makes me smile. I wish I could see it, how he would be in those moments. What his voice would sound like.

"Here we are..." he murmurs. "We'll just say a quick hello."

I'm introduced to two men and their wives. Tristan, Carter, Audrey, and Frederica, whom everyone calls Freddie.

They're seated around a low firepit with an assortment of drinks spread out in front of them.

"Isaac," one of the men says. He's got a distinguished look, not unlike Isaac's, but the smile he gives us is open and friendly. Tristan, I think. "It's good to see you again. You're remembering to do other things than just work?"

His wife bumps his shoulder with hers. "I don't think you're the best person to lecture anyone else about workaholism," she tells him.

Tristan laughs. "Maybe not."

"I know for a fact that none of you are," Isaac says. "Case in point, Audrey, I saw your latest piece for the *Globe*. It was excellent."

The woman with beautiful curly hair lights up. "Thank you! It was a lot of fun to write."

"You're a journalist?" I ask.

Isaac and I have a seat with the group, and the conversation spins on, genuinely interesting. Audrey's job is fascinating, and it doesn't take long until I learn that Tristan was Exciteur's CEO before St. Clair, before I worked there.

The conversation comes to an abrupt halt when a party photographer stops by our table, camera in his right hand. The others rise, familiar with the practice. Isaac's arm lands around my waist.

"Thanks," he murmurs.

"For what?" I whisper back.

He's looking straight ahead, at the camera. "For being here."

Right. For ensuring his family stops nagging him about dating. Driven by adrenaline and champagne, and maybe something less, something I'm not brave enough to put a name on yet, I press my lips briefly against his cheek.

The photographer's camera makes a few audible snaps. "Excellent," he says before wandering off in search of new victims. "Thank you."

The reality of what I've just done hits me. "I'm sorry, Isaac. I shouldn't have done that."

"It's fine."

"No, that was crossing a line. I'm sorry."

His eyes darken. "Sophia," he says. "Never apologize for kissing me."

"Oh. Okay."

"Now," he says, looking over my shoulder, "someone just arrived that I think you'd like to meet."

A couple has just arrived. The man is familiar. Not from seeing him in person, God no, but from pictures and company memos. The woman beside him must be his wife. She's beautiful in an understated way, wearing a simple white dress that accentuates her hair.

"Oh," I say again. "I don't think he'll know who I am."

"Probably not," Isaac says, the picture of honesty. "He's not the best at remembering faces. Or names, for that matter. You're fine."

"He controls my fate, in a way. At least my professional one, at any rate, and that's everything to me right now. And he doesn't even know who I am." I shake my head, my mind racing. "Maybe that's how your employees think about you."

Isaac takes a moment to answer. "Maybe so."

"I'm sorry. That might not be true."

"It probably is," he says with a sigh. "I don't like the idea of my employees thinking that way, but I can't deny they probably do."

"It's the nature of the game," I say. "If it helps, I've spoken to a ton of your employees over the past few weeks, and not a single one has had anything negative to say about you or the executive team."

He raises an eyebrow. "That might just prove how scared they are to talk."

"Do you genuinely believe that?"

"No," he says, looking at me. "And you have nothing to worry about with St. Clair, or your job for that matter."

"Well, the pitch I'm preparing for your company is a pretty big one for me," I confess. "For my career, too, if we were to nail it."

His face is serious. "So I've gathered."

"That's why I can't resist picking your brain whenever I get the chance to."

"It's yours to pick," he says.

"Until midnight, at least?"

"Until then," he agrees, lips curving. "But I suspect I'll—"

"Isaac." There's a shape at our side, and then Anthony comes into focus. His eyes are intense on his brother. "She wasn't on the guest list, but she's here regardless."

"Who?"

"Cordelia. Summer just saw her come in with her parents."

Isaac doesn't look any less composed at this news, his face set in the usual lines of competence and command. "I see."

"Her parents were invited, at our parents' request."

"Naturally," Isaac says. "They'll be the ones to spend time with the Jacobs tonight, too."

"Cordelia must have come with them, but honestly, I have no problem telling her to fuck off," Anthony says.

Isaac huffs out a half laugh. "And ruin the hard work this party is doing to change your recluse reputation? Absolutely not."

"I don't care."

"I know you don't," Isaac says and puts a hand on his brother's arm. "But I do."

"Fine." Anthony looks over his shoulder. "This is when I wish I could see clearly at a distance."

The brothers exchange a few more heated sentences, and then Anthony disappears, weaving his way through the crowd. For the first time I notice that one of the dogs is glued to his side. Must be the one who passed the exam.

"So," I say carefully. "Would it be too intrusive of me to ask?"

Isaac's eyes roam the crowd, almost like he's trying to spot the mystery woman. But then, he takes my hand and pulls me into the comfort of the pool house. We're in full view of the crowd, but the music is quieter here, the sound of a dozen conversations dampened.

"She's someone from my past," he says.

"An ex?"

"Yes." He looks down at my empty champagne glass and, almost like his chivalry is on autopilot, takes it from me. He sets it and mine down on the empty bar. "We were engaged, years ago."

My eyes widen. "You were engaged?"

"Yes. We ended it a few months before the wedding."

"Why?" The question slips out of me of its own accord.

Isaac takes a moment to respond. "My brother saw her with someone else."

The words hit me like a weight of bricks, a realization and an understanding. He's gone through the same thing I have. *I made his check-out hell,* he'd said about Percy. It all makes sense now.

"Oh," I whisper.

Isaac sighs. I've never seen him run his hand through his hair in agitation, but he does it now. "It was a long time ago."

"Do you miss her?"

"No," he says. "I haven't for years."

"And she's here?" Irritation burns in my chest. "Your family invited her and her parents despite what happened?"

"Just her parents. They're... well, the Jacobs own golf courses and a few smaller hotels."

Several things flash through my mind at once. *It was a marriage for the business,* I think. He chose a partner who he thought could help the company. *And his family still considers them more important for networking purposes than their son's feelings.*

He watches me process his words, eyes unreadable.

"Have you dated since?" I ask. My voice comes out heated. "Has she seen you with someone else?"

He shakes his head. "Not that I know of."

I grip his wrist and pull him toward the archway, ensuring we're in full view of the crowd. Slowly, giving him time to pull away, I reach up and grip the lapels of his suit jacket.

"Look out over the crowd," I say. "Do you see her?"

Isaac frowns at me, but does what I've asked him. He's close enough that I can make out those golden flecks in his eyes again. "Yes," he says. "She's spotted us."

"Good. I hope you meant what you said earlier," I whisper, and then I press my lips to his.

They're soft and still under mine. I get the distinct impression that I've shocked him, and the only thing stopping me from pulling away is the knowledge that his ex is watching.

Damn, I've messed—

But then, he kisses me back. The hand resting on my waist grips me tight, and then he tugs me against the length of his body. Our heights are a perfect fit.

Neither of us has to bend.

He tastes good, like warmth and champagne and determination, and I shiver when his fingers dig into the soft flesh at my hip. I'd forgotten how nice, how heartbreakingly lovely, it is to be kissed like this.

Isaac lifts his mouth from mine, but I'm not ready to let go quite yet. My hands tighten on the lapels of his suit jacket, and he stays close, brushing his lips over my cheek.

"What," he murmurs, "was that?"

"You've helped me with Percy," I whisper. "It's only fair I help you get some payback on your ex, too."

It's the truth and the reason I'd pulled him here, indignation like a second heartbeat beneath my skin. That he'd experienced what I'd experienced and had to face the person who did it at his own family's parties over and over again.

But I'd forgotten about that the second he kissed me back.

Isaac's hand loosens its tight, comforting grip on my

waist. "Well..." he murmurs, his eyes darker than usual. "That's considerate."

"Yeah. That's me."

His mouth curls into a half smile. "I suppose that means I should thank you, Bishop."

"Bishop," I repeat. "You've stopped calling me Sophia. Why?"

He grabs a tendril of my hair and lets it run through his fingers. The back of his palm brushes my cheek. "It's too-beautiful a name for too-beautiful a woman," he says. "Bishop is safer."

13

ISAAC

The new resort development in the Caribbean had stalled. Amanda had flown down, and I had to join her, together with a few others from the executive team.

But the negotiations take hours. More hours than I have, and by the end of the third day, I'm cutting it too close. I've missed my flight back to New York. And while it might be a crime to be on this island and not look twice at the brilliant turquoise waters, there's no time. I've already used too much of mine.

I call my assistant. "I need to be in Midtown by noon tomorrow. Put together a few flight plans and book what you can."

It ends up being an evening flight to Miami, where I spend miserable few hours at an airport hotel before my morning flight. I should be tired. Should have no problem getting a few hours of sleep. But memories compete in my head, each wanting a center stage.

Sophia had kissed me in front of my ex.

The sentiment had been kind, but it's been years since Cordelia and I ended, and I doubt she'd care about me dating. I know I don't give a fuck about her love life.

But Sophia didn't know that.

Her lips on mine had been the best thing I'd experienced all summer, all damn year—soft and determined, and with just a hint of shyness because she wasn't sure how I'd react.

And then, she'd taken it all back in the next breath and reclaimed the kiss as a favor. Just simple quid pro quo for what I'm helping her to do to Percy.

Painful to the ego, sure. But it shows her character. Kind and fierce, in the same clever package.

I run a hand through my hair and look up at the dark ceiling. She wants a math teacher and not another member of the social circle Percy belongs to. Not another him, in effect. I suspect she feels like she doesn't fit in.

But she does, though. That's the thing. She *does*, and I've seen it.

Percival Browne had been so damn lucky and then so damn stupid to have thrown it all away.

I turn onto my side, staring at the numbers on the alarm clock. She should be asked out properly. Not this half dating, just-for-show kind of thing. My instinct is to do just that, but I know it would only take me further away from her. I doubt Sophia is ready to date, and even if she was, I'm a damn far cry from a high school math teacher.

I flip onto my back again and force my breathing to slow. There's only one solution. After the tournament tomorrow, and after I've gotten some illicit pleasure from winning against her ex, we'll end this little fake relationship. It's run its course. Percy is jealous, and I can tell her that my family is mollified.

It's time to avoid the temptation who's made it very clear she isn't in the market to be tempted.

The next day, I arrive at the Grandview Club straight from the airport. My assistant is waiting outside, holding a bag with newly bought workout clothes, and I can see the handle of a tennis racquet peeking out.

"I've registered you for the tournament," he says. "Your

partner is on court four, and the two of you are playing your first game in fifteen minutes."

I change and catch a brief glimpse of myself in the mirror. No sleep and two flights haven't been kind. My eyes look haggard, and I need a shower.

But what I really need is to win. Despite the sleepless night, competition burns in my veins. It's all too easy to remember Percy's face and the expression on it when he'd taunted Sophia about his new relationship.

The club is buzzing, with the makeshift stands around the tennis courts selling lemonade and drinks. A lounge area has been erected, and in the distance, I see a band setting up.

Of course. A tennis tournament, but also an excuse to mingle and day drink, just like every event in the city. A few people cast curious glances my way. I've never frequented the Grandview, never wanted to mix my networking with my workouts.

"Winter?" a man says, someone I vaguely recognize from my father's golfing days. "I didn't know you'd be here!"

I nod hello with a polite smile and make my way to court four. Sophia's already there, waiting.

She's in a navy-blue outfit, a contrast to all the people wearing white. The tennis skirt is pleated... and short. Very short. I catch the full length of her toned legs and the perky swing of her ponytail.

She lights up when she sees me. "Isaac!"

"Hey, Bishop."

"You made it. I was worried there," she says and frowns. "Are you okay?"

"Yes."

"What happened?"

"There was a hiccup in the building of our Barbados resort that needed my attention," I say, shaking my head. "But it's been ironed out. Mostly."

"You were just in Barbados?"

"Yes, briefly. We're almost finished building."

"I know," she says, nodding slowly. "I've done my research about that. But I didn't mean to pull you away from work, Isaac. If you need to be somewhere else, you know, you're free to go."

She says my name easily, rolls it off her tongue like we've known each other a lifetime.

"I promised I'd be here."

"Isaac..." she says.

I hear what she's not saying. That it would've been okay, that she would've understood, that she never meant for me to go to these lengths. *But I wanted to,* I think. *I will never be the one to let you down.*

I clear my throat. "So, what's the score?"

"The first set of matches has been played. All their scores are being recorded over there." She nods to a giant chalkboard on wheels, complete with drawn brackets of teams. All of them are listed, and there's a clear path to the two empty spots in the center.

"We're playing the second round of starters."

I raise an eyebrow. "And who are we playing?"

"Them," she says grimly. "Percy knows the guy who runs the club pretty well."

"Ah," I say. So he'd made sure he would play his ex-wife. I flex my hand and reach into my bag, gripping the handle of my racket. I can't wait to beat him.

Sophia takes a deep breath. "I think we should've practiced together beforehand," she says.

"We could've," I say and regret not having that idea myself. It would have been another reason to spend time with her.

"I emailed your assistant about it," she said. "With some proposed dates. But I think you were busy on all of them."

I pause. "You did?"

"Yes."

"I didn't know about that."

"Oh, well, I thought maybe you didn't."

"You could have called me," I say. "Or texted."

"I didn't want to overstep. You're busy," she says and reaches for her own racquet. "Besides, I'm already grateful for your help with this."

"You came with me to the Montauk party," I say. "You kissed me in front of my ex."

A faint blush creeps up her cheeks. "I did, yeah."

"So, consider this me returning the favor."

She smiles, and it sets the world to rights. "Literally?"

"If you'd like, yes," I say. "If you want to rub Percy's nose in us, make it clear you've moved on... then you can. What I said at the Montauk party still stands."

"You mean that," she says. It's a statement, not a question.

But I nod anyway. "I do."

"I was worried I'd overstepped."

"You didn't. I don't say things I don't mean."

She chuckles. "No, I suppose you don't. It's refreshing. So many people do."

"Yes, and then they pay the price for it," I say and pull out my racquet.

Sophia eyes it. "You've played before, right?"

I hold the racquet like a frying pan. "Which way is up, again?"

She laughs. "Okay, so you have."

"Yes. Anthony and I played growing up."

"So, you're good?"

"Good enough," I say. It's been years since I played just for fun. Years, really, since I made the time and effort for things of any nature, just for fun.

"They're here," she murmurs. I look across the net to see them, Percy and Scarlett, step onto the court.

He's in all-white, and so is his girlfriend. They both smile and wave to us like all is normal and right in the world, and as if this won't be a fight to the death.

"Oh my God," Sophia murmurs.

"You're not playing him," I say. "You're just playing the game. Don't focus on who he is."

She takes a deep breath. Fire flickers in her eyes, so clear I can almost see the flames. She doesn't need to be talked down from her nerves, I realize. They're giving her fuel.

"I have to win," she says fiercely. "I *want* to win."

"We will," I say. "You will. But you know what will be a true victory?"

"What?"

"Walking away from here and looking happy, regardless of what happens during the game. That's what'll hurt him the most. You, thriving without him."

Her mouth curves into a smile. "You're good, you know. Very good."

"It doesn't take a genius," I say, "to imagine how it would feel to lose you."

Her smile falters, and the eyes on mine turn questioning. Damn. Too much, and if it wasn't for my lack of sleep, I wouldn't have let those words slip.

The game begins and saves us from the silence. The first few serves make it clear that Scarlett is a competent, if not a particularly ambitious, player.

Percy, though? That's a different story. He's not a wild talent, but from the very first ball, I see the hunger in him. He's playing to win this, just like I am.

And just like Sophia.

They net the first two points, but we gain the next four. Then we miss the point because of a failure in communication. I curse. Sophia curses. And after that, we make sure to call it—always, and it doesn't happen again.

She's good. Great even, especially her backhand. It's hard to master, but she makes it look effortless. The ball becomes a blur over the net, flying in quick crosscourt shots.

Playing feels good, the forehand swings and the twang of the ball great. We win the first set, but it's close, and during the water break, I watch Percy give animated pointers to Scarlett.

Sophia gives me a fierce look over her water bottle. Her skin glistens beneath the overhead lights. "You're really good," she says. "Those serves? Damn."

I shrug. "Anthony and I were forced to work on serves until we could do the movement in our sleep."

"They're hard. I can never quite get the ball toss quite right."

"I'll show you sometime," I say.

She knocks my shoulder with hers. "I'd like that."

The second set is far more intense than the first. Percy has kicked into a higher gear, and I find myself responding in kind, sending balls as hard as I can back to the other side. For a few glorious seconds, it's just him and me, crosscourt forehand shots and the ball clearing the net by mere inches. I flick my wrist slightly on the next impact, and it skews just out of his reach on the other side.

Point us.

The game reaches a fever pitch. I can feel it on the court, playing beside Sophia, who hits every ball like it's a tie-breaking shot. I can feel it in the sounds of the onlookers, too. For a brief moment I feel sorry for Scarlett, who'd likely signed up for a fun day of tennis and not a death match at the Colosseum.

But then I remember what she'd done to Sophia, and the pity fades.

The final set is close. We lose points three times in a row, but in the last second, Sophia plays a drop shot. Scarlett sprints but it's too late, point us, and the game shifts in our favor.

And they never recover.

We win the final point with one of Sophia's backhands, and it's all over. The referee calls the game over and, absurdly, the people around us applaud. I wipe sweat off my forehead and meet Percy's gaze from across the court.

He looks like he wants to lob his racquet at my head. I give him my most polite of smiles.

Sorry, asshole. You lost.

"We won!" Sophia says, and I tear my eyes from Percy's scowl. She's flushed and stunning, and she drops her racquet on the court floor. Then, she throws herself into my arms.

I swing her around. She smells good, like warm woman, and shampoo, and victory. "We won," she murmurs into my ear. "Thank you, thank you, *thank you.*"

I tighten my arms around her waist before I let her sink back down to the floor. "My pleasure."

Her smile is a beautifully bright thing. "Incoming," she says, and then she kisses me again.

I ignore the people looking at us and, selfishly, take my time. It's impossible not to with the softness of her lips against mine and the lithe waist beneath my hands.

But most of all? I ignore that she's only doing this to get back at the man across the net.

Sophia pulls away first. "Now," she murmurs, "we're even."

"You know," I say, with the taste of her still on my lips, "I think I might enjoy being in your debt."

She smiles, alight with life and victory. "Really? Help me win another game, then."

14

ISAAC

By our third game, my shoulder ached, and the bloodlust in Sophia's eyes turned into a satisfied simmer. We place fourth overall in the tournament. She doesn't want to stay for the after-tournament drinks, or to collect our prize, and I couldn't agree with that decision more.

We won against her ex-husband, and that was victory enough. So we leave the club together. The early September air is still warm but lacks the sting of heat the summer had carried. I won't miss that.

"That was such a rush," she says as we start to walk downtown. "I feel like I've just graduated high school, and won the lottery, and maybe, it's also Christmas morning and I'm eight years old."

I laugh. "I take it you're feeling good?"

"Absolutely amazing. I think I could do anything right now," she says, her ponytail bouncing. She's thrown a sweater on, but she's still bare-legged beneath it, long legs easily keeping up alongside mine in the afternoon sun. "God, I love that sport."

"Did you start playing recently?"

"A few years ago," she says. Then she laughs. "Percy got me into it, but then he started to hate how seriously I took it. I found a great trainer and started spending two evenings a week with her, and he thought that was too much. You know, on top of my incredibly packed and unnecessary work schedule."

"Your work schedule?" I murmur.

She shakes her head. "Yeah. But it doesn't matter, ultimately. Thank you for making it here and for being on my team."

I nod and think about the unmistakable anger written in every line of her ex-husband's body. "Looks like he took it pretty seriously back on the court."

"He hated seeing you there with me, I think," she says. Then, she gives me a sheepish smile. "Sorry. I don't think it's personal or anything."

I chuckle. "Percy Browne hating me," I say, "doesn't feel like much of a problem."

"No, I don't suppose it would. So you played growing up?" she asks. "What was your childhood like?"

"Interesting question," I say, and she chuckles again. I don't think she's laughed this much around me before. It must be the adrenaline, the excitement. The thrill of victory.

"Well, I'd be lying if I said I wasn't curious," she says. "So, you grew up playing tennis with a trainer?"

"Yes. My parents made my brother and me try a bunch of different sports to see if we had a natural aptitude for any of them."

"Let me guess. You were great at team sports, and he did better at solo ones?"

"Yes," I admit.

She smiles. "But you weren't just any old team player, no —you preferred the role of team captain. Am I right?"

I look at her for a long moment.

"What?" she asks. "Am I off base?"

"No, you're a little too spot-on."

She chuckles. "Okay, so you played a lot of sports. Was winning important in your family?"

"At times," I say. "It depended on the sport and the time. What mattered to my parents was that we always gave a hundred and ten percent to whatever we chose to pursue. Anything less wasn't acceptable."

"I can imagine that," she says. "Your father must have been busy while you were growing up. He was the head of the Winter Corporation before you, right?"

I tug at the rounded collar of my T-shirt. "Yes," I say. "He was. But he wasn't as involved as my grandfather was before him, or like I am now."

"No?"

"No," I say. There's no need to elaborate on that. My father is who he is, a man with good stewardship skills but no vision. Life happened, and he became the CEO; and when life allowed him to, he stepped down.

But I find, to my surprise, that I *want* to tell her more.

"My aunt was actually supposed to take over after my grandfather," I say.

"Really? I didn't know that."

"Yes. She was his eldest kid, and she had a real knack for the business," I say, and then I chuckle. "You know, she drew up these wild expansion plans for the hotel when she was fourteen and presented them to my grandfather one evening. They were so unrealistic that it became a running anecdote in the family. Rooftop pools and underground valet parking in every hotel. But it showed spirit. It was assumed she would be the one to inherit."

"Wow," Sophia says, and then her voice softens. "What happened?"

"She died at thirty-six while she was working as my grandfather's right-hand woman at the company."

"Oh, I'm sorry, Isaac."

I had known her only a little, being a small kid when she passed, but her story is so ingrained in my family that it's like she's a living legend. "My father was my grandfather's only other child. He took the job."

Her voice turns curious and a tad cautious. "Was there ever talk of hiring someone else? The family doesn't technically *have* to run it, right? You could just be on the board."

My lips twist into a half smile. "People suggested it, yes, and my grandfather threw them out of the room when they did."

"Oh."

"He was a man of hard-held beliefs."

"Did he expect you to present your ideas to him, too? When you were fourteen?"

"No," I say. "But I did it, anyway, when I was sixteen."

There's a smile in her voice. "I can almost picture that. Did you impress him?"

"Mine were less visionary," I admit. "More numbers-based. But I think he enjoyed them. He was less impressed and more... content. Happy that the family legacy would continue, and that my generation wouldn't be the one to sell out."

Sophia gives a slow nod. She doesn't say anything, and I'm glad for that, too. Because I can hear how it sounds when it's spoken out loud.

"Is he still alive?" she asks.

"He died almost a decade ago."

"I'm sorry to hear that," she says. "He sounds like an extraordinary man."

He had been. And as blasphemous as it is to think, it's easier now that he's gone—when he's a legacy to live up to rather than a difficult person to appease. It had been hard to deal with his opinions when he visited the Winter Hotel in his eighties, and hard to handle the phone calls when he was disappointed with some aspect or another.

Now I can honor him and the generation that laid the groundwork before him without being beholden to them all.

But it's not a thought I've ever spoken aloud.

"Tell me about your family," I say. "How proud are they of your career in the big city?"

Sophia doesn't seem to mind the abrupt change of topic. "Not very. No, that's unfair of me. I think they are, but they don't understand it or why it means so much to me."

"Right," I say. "Seeing as they're trying to get you to move home and marry your high school sweetheart and all."

"Gosh, yes. Apparently, the cure to a case of post-divorce blues is a solid few months living in my childhood bedroom."

"With a rebound and some family time," I say.

"Exactly," she says. "They mean well, but leaving New York... maybe that's the right move for me. But I can't see it yet, anyway."

I make a low humming sound. She feels like the city. Pulsing with energy, sharp and smart, and always well-dressed, with a hunger that's clear in her eyes whenever we talk shop.

"The city would be worse off if you left," I say.

She's quiet for a long moment, and when she speaks again, the words are unexpected. "There's a place up this road that makes the best ramen," she says. "Do you want to grab some? I'm starving."

I know what my answer should be.

But I can't bring myself to say it, not just yet.

"I live on this block, so we can eat at my place. But I understand," she says, "if you want to go home. You just got back from an overseas trip, after all."

So I did, and just in time. Perhaps that's why I have no resolve. The last of it slips away, not even leaving rings on the water in its wake. "I'll come with you."

We end up in the short line for ramen. She looks at me over her shoulder once, and then again, longer this time.

"What's wrong?"

"Nothing," she says with a smile. "It's just... you're here. It feels like I'm living in a parallel universe. You, in casual clothing, here—at my ramen place."

"Well, I don't always wear a suit."

"You know, somehow, I *knew* that was true intellectually, but I didn't really believe it until today."

That makes me smile. "Sorry to disappoint you."

"Oh, I'm not disappointed," she says. We're close, standing in line like this, and my eyes flick to her lips. I know exactly how they feel against mine.

"The miso ramen is the best one," she murmurs. "It's not made by a Michelin Star chef, of course, but it's… good."

I fight the urge to brush a tendril of hair back from her forehead. "I trust you."

We order, pay, and head to her apartment. The building is anonymous and simple, but it looks recently renovated, complete with a double-code system for entry.

"My place is pretty bare," she says apologetically. "And I hope you're not allergic to cats."

"I'm not," I say, *and I wouldn't turn around now, even if I was.*

As if I even could at this point.

Her apartment is bright and neutral. It's neat, but not clinically so, and little parts of her are sprinkled across the surfaces. It's there in the sweater hung over the back of a kitchen chair and in the book tossed on the sofa with a bookmark sprouting from its pages.

She sets the takeout down on the kitchen counter. "It's a bit messy, I'm sorry about that."

"It's not. You have a lovely place."

She reaches up to tighten her ponytail, and her skirt rides up another inch. "Thanks. I figured Milo would come and say hello, but he's probably hiding. I haven't had a lot of visitors since I got him, you know. He's not used to company."

"Makes sense," I say. But all I hear is the implication that she isn't seeing anyone, not even casually.

This feels like the evening we spent in the penthouse suite when I sat opposite her, with her wet hair and bright eyes, sharing a drink and making conversation. Behind a closed door, the veil of professionalism melts away, and it's just the two of us. It makes it too easy to forget myself.

Only this is worse than the hotel because there are no reminders of work here. She's everywhere in this apartment.

"Hungry?" she asks.

"Starving," I say. We eat at her kitchen table. It's small, and beneath it, our knees brush against one another. The silence feels heavy. Not because it's uncomfortable but because it's not, and there's something even more significant about that.

I clear my throat. "How was your marriage?"

She pauses, chopsticks in hand. "Where did that come from?"

I take another bite to gather my thoughts. Sleep deprivation, exercise, the desire to crush her ex into a pulp... and now this—prolonged exposure to her—has thrown me off-balance. I've lost all sense of propriety. "You mentioned that he didn't like your career. I'm curious."

"He didn't. Well, he did in the beginning, but the way he was raised made itself known soon enough."

I frown. "How so?"

"His mother is very... traditional," she says. "She was a stay-at-home mom; but also a homemaker, a philanthropist, on the school board, organized charities, and ran three households. So, I think he expected the role of wife to be a full-time job."

"I see," I say, because I do. She had a hunger for a career, for advancement, and for things bigger than a country club social ladder.

"I love my job," she says, "and I think I'm good at it. It took me years and a degree to get to where I am, and to think I would give all that up? He wasn't planning on giving up his golf or squash or ski trips with his friends, or his job, for that matter, even if he never liked it that much."

Fuck, I think. I'm in so much deeper than I thought. Miles deep, with no way out, because every word she says rings true for me as well.

"Sorry," she says. "I didn't mean to get so heated."

"It's a topic worth getting heated about."

"He's not," she says, and takes a big bite of her ramen. "Don't think I won't ask you about your past relationship some day."

I lean back in the chair with a groan. "Must you?"

"Yes," she says. "That's how you and I work. We're strictly quid pro quo."

"I can think of a lot more fun things to apply that to."

Her eyes flick to mine. The innuendo just slipped out, and it hangs in the air between us. "Maybe so…," she says, "but that doesn't get you out of this."

"Maybe not today," I say. "But I'll answer your questions eventually."

"Eventually?"

"Yes. Let's put a pin in that topic."

Her eyebrows rise. "How many business negotiations have you been in where you've used exactly those words?"

I grin. "A few."

"Fine, *eventually*. But I have an excellent memory."

"I don't doubt it."

"You know," she says, raising her chopsticks high, "you're more interesting than I think you give yourself credit for. I can't think of a better man to fake date."

I snort. "Well, that's a compliment I've never gotten before."

That makes her laugh, and fuck, I should say it now. That our mutually beneficial fake dating needs to come to an end. It's run its course, and I can't have these situations happen again and again. The temptation is too much.

And yet, the words won't come.

When we're done, she grabs my bowl and hers, walking to the sink. My eyes track the short skirt and her bobbing ponytail, the graceful lines and the fierceness that radiates from her.

I shift my focus to the clock on the wall instead. The second hand ticks with steady, unyielding movements.

Time stops for no one.

"I should leave," I say.

She takes a deep breath. "There's something I'd like to say first, though, if that's all right."

"Yes?"

"I know you said never to apologize for kissing you, and you also said that you always mean what you say. But I feel like I should apologize, anyway. I need to make sure that I haven't... broken anything or messed up what we have going on here—being the pretend dates. Or worse, injured our professional relationship. I'm sorry, Isaac."

She's looking at me with caution and hope, the brilliantly blue eyes clear with honesty. I can't remember the last time I was close with someone who spoke their thoughts and feelings this freely.

My hand clenches into a fist at my side. "I don't think we should do it again, even if it would help the pretense."

Her smile disappears. "Of course! It's probably for the best. I'm sorry I ever did, really, and I hope you don't feel like I took—"

"No, Sophia... Don't," I say with a sigh. "The problem is that I liked it too much. More than I should."

Her face goes perfectly blank. "Oh."

I get up from her kitchen table. She's only a few steps away. But so is her front door. "I don't mix business with pleasure," I say.

"Well," she says softly. "I don't date Upper East Side men."

There's a long, heated silence between us. I've got one foot in either direction, and she's there, leaning against her fridge, looking painfully beautiful and present.

"I have leftover tiramisu in the fridge," she says. "Want to stay for dessert?"

It takes me a moment to nod, just once, and she sighs. Like she's relieved. The sound travels through my body, so when she turns around, when she takes out the box from the fridge and sets it down on the counter, I cross the distance between us.

It's impossible not to.

I look over her shoulder, down at the dessert in a takeout container, and feel the softness of her ponytail brush against my neck. Her hands fall flat on the counter. "Oh," she says again. And just as slowly as I'd come up behind her, she leans back against me.

"I liked kissing you, too," she murmurs. "More than I should've."

The long line of her neck is right in front of me, bared by her ponytail. I lean down and touch my lips to the skin. Once, twice, following the column up toward her jaw.

"I'm sweaty," she murmurs.

I smile against her skin. And I'm not? The idea of breaking this magic spell because of something so mundane feels like heresy.

"So am I," I say against her skin. She exhales shakily, her head dropping back to rest against my shoulder.

"Wow," she breathes.

My hands wrap around the curve of her waist, my fingers stretching to find the press of her hipbones through the tennis skirt. *Just this,* I think. *Just let me have this moment with her.*

Sophia lets me explore her neck, lets me listen to her breathing becoming rougher. And I'm fine to do just that, to stay like this, but she has never been anything but an equal partner in the games we've played.

She turns in my arms. "Hi," she whispers. Her lips are only inches from mine, and all the reasons why I shouldn't do this feel like driftwood against her current.

"I can only do things a hundred and ten percent," I say.

Maybe it's a warning. Maybe it's a question. My hands tighten on the smooth skin of her thighs.

Her lips lift in a smile. "I remember."

I kiss her.

Surrendering to the moment feels like the easiest thing I've done all week. Sinking into Sophia is effortless.

She kisses me back, lips soft and open, and achingly smooth. Her hands find my shoulders and then my hair, and her tugging sends a ripple of sensation through my body. I kiss her the way I've wanted to since the beginning. The way kissing her should be done, in private and thoroughly, not like our kisses in front of others. Those had been brief and performative.

This? It's just for us.

I lift my head. "I'm not a math teacher," I say. "Don't think I ever will be."

"Good thing I'm not ready to date again, anyway."

"Mmm, yes. There are so many reasons why we'd never work." I look down at her legs, splayed on either side of me. The short tennis skirt has risen up along her tanned thighs. My hands grip them of their own accord, and I lift her up, setting her on the counter.

"Yes," she murmurs. "But that doesn't mean we can't have fun together."

Have fun together. My fingers dig into the soft flesh of her thighs, and I look down, focusing on the skin rather than the soft mouth in front of me. "I should at least buy you dinner first."

She chuckles. It's a breathless sound, and something about it, about Sophia unbound like this, makes my chest ache. Her bedroom is only a few strides away. It would be easy, so damnably easy, to ruin it all.

"Well, you bought me ramen," she says and kisses me. Her arms tighten around my neck, the edge of the counter digs into my lower stomach, and I yearn to be closer still. Her mouth is warm and familiar, and fuck if I don't want to do all

134

kinds of things I know I shouldn't. My fingers inch the skirt upwards, sweeping across the smooth skin of her thighs.

But then, I encounter tight fabric.

I look down. "You have shorts on?"

"Yes," she says with a little laugh. "They're built-ins."

"Clever," I say and wrap my hands around the outside of her thighs, minishorts and all. "Did you see us doing this?"

"Definitely not." She braces her knees on either side of my hips. With her hair up, there's nothing to distract from the beauty of her features. I can't look away from the freckles and the fierce eyes and the soft mouth. "Not complaining about it though," she says.

I raise an eyebrow. "High praise."

She chuckles. "I've never been very good at giving praise. I'm much better at constructive criticism."

"Really?" I say. Conversation is good—conversation distracts. "The members of your team must love you as a boss."

She knees my side. "Hey, I make it a point to only work with people who *like* clear communication."

"You'll have to tell me where you find them," I say.

Her hand slips beneath the collar of my T-shirt, and warm fingers brush over my shoulder. "Well, I have two team members. How many employees do you have?"

"Don't know the latest count." I rest my head against her neck and take a deep breath. "Sophia…"

"You think too much," she murmurs. "We both do."

"I'm not thinking at all right now," I say and kiss her again. It's deeper this time, longer, and I sink into her loveliness. I slide one of her sleeves off her shoulder, revealing tanned skin and the harsh line of a sports bra strap. The elastic looks almost bruising.

"Wow. You're very…"

"Locked in?" she says with a smile. "I know. I dressed to win."

"And win you did," I murmur. Her skin beneath my

hands is a live wire I can't stop touching, electrifying my entire body.

"Come," she says and slides off the kitchen counter. Hips to hips, and chest to chest.

"Come where?"

"We should shower," she says and backs away from me. There's a crooked smile on her face that speaks of reckless-ness and confidence, of pleasure to come, and intimacies to be shared.

I close my eyes. "Sophia," I mutter.

But she reaches for the hem of her top anyway.

15

SOPHIA

I drop my tank top on the floor.

"Sophia," he says. There's a pained expression on his face. "Please don't."

I watch him across my living room. Recklessness and something else, something wild, claws beneath my breast-bone. "And why not?"

"You know why not." He's not looking at me, like my sports bra and bare stomach is as dangerous as Medusa. His face looks carved in stern lines.

"Because you don't mix business and pleasure," I say, "or because you don't want me?"

He shakes his head. "You know that's not it."

"Do I?" I walk backward through my living room, my feet sinking into the plush carpet.

His hand turns into a fist at his side. "You deserve much more than this. Proper fucking dates, over candlelight. Flowers and gifts, and a slow seduction."

"I don't want that. I've *had* that."

"I know," he says and curses again. I've never heard him swear this much before. "You think I don't want you? You're all I goddamn think about these days, and it's been that way for far too long."

My skin feels hot. "We're not breaking any rules."

"Only all of them," he mutters, and for the first time since I took off my clothes, Isaac lets his gaze drop.

His eyes warm every inch of my skin they touch. There's always been a leashed quality to him, but it's fraying now, coming undone at the edges. His hair is mussed from my fingers, and I want his hands on my bare skin.

He flew in just to make our tennis match.

"Fine," he mutters, an angry furrow between his brows, and then he crosses the distance to me. He kisses me the same way he did in the kitchen. Thoroughly and deeply, and I lose myself in it. It feels so good to just *feel* again, to forget about myself and my ruined life, and Percy dating Scarlett.

I reach for his shirt, and he breaks our kiss just long enough to tug it over his wide shoulders. His chest is clearly defined, and there's a hint of ab muscles beneath a smattering of dark hair. It disappears down his shorts.

My stomach tightens at the sight, and when I run my hands over his chest, he groans against my lips.

"Where is—"

"Behind me," I say. He starts walking me backward toward the bedroom, but then I remember what we've just been doing.

I grip his shoulders. "Shower first."

He groans. "Do you want to kill me?"

That makes me chuckle. The sound is tinged with nerves and anticipation, and the remnants of my adrenaline high from our victory earlier. I haven't had sex since Percy, and it's been many years since I had sex with anyone else.

Isaac's hands tighten around my waist, and he lifts me up with a grunt. I lock my legs around his hips. "You didn't have to do that," I say with a grin.

He walks us toward my bathroom. "Trust me, I didn't feel the least bit forced."

"Oh? What is it then, a privilege?" I tease.

He sets me down on the bathroom mat but keeps our

bodies tight. "An honor." His hands slide down my sides and over my tennis skirt, and I shiver at the slow touch.

"I always thought we'd do this in a hotel room," I say.

He raises an eyebrow. "You've thought about this, too?"

I like the word *too* more than I should.

"Maybe." I undo the zipper in my tennis skirt. "Not once did I think it would be in my apartment, though."

His gaze is on my body and the slow shimmy of my skirt and built-in shorts down my legs.

"Stunning," he murmurs. "Let me…"

He tugs at my ponytail until it unravels, my hair falling over my shoulders. "First thing I noticed," he says and bends to kiss my neck. His free hand runs through my hair.

I close my eyes at the sensation. "First thing you noticed?"

Isaac kisses along my collarbone and takes a very long time to answer. "What was that?" he asks, voice hoarse.

I chuckle. "Never mind."

His lips stop at the edge of my sports bra, and then, his eyes shift with a focus that makes me shiver. He reaches behind me for a clasp.

But it doesn't have one, and I lean back in his arms to pull my sports bra over my chest. My breasts pop free, and Isaac groans, the hands supporting my waist tightening almost painfully.

"Jesus, you're so fucking beautiful," he says.

The expression on his face heats my skin as much as his words do. My chest is average, not big or small, and not very noteworthy. But his expression says anything but *average*.

We step into the shower. I reach behind him to turn the knob, and cold water sprays from above.

"Shit," he says, and I yelp at the sudden spray. "Sorry!"

He pulls me into his arms and into the corner of my small shower. Chest to chest, my cheek against his. He reaches behind me to adjust the temperature.

"I might not be a math teacher," he murmurs, "but I know degrees."

I pretend to shiver in delight, and he laughs. "Yeah. Just don't make me do calculus, though."

"Please don't," I say and fan myself with my hand. "That would bring me over the edge."

He glances down, and the humor on his face fades, leaving behind concentrated awe. "Cold water does have its perks, though." He smooths his hands up my ribs, his thumbs brushing a peaked nipple. "Would you look at that," he murmurs.

It's been so long. So long, and never here in my shower in the apartment I got to start over. He bends his head and kisses my skin, his mouth hot, warmer than the water at my back. I close my eyes at the sensations.

I twine my fingers through his hair, the short, dark strands unusually mussy. He adds his teeth, biting lightly at my nipple.

"Isaac," I say. My free hand finds his shoulder, curving around it. "Please."

He lifts his head. "Please what?"

"I need more. I need…" I wrap my arms around his neck and pull us under the warm water. The nerves in my body feel electrified, my stomach alive.

"What do you need?" Isaac asks and bends his head to kiss me. They're long, warm kisses beneath the onslaught of water; kisses with his hands on my waist, on my breasts, on the wet fabric of my underwear.

You, I think.

"Sophia?" he reminds me in a deep voice.

I rest my hands on the waistband of his shorts, now soaked through. To pull them down? To pull us both out of this shower?

I don't know.

I open my mouth to tell him that I want him. That I want fun, and easy, and for us to forget ourselves in one another. But that's not what comes out.

"It's been so long since I did this," I whisper.

His hands pause at my hips. "I see."

"But I want you," I say. "I want *this*."

Isaac makes a low humming sound, a thoughtful agreement. The water runs in rivulets down his lightly stubbled cheeks and over wide shoulders. The silence between us feels taut, and I wonder if I've ruined the moment. Broken the magic spell.

But then, he turns me around, my back to his chest, and his hands move down my body. They grip my underwear. "These need to come off," he says and pulls them down my thighs. Soaking wet, they fall the rest of the way, leaving me naked.

"You said you liked clear communication," he murmurs in my ear and slides his hand down my stomach. "Go on, then. Tell me what you like."

The first touch of his fingers makes me catch my breath. It's so foreign, being touched there, and I can't help but look down. At the thick forearm draped around my chest.

His free hand cups my breast. "Sophia," he says. "Talk to me."

His hand moves, and it's almost obscene, watching him touch me. "That's nice," I breathe.

"Just... nice?"

"Mm-hmm. I think you could—oh." He finds a spot that has me reaching out to the tiled wall to brace myself.

"Here?" he asks and presses his lips to my neck. The kisses, the fingers between my legs, and the hand on my breast...

I'm so turned on, I have to focus on breathing through my mouth, in and out, to stop from moaning. "Yes," I say. "That's it. Right there."

His fingers circle, and speed up, and I grip his forearm to make sure he doesn't pull away. He chuckles and tips my head back to rest against his shoulder. "So, it's been a long time, huh?"

"Screw you," I whisper, and he chuckles again. The sound

echoes against the tiles, and I spread my legs wider, holding on.

"That's it," he mutters, fingers speeding up. "Do you know how long I've wanted to do this?"

I shake my head. The words ricochet through my mind, but it's impossible to hold on to them, to hear anything but the pounding of my blood. I'm close, and it hasn't been this good by myself, not for months, not for—

Isaac takes his hand off me. I open my mouth to protest when he brings it back sharply in a smack, right *there*. I gasp, and then he does it again, and one more time, and on the fourth, the orgasm erupts inside of me.

My legs freeze up, and I moan at the liquid heat pouring through my limbs, almost unbearable. His hand returns between my legs to stroke me through it.

When the last tremors leave me, I rest my head against his shoulder. "Oh my God," I whisper. "I didn't expect that to be so…"

"Satisfying?"

"That, too. But not so quick. It's not like that happens every time."

His hands stroke up my stomach and return to cup my breasts. My body feels languid and liquid, like it's becoming one with the water pouring down from above.

"Every time by yourself?" he asks. "Or every time with… someone else?"

We both know who he's referring to. I close my eyes. "Someone else," I say. "Any someone, really."

He reaches past me to grab a few pumps of soap and starts stroking down my body. I give a satisfied sigh and turn in his arms. "Thanks."

His smile tips up and to the side, wider than I've ever seen it before. "I should be the one to say thank you. You're beautiful when you come."

A flush creeps up my cheeks. "Thanks."

He looks down my body, at his hands and at my own,

resting on one another. Soapy bubbles have started to form at the peaks of my nipples.

He kisses me slowly, softly. "Thanks for today," he murmurs. He runs a hand through his hair, squeezes out some of the water, and then steps out of the shower.

"Isaac?"

He reaches for a towel and runs it over his head. "Yes."

"You're leaving?" I look down, at the clear imprint of his length against the wet workout shorts. The sight makes my stomach tighten again, and I feel hyperaware of my naked body, and of how close it is to his. To *that*.

"Do you have a condom?" he asks, the look in his eyes wry. "Because I didn't bring one with me to the tournament."

"Oh," I breathe. "Shit, no, I don't."

I'm not on birth control anymore. Three months after I'd left Percy, it was time to renew my prescription for the pill... and I just hadn't. What had been the point? I wasn't looking to date. Ever. Only a small, gray-striped kitten had forced me out of bed in those early weeks.

"Didn't think so," he says and bends to grab his shirt. "I would never impose on you like that."

Impose. The old-fashioned word makes me smile. It's so him, the glimpses of chivalry bred into him. As if having unprotected sex with me would be an *imposition.*

"Stay," I say. "There are other things we can do."

His eyes are filled with heat. "Don't tempt me. It's been a very long twenty-four hours, and resisting you is more than I have in me right now, sweetheart."

My mouth opens. "Oh."

He kisses me goodbye and looks me over one final time with eyes glowing with appreciation. He smiles in farewell and leaves, and a few seconds later, I hear the door to my apartment close behind him.

I lean back against the shower wall. *Sweetheart.* Percy had never called me anything but Soph for our entire relationship. When I once asked him why he never called me any pet names, not even baby, he'd laughed and said that I was nobody's baby. *You're way too… strong,* he'd said, phrasing it like a compliment. *Too smart. Baby doesn't fit.* I'd tried to take it as a compliment, even if the words hadn't made sense to me.

Sweetheart. I let the warm water wash the remnants of the soap away, and every single part of me feels clean.

16

SOPHIA

"If someone had told us fifteen years ago," my sister says, the sound of a toddler wailing impatiently in the background, "that we would be talking on the phone before seven in the morning, we would—"

"Never have believed them," I finish. "I know. You used to be so grumpy in the mornings."

"You weren't such a peach, either," Rose says. There's happiness in her voice, beneath the tiredness. "Imagine how good it was for our relationship to stop fighting over the shower."

I chuckle and look both ways before jaywalking across an empty side street. New York is glorious this early. Some passersby are heading home from a wild night out, and others are out on their morning coffee runs. The city is alive with people's ever-clashing lives and routines.

"How's my favorite niece?" I ask.

"Your *only* niece is stuffing her face at the moment," Rose says. "Which is how I got these precious minutes with you in peace. So—"

"I haven't killed the cat," I say. "Don't worry."

She laughs. "I knew you wouldn't. You're great with animals. Is he a keeper?"

"Well, he sure is keeping my apartment wonderfully mouse-free."

"You have mice?" she says. "In that fancy place?"

"No, that's what I just said."

Rose groans. "It's too early for your sarcasm."

"I couldn't resist."

"Are you working too much?" she asks. "That was going to be my annoying question, not about the cat, but I'm always interested in updates about Milo, too. I don't want you over-working yourself."

"I love my work," I say. "You know that."

"Do I ever! But I'm just afraid that it's become the *only* thing you love after the divorce."

"Not true," I say. "You know I love you, and little Mia. Mom and Dad, and our first family dog, may he rest in peace. I love Grandma and—"

"Yes, yes, you master deflector, but I won't be distracted off the topic."

"I play a lot of tennis."

"Right, so not only are you working yourself to the bone, you're now exercising yourself to the bone, too." Rose sighs. "Just... try to find balance, okay? Make some friends at work, or join a club, or... just do something else."

"Balance," I repeat and rummage through my bag for my keycard to Exciteur. "Definitely. That's really important."

She sighs again. "You're still coming home in a few weeks, for Mia's birthday party, right?"

"Of course, I am."

"Excellent." Her voice brightens. "Robbie is invited, too."

I groan. "Why on Earth did you invite my high school boyfriend?"

"Because he and his brother helped us repaint the garage, and I wanted to be nice," she says. "Also, I want to set you up with him."

I sit down on the bench opposite Exciteur and reach into my bag for my pumps. Methodically, I unlace my ergonomic walking shoes, one at a time. "You can't set me up with someone I've already dated. That's now how set-ups work."

Rose lowers her voice. "Just flirt a bit. Have a nice little fling. Backslide."

"Backslide?"

"Yes, I think that's what the kids call hooking up with an ex. I think. Anyway, he's safe and familiar, isn't he?"

"Yes," I admit and fasten the clasp to my slingbacks. "I suppose. But—"

"All I'm saying is, don't close off the possibility of having some fun, or just getting laid. It's been a long time, hasn't it?"

"Rose, I don't—"

"Be open-minded," she says. "That's all."

"Rose, I think I might be close to sleeping with someone already."

There's absolute silence on the other end. Then her voice, no longer hushed. *"What?"*

"It's complicated."

"Start from the beginning," she demands. "No, scrap that, Mia's almost finished with her food. Start from the middle. Don't leave out any of the important stuff, and text me all the unimportant stuff later."

I laugh and pull out my headphone case. I need to go to work soon, too. "It's with someone I'm working with."

"An employee? Oh, I can see where this is going," she says.

"No, he's a client."

"A client," Rose repeats.

"Yes. He's not really my type anymore, but... well, I guess that's not true," I say. "He's definitely my type. But after Percy, I can't date those kind of men anymore."

"Soph..." she says.

"No, no, he's not *like* Percy. They're night and day, person-ality-wise. But they have similar backgrounds, if you know what I mean."

She makes a humming sound like she really does. "And something's happened between you two?"

"Flirting, and definitely more conversations than are appropriate."

"Oooh."

"He also helped me make Percy jealous at a few parties."

"Yes! I love this guy!"

I chuckle. "Yeah. Also, we sort of made out a couple of days ago. In the shower."

"Oh my *God*," Rose says. "Why am I just finding this out? No, honey, don't throw that on the floor."

"I'm not throwing anything," I say because I can't resist.

"Please. Mommy just has to talk to Auntie Sophia," Rose says, voice away from the phone. Then she's back. "I'm all for it. That's all I have to say. Absolutely all for it. Hooking up with someone means you're living a more balanced life."

I laugh. "Right, well, I'm glad."

"Will you see him again?"

"Professionally, yes. Privately... I don't know. He just kinda left after we made out."

"Oh," she says. But then her voice brightens. "Then you make the first move. You're free to live your life however you want to now, Sophia." Sounds erupt on the other end, suspiciously like plastic hitting a wooden floor. "Darn. I have to go. Text me more details, okay? I'll badger you if you don't. See you in a few weeks!"

"Love you," I say. But Rose has already clicked off to take care of my niece's high-pitched wailing, who is as adorable as she is demanding.

I tuck my sneakers into my bag and the conversation into the back of my mind. Exciteur and the work I do deserve my attention, and not Isaac or what his hands had done in the shower.

Nor the absolute silence I've had from him in the three days since. Not a word, a text, an email, or a call.

There's a mild humiliation along with the memory,

dimming its shine. He had been so controlled, so natural through it all, with the sound of his deep voice murmuring in my ear while he... well. It had been one of the hottest moments of my life. But he hadn't *lost* control.

Not that I think Isaac Winter ever truly does. It's not in his character, and that's a good thing, but I'm still embarrassed.

Because I had.

That day had been an intense one. I'd been high off the victory, bitter from seeing Percy and Scarlett, delighted over spending time with Isaac, and then the sudden presence of him in my apartment. There, in a place that's just mine. His body in my kitchen, and his eyes on me.

And then his hands and body against mine.

But he'd been in control enough to remember condoms, and composed enough to leave.

I let myself think about it for twenty-eight more seconds, the exact time it takes for me to ride the elevator to my floor in the skyscraper Exciteur calls home. Then, I leave thoughts of Isaac behind... and get to work designing a pitch for his hotel business instead. That's what I do best, and that's my comfort zone. At least it used to be before it was his name at the top of all my work documents.

I'm reviewing the color schemes Toby sent over for the traditional pitch when there's a knock on my door. Toby and Jenna swing by all the time, and sometimes, the head of our department does, as well.

So I don't look up from my screen when I answer. "Come in!"

"Sophia," a familiar voice says.

It's not an Exciteur employee.

Isaac's in a navy suit, unbuttoned jacket and clean-shaven jaw, and is looking at me across the familiar space of my office with those dark eyes.

"Oh," I breathe. "Hello."

"Hi." He gestures to the chair opposite mine. "Do you have a minute?"

"Yes, absolutely. Is this about the pitch?"

"That was my reason for coming to Exciteur, yes. I just spoke to Victor about it."

"Oh," I say again. The big, big boss. His brother's business partner and probably also a personal friend. I've never been up to the thirty-fourth floor where he conducts business. "Interesting."

Isaac's lips curve into a half smile. "All good things."

"I'm glad to hear it."

"I also told your department head I'm only popping by to chat with you about how it's coming along and to touch base. Everyone's aware it's a professional visit."

I knit my hands together on the desk. "Of course. What do you want to know? Things are coming along great, and I'm confident we'll have it ready in time."

He leans back in the chair, and beneath my desk, I feel the brush of one of his long legs against mine. "How have you been?"

"Since the weekend?"

"Yes," he says.

"Great, actually," I say. The memory of what happened in the shower must play across my face, evident in my gaze.

His eyes warm. "Great? Funny. So have I."

"Really?"

"Yes. I must have had a relaxing weekend."

"I can't imagine you did," I say. "You flew in from another country, were forced to play in a tennis tournament with a crazy woman you work with, and then you..."

"Then I what?"

I shake my head. "Never mind."

The words that had come to my mind aren't fit to be spoken in the office, and I can't bring myself to say them. *And then you got hot and heavy without the reward.*

Isaac runs a hand along his jaw. "Because I couldn't... finish what I started?" he asks. "I'll admit that was frustrating at the time, but it was still worth it. Overall, a very pleasant experience."

"I'm glad," I murmur. "Because it was for me, too."

He gives a wide smile. "I noticed. So, I've been thinking about the rules."

"The rules," I repeat. "Which ones? Oh, that I don't date Upper East Side men? And you don't…"

"Mix business and pleasure, yes," he says. "They've been on my mind quite a bit since your shower."

Heat rises beneath my blouse, inching toward my neck. *Bad idea,* but it's so well-packaged, and sitting right in front of me. I remember the feeling of his hand, strong and broad, sliding down my stomach to find what it sought.

I swallow hard. "And what have you decided?"

"Well, that's what I wanted to talk to you about," he says.

"So, stopping by to see St. Clair was a ruse?"

"Yes, but don't tell him that. His ego would never recover."

"I'll keep it between us," I say.

Isaac braces an arm against my desk. "You're pitching my executive team in two weeks. Correct?"

"Yes," I say. Then I start to smile. "And it's only *after* the pitch that your team has to decide about hiring us to manage the project or not."

"Exactly. Which means we're not technically in business together until that decision is made," he says. "The pitch is like an audition."

"Airtight logic."

He chuckles. "Well, it takes care of the business and pleasure part. Now, you want to avoid dating men from New York, right?"

"Not from the entire city," I say. "That'd make life pretty hard. But from Upper East or West Sides. Anyone who's ever been to a country club is automatically ruled out."

Isaac nods like my logic is equally sound. "That's right.

Well, if we only have two weeks, and a clear time limit, would it even qualify as dating?"

I start to smile. "No."

"My thoughts exactly," he says.

"Great minds think alike."

"So it seems," he says, and then he smiles, too. "You look beautiful today."

"Thank you."

"Does that skirt come with built-in shorts, as well?"

I laugh. "No, it definitely doesn't."

"Interesting," he says, voice warm. "Come to Connecticut with me this weekend."

"Connecticut?"

"We won that spa and hotel night."

"You won it," I correct softly. My mind is wheeling at the idea of slipping away from the city and everyone who knows us, from our everyday life with Exciteur and the Winter Hotel...

"Come with me," he says again. "One night, two days."

It's a possibility that shouldn't even exist but now just might, a brief window into what life might have looked like if things were different. I look at the man across from me. The man who's looking back at me with tension in his shoulders, waiting for my decision. Caring about what I decide.

"Okay," I say. "Let's do it."

"Great. I'll pick you up on Saturday," he says, and then he smiles, a wide grin spreading across a face that seems unused to it. "They have a tennis court at the hotel."

"They do?"

"Yes. Bring your racket."

He stands and extends a hand across the table. I take it, warm fingers closing around mine. "What's this?"

His eyes are alight with humor. "Always a pleasure working with you, Miss Bishop," he says.

"Likewise, Mr. Winter."

"It's rare to find someone who appreciates such... clear communication."

"Definitely. Not to mention someone who plans ahead."

He lifts my hand and presses a kiss to the inside of my wrist, warm and brief. The gesture catches me off guard. "I'll plan ahead for this weekend," he murmurs.

A shiver sends goose bumps along my arms. "Good," I whisper. "Would hate for you to end up... unsatisfied again."

He smiles and drops my hand. "Until Saturday, then."

"Until Saturday," I say.

17

ISAAC

The drive takes us away from high-rises and industrial buildings and into dark green forests. September is upon us, and leaves have just started to hint at a shift, not yet committing to the brighter colors. But the air has lost all the intense August heat, and Sophia has rolled down her window a few inches, her face turned toward the landscape passing outside the car.

It lets me glance at her as often as I'd like. Mile by mile, all the concerns I left back in the city slip away, leaving only the two of us and a weekend full of possibilities.

"What are you thinking about?" I say. She'd asked me the same only a few minutes earlier.

"That this will be our only weekend away together."

I drum my fingers against the wheel, once, twice. "Might be, yes."

"Might be?" She crosses her legs, clad in beige suit pants, while the matching blazer is tucked into the backseat.

"Might be," I say. "The future is unwritten."

She hmms. "As long as that doesn't make you reject our pitch, you know, just to ensure we don't have to work together again."

"Oh," I say, "I would never put my own desires in front of what's best for my company."

Sophia chuckles at that. "God forbid!"

We pull up on the long gravel road a few hours before sunset. The hotel is made up of a collection of cabins, surrounded by old, tall trees, and beautifully situated on the shores of a lake.

Sophia sighs. "God, this place is so pretty. Imagine when the leaves fully turn."

It is pretty, built in harmony with nature. I put the car in park, and a man from the hotel comes forward immediately. Valet. Nice touch.

We're escorted through the lobby, welcomed with a drink, and the check-in process is smoother than silk. Sophia stands beside me with a small suitcase in front, her hand curved around the handle. She gives me a smile.

"Mr. Winter?" the receptionist says, pulling my gaze back across the desk. "I'd just like to say that it's an honor to have you stay here. Please let us know if you need anything at all."

"Thanks," I say and bend to take Sophia's bag from her. We head down a corridor, and her smile widens, turns conspiratorial.

"What are you smiling about?" I mutter.

"Nothing," she says.

"There's definitely something."

She glances at the attendant before leaning her head toward mine. "You must be used to this when you travel, right? Impeccable service and overly nice staff."

I frown. "Impeccable is a high standard, but good, yes."

"Most hotels must be scared shitless of having you stay with them," she says, her smile smug. "You probably get the best treatment everywhere."

"Absolutely not."

Her smile widens. "Totally. The receptionist out there? Did you notice that she called for the hotel owner to join us?"

"No."

"Well, she motioned for him to come out of the office. Anyway, all I'm saying is, when we check out? If you give them a compliment on their suites or their service, I think they might faint with happiness."

I roll my eyes at her exaggerated teasing. "Right. Do you want me to write them a glowing review online, too?"

"They'd frame it if you did."

"You know, the vast majority of people have absolutely no idea who I am," I say. "I've never sought fame or notoriety, and I can promise that no one staying at this hotel will recognize me."

"Yeah, but they're not in hospitality. They're—"

"Here we are," the attendant says and pushes open the door to the suite. It's finished in wood paneling but understated in furniture. The real showpieces are the windows, opening on the silvered expanse of the lake and illuminating the king-size bed in the center of the room.

"Everything to your satisfaction?" the attendant asks.

"Yes," I murmur and reach into my pocket for a tip. "Thank you."

"Dinner and breakfast are served in the restaurant downstairs, but we also have room service. You'll find everything you need for the spa experience in the bathroom. Give us a call if you need anything."

The door shuts behind him, and then we're alone. Sophia runs a hand over the elaborate bedding, her form gilded by the golden sun setting outside the windows.

Just us again. Alone.

"Nice room," I say.

She nods. Her hair had been in a bun when I picked her up, but somewhere along the ride, she'd unraveled it, and it now hangs in glossy brown waves down her back. "It's lovely here."

You're lovely, I think.

She looks at me over her shoulder. "So, what do we do now? Have dinner?"

"I could eat," I say. I've been hungry for days.

Her eyes heat. "Me, too."

We make it down to the restaurant, with candlelit tables and bouquets on every table. We drink wine and order pasta and filet mignon, and then more wine, and I spend my time trying to make her laugh. A flush colors her cheeks, and the blue of her eyes glitters with every chuckle. *Beautiful,* I think, and it hurts to look at her.

"Anyway," she says halfway through a story, "that's how I got the internship."

"You didn't."

She nods and sets down her wineglass. "Oh yes, and I can't believe they hired me. I called the CEO's *landline.* Her fourteen-year-old-son picked up!"

I chuckle. "To be fair, they had to hire you at that point. You were basically threatening to stalk the CEO until they did."

"Yes." Sophia covers her face with her hands. "I can't believe she gave me a solid recommendation letter after-wards, too."

"Well, I can. You did a great job, didn't you?"

"I don't know about that," she says and shrugs. "I hope I did, but I was young."

I shake my head. "Don't do that with me."

"Don't do what?"

"Downplay your accomplishments," I say, "or feign humility. You were the best damn intern they ever had. Weren't you?"

She taps her fingers against the table. "Yes," she admits. "I created a new system for their internal filing. The CEO called it genius."

"I'm not the least bit surprised."

"You know me that well?"

"Yes," I say, "and you don't ever have to pretend you're anything but the best around me. Don't make yourself smaller."

It takes her a long few seconds to answer. "Thank you," she murmurs. "That's a rare thing."

My chest tightens at the thought of her dimming her shine for anyone, let alone Percy, with his dislike for her career. "It shouldn't be," I say. "Fuck anyone who makes you feel like you need to make light of your accomplishments."

She gives a rueful smile. "You've never apologized for being ambitious."

"Of course, not."

"It was probably expected of you. Maybe even encouraged, right? By your grandfather?"

I nod. "Yes. The Winter Corporation did well under my father. It didn't grow, but it didn't falter, either. But I have always wanted to expand it."

"Where does that come from, for you? The desire to... to..."

"To be the best?"

"Yes," she says, nodding. "And to want to make things around you better."

"It's always been there," I say, but then I frown and consider it. "There's also an aspect of supporting the family, I suppose."

"Supporting?"

I look at her across the table. Interested, intelligent, and eyes like crystals. And I say things I know I shouldn't. "The entire family draws an income from the company."

"Oh," she says. "I see."

"It's minuscule in comparison to the overall profits, of course. Basically, just dividends on the shares. But it's substantial for the family. My great-uncle, my cousins, the extended family." I sigh. "They're all invested in the future of the company. If it were to fail, if we had to close shop, every single one of them would see it as a failure."

"But none of them want to help keep it running?"

I nod, my hand tight around my wineglass. "No, they've all made that very clear. At this point, I don't know if I'd even trust anyone else with it. It's my family's legacy, and it was my grandfather's wish that it stays in the family..." I shake my head. "I just can't see it fail."

"I see," she murmurs, and it's clear in her eyes that she does. "It's your cross to bear."

For life, I think and feel the familiar weight of that responsibility, the knowledge I've lived with since I was a teenager. It's been a long time since I resented it. But I resent it now, sitting across from a woman who has sworn off Upper East Side men and the superficiality of the world we come from. It's a world I can disdain, but never leave.

I clear my throat. "Anyway," I say, "don't feel any pressure for the pitch."

She laughs. "Oh, of course, not! After hearing how you'd give your life rather than seeing it fail?"

I grin. "Yes. I'll be honest, but fair."

"Oh, I know you well enough to know that, too," she says and stretches her legs out beneath the table. Her ankle brushes mine. "Can I ask you a really intrusive question?"

"I'm intrigued now."

"I think it's finally time for you to tell me about your previous relationship."

I close my eyes. "So disappointed."

She laughs again and nudges my leg beneath the table. "That was an easy one! Get me another drink and I can switch to really intrusive ones."

"Oh? Now that's a game I can play."

"Later," she says. "Now tell me."

"What do you want to know about it?"

"How long were you dating before it ended?"

"Three years," I say. "Engaged for one."

She nods and tilts her head. "Why did your brother invite her parents? I've been trying to understand that, but it just seems so rude to me. Against you, I mean."

I shift my thumb so it rests against her palm. Of course, she's curious. There's no pain talking about Cordelia, no regrets, so I give her what she wants. "I told you that her parents build golf courses."

Sophia's eyebrows rise. "Oh, that's right."

"They build and manage them all across the world. I'm technically in business with Cordelia's parents in the Caribbean, for the new resort."

She blinks a few times. "Seriously?"

"They aren't involved with the day-to-day, and the CEO isn't a member of the family," I say and shrug. "But yes. There was a fair bit of speculation at the time, if it was…"

"If you two were getting married for the companies."

"Yes," I say. "Wasn't true."

Her smile softens. "Not even a little bit?"

I narrow my eyes at her, but she narrows hers right back. "No," I say again. "Although… you're not wrong, either. I did consider it a perk."

She shakes her head. "You're ruthlessly ambitious."

"Ruthless?" It's not a description I've strived for.

"With yourself, I mean. You're ruthless with your own happiness."

I have nothing to say to that, my mind blank. That's not a perspective I've ever applied to my own life before. Her gaze is warm on mine, and beautifully honest.

"I'm sorry about the way it ended," she says. "No one deserves to be cheated on."

"No. I'm sorry about the way your marriage ended, too."

Her mouth tips up. "This got more serious than I suspected."

"You're the one who asked the question."

"I did, didn't I?" She sighs and rests her head in her hand. "You know, I can't believe I'm here with you."

"Hmm?" My hand moves on its own, finding the curve of her elbow. I smooth my thumb over the soft skin beneath the short sleeve of her dress.

"Just last weekend, you were in my apartment," she murmurs. "Eating at my table and taking a shower with me."

My smile widens. "Yes. Is this when the more intrusive questions start?"

"It might be. Brace yourself."

"I'll consider myself warned."

"Last Saturday," she says. "You were… very controlled."

I raise an eyebrow. "Was I?"

"Yes."

"Didn't feel that way," I say. The need for her had been a second pulse beneath my skin, my shorts painfully tight around my erection. "Is this because I left?"

"Might be," she says. "It was pretty… abrupt."

I chuckle. "Trust me, it needed to be, or I wouldn't have left at all."

"Oh."

"I told you I wanted to buy you dinner first."

"That was it? I thought it had to do with the lack of a certain… garment."

My smile widens. "A condom is a garment, now?"

She looks over her shoulder, but no one is close enough to overhear. "Technically speaking, yes. Did you bring one this weekend?"

My entire body tightens. "Yes."

"Good," she murmurs, blue eyes glittering.

I motion to the waiter. Across the table from me, Sophia laughs. The sound is breathless. "What are you doing?"

"Wrapping this up," I say. "You can keep asking intrusive questions up in the room."

18

SOPHIA

The door to our hotel room closes behind us, falling shut with a sound of finality. Isaac turns on the lights. They're set for the evening and cast a dimmed shine over the tastefully decorated room. Minimalist and comfortable.

I step out of my heels and watch as he opens the door to the minibar. "We haven't tried the spa area yet," I say. My throat feels dry.

He closes the door again. "Is that what you want to do?"

"No, not really."

His mouth curves. "Me neither."

"We'll have time for that tomorrow."

"Plenty of it," he agrees.

"Are you making a drink?"

"Looking at the options," he says. "But I'm not sure if more alcohol is the best route for us now."

"Well, it's been known to... ease the way."

"Do you think we need it?" he asks. "The last thing I want to be tonight is too buzzed to savor you properly."

My stomach tightens. "Oh."

His mouth tips up again into *that* smile, the one so unlike the professional ones I've seen him exploit in meetings, at conferences. It makes it hard to breathe.

"Too much?" he asks.

I shake my head and sit down on the edge of the bed, bracing my hands against the soft cover. It takes me a few breaths to speak. "Isaac," I say.

"Yes?" He's watching me like he's been from the very beginning. Sometimes casually, sometimes intensely, across his hotel lobby and conference rooms and suites. And now I finally understand what his gaze means, and the weight of it is delicious.

"Do you feel like having a shower?" I say.

"You know what, I wouldn't mind one, if you're in it."

"Me neither." I get up off the bed, nerves and adrenaline pounding through me. The world feels slightly off-balance. "It's best to be thorough, you know, in evaluating the hotel."

He reaches out, curving a hand around my waist. "Sophia," he murmurs.

I rest my hands on the lapels of his suit jacket. The solidity of him is reassuring, anchoring, bringing me back to Earth. "Yes?"

"Are you okay?" he says. "We don't have to do this."

I shake my head. "It's not that."

"Then what is it? Talk to me."

I shake my head again. The words flashing through my mind aren't ones I want to share. That it has been a year, that the last person was Percy, and only Percy. That I know he was never faithful, but I always was, and this feels like I'm leaving him behind, finally. And that I want that so badly, but I'm also scared of it.

But I don't say that because I don't want Percy anywhere close to this hotel room.

"Just the past," I say and slide my hands up to wrap around his neck. "But it belongs right where I left it."

His eyes are hard to read, thoughtful and intent on mine. He runs a hand along my jaw and slowly tips my head back. "You don't need to pretend around me."

"I know," I say, because I do. "That goes both ways."

He kisses me. It's slow, a brush of lips against mine. Another step in the conversation we're having.

"I know," he murmurs. "It always has with you and me."

I tug at his lapels, and Isaac shrugs out of the suit jacket, letting it drop to the ground. Then, his hand is back, cupping the side of my face, and he kisses me again.

This time, his mouth slants over mine, and I sigh into the warmth, my lips parting. He's there with a sweep of his tongue, and heat spreads from the touch. It's heady and liquid, softening my muscles, and I sink into the embrace.

Isaac's fingers find the zipper of my dress. Slowly, inch by inch, he pulls it down my side. The touch of his skin follows, his hand slipping into the hole to touch the bare skin of my back.

"You have no idea," he says, "how long I've been thinking about this."

"You have?"

"Yes." His hand fits itself under the strap of my bra. "The shower was just an appetizer."

I chuckle, feeling drunk on the scent of him—his cologne and clean, warm man. "I was offering you the main course on Saturday, you know."

Isaac makes a sound, somewhere between a growl and a groan. "Leaving you in that bathroom was the hardest thing I've ever done."

He tugs down the shoulder straps of my dress. The fabric cascades down my body, and I shimmy my hips to let it fall to the floor.

Isaac looks down. "No shorts this time."

"No." I feel naked, in only my black bra and lacy panties. And I feel beautiful, vulnerable yet strong, choosing to do this again with a man I know understands me.

His hands trace the shape of my body. There's such heat in his gaze, it burns. "The shower," he says, "let me look. But I didn't get the chance to linger."

I take a step toward the bed, but Isaac has a different goal in mind. He sits down in one of the armchairs and pulls me on top of him. I brace a leg on either side of him, gripping his shoulders for support.

"And lingering," he says and pulls down one of my bra straps, "is my favorite part."

He peels the bra off me. Strap by strap, and then cup by cup, until I'm bared to his gaze... and his touch.

He leans in, mouth closing over a nipple. His dark hair is a stark contrast against my skin, and I weave my fingers through it, trying to breathe through the building heat. His body is beneath me, separated only by fabric, a few insubstantial layers.

He bites down on one of my nipples. "Oh," I say. "*Oh.*"

He chuckles softly, his hands gripping my hips. I start rolling them into his hands, pushing my lower body against him in a slow grind until I feel the hard outline beneath me.

"Sophia," he mutters. His thumbs dig in sharply at my hipbones as if torn between slowing down my movements and egging me on.

I find the buttons of his shirt and open them one by one until I can rest my palms against the warm skin of his chest. "You're so gorgeous," he says, dark eyes nearly black.

"Tell me," I say. "Tell me how long you've wanted this."

A smile cuts through the tension on his face. "You like praise, sweetheart?"

My cheeks flare with embarrassment. The sentence had just slipped out of me, and now I can't take it back.

But Isaac doesn't miss a beat. "When you walked into that conference room," he says and tweaks one of my nipples, "the first thing I imagined was how good your body would feel against mine."

My breath is coming fast. "Oh."

"I knew it was inappropriate, of course. But that's where my mind went on its own. And when I saw you on the tennis court in that skirt and ponytail?" He trails his hand over my hip and rests it between my legs, his hand cupping me over the lace. "My first thought was what you looked like beneath it."

"Not winning?" I ask. The words sound breathless.

He curls his fingers, brushing them against sensitive flesh. "You know I love to win."

"Mm-hmm," I say. "So do I."

"But I wanted you more," he says and tugs the lace of my panties aside. His fingers brush against my bare skin, and he gives a hoarse groan. "This still feels like victory, though."

He's touching me like he had been in the shower, only now he's watching me as he does it, his eyes roaming between mine and the movement of his fingers.

It's intimate in a way the shower hadn't been.

His fingers circle, finding the spot he'd so expertly manipulated last weekend. "That's it," he murmurs. "God, you're so soft."

I roll my hips against his hand. He taunts and teases, sends me rising. Lingering, as he put it, until I can't take the teasing hands anymore. I reach between us for the belt on his pants.

He lets me undo it, his hands drifting up to my hips.

"You wouldn't let me take off your shorts last weekend," I say.

He groans when I pull the zipper down over the distinct hardness beneath. "No, because condom or no condom, I would've wanted to get inside you if you had."

I run my nails over the bulge in his boxer briefs. "You've teased me a lot," I say.

"Only fair," he murmurs.

I slide down from the chair between his splayed legs. My hands have a goal, and he must be anxious to help because it takes us less than five seconds to tug at his pants, to pull the elastic down, and then he's there.

Bobbing hard and big in front of me.

"Sophia, I—"

His words end when I start to stroke, and when I close my lips around him, he draws a sharp breath. From the corner of my eye I see his hands curving around the armrests of the chair, the knuckles turning white.

Excitement races through me at the sight.

Knowing he's coming undone by me, *because* of me, is thrilling. Losing control, being vulnerable... I know without asking him that's not something he allows himself often.

His hand runs over my head, strokes over my bare shoulder. It tightens over my skin when I add fluttering strokes of my tongue.

"Fuck. Okay, you're too good at this," he says. "Like you are at everything."

I want to smile. I want to laugh, I want to live in this moment forever, but I sheath my teeth and grip him tighter instead.

He groans, and his hips flex, involuntarily, beneath me. "No more," he breathes, and hands beneath my arms tug me upwards with too much strength to resist. "Come, I need... here, sit on me. Let me—" Then his hands pause on my waist. "Fuck, the condom."

I chuckle. "Not again."

He sighs like a man settling down to a task, hard and cumbersome, and stands with me in his arms. "Waiting," he mutters, "for a good thing is getting old."

I brush his hair back as he carries me to the bed. "Where is it?"

"My wallet," he says. I stretch out on the bed and luxuriate in the heat of his eyes. He barely looks away from me as he fishes the wallet out of his back pocket and shucks his pants off entirely.

His eyes trace every part of me. The modest size of my breasts, the stomach I can never quite get flat, and my long legs. While he takes me in, I watch as he rolls on the condom. There's not a single trace of hesitation in his movements.

Isaac gives himself two slow strokes before he climbs onto the bed. "Finally," I say. It's meant to be half-teasing, half-sincere.

But the look on his face takes all the amusement out of me. Need, so sharp it's almost painful, marks his stark features. He pushes my leg to the side and lifts the other up along his chest.

We both watch as he takes himself in hand and aligns us. He pushes in slowly, disappearing inch by inch inside of me. The view is delicious and the stretch even more so. We both exhale in relief when he's fully in.

He grips my hip. "Finally," he breathes and starts to move.

The need has been building inside of me since we entered the hotel room, and longer still, lingering from the shower last weekend. It's been heightened by the dinner and the knowledge that he's here, with me, without time restraints or pretense. Anticipation has kept my body in a constant state of readiness for just this moment.

Isaac rolls his hips in deep, steady movements, and his hands never stop touching me. I can't look away from his eyes, and it doesn't take me long to hover on the edge of an orgasm. I feel full, and half-sated, half-needy.

"You're close," he mutters.

I nod. My breath is coming fast, and I'm holding on to the sheet, to him, to anything I can grab. His eyes glint, and then he sits up, spreading me wider, and his hand speeds up its tight, small circles between my legs. It takes me four more seconds to explode. My back arches up off the bed, and I stare unseeing at the ceiling while pleasure flares out from the spot where we connect.

Isaac groans at the feeling of my body convulsing around his. He lowers himself down, arms resting on either side of my head. It takes him a few more thrusts, and then he's there, too, his hips sharp against my inner thighs when he explodes.

I close my eyes and luxuriate beneath the delicious weight

of him. *Only one weekend,* I think and tighten my legs around him. *I have to remember every detail.*

He lifts himself onto an elbow. Dark hair falls mussed over his forehead, now unlined, his brows unfurrowed.

"Hello," I whisper.

Isaac smiles. "Hi."

19

SOPHIA

I wake up in a bed much larger than my own. Cotton is soft against my skin, and I stretch my legs, finding that my muscles ache. There's a heavy arm around my waist, beneath the cover. A warm body is lying behind mine.

Isaac.

I blink my eyes open and look at our surroundings. The hotel room, the sparse decor, the scent of citrus from their diffusers. We must have forgotten to draw the blinds, and soft light filters in through the giant windows. The sun is rising over the lake. It sets the rippling water ablaze in soft morning colors, and the dense foliage around hints at fall. It's beautiful.

I hadn't realized how much I needed an escape from New York, and an escape from the ingrained routine that's became my lifeline over the past year. Possibility feels thick in the air here. A different life, and a different outlook.

And I hadn't realized how much I'd needed last night.

My eyes fill with moisture. I blink to clear the tears away, but they don't stop, my emotions rising within my chest. It's been a few intense weeks, and an intense weekend.

On top of the most intense year of my life.

And now this beautiful sunrise outside the window,

setting off the fall colors. Another season is changing, and I'm here to witness it, and maybe I haven't noticed the seasons changing, not really, not for an entire year. Maybe I can find something good again. Not like how it was with Percy, and not like how it was after him. But maybe I can create my own future, and it won't be what I'd imagined, but it can still be a beautiful thing. I'm grateful that I get to see it all, and for the first time in months, the thought of the future fills me with excitement.

The warm arm around me flexes. "Morning," he mumbles into my neck. His voice is rough and hoarse, and my silent tears flow faster at the sound. He's so unguarded here with me, and I'm grateful for that, too.

You're so silly, I think and blink rapidly to clear the tears before he notices. They've always come at the most inconvenient times. When I'm furious, or humiliated, or overwhelmed with emotion. Always and forever in situations where I feel the least comfortable crying. It's an aspect of my body I've never been able to control.

"Good morning," I murmur.

His body shifts behind mine. "Have we slept in?"

"No clue." The only alarm clock this wellness retreat has is the sun, apparently.

"I can't remember the last time I did that."

"Me neither." My voice isn't wavering, but I'm not speaking above a whisper, either. The emotions inside have started to ebb.

He clears his throat, but it's still hoarse with sleep. "You know what I just realized?"

"No?"

"You didn't ask me any intrusive questions last night. Not a single one."

I turn my face to the pillow, hoping it soaks up some of my tears. *I'm proud*, I think, *that I dared to do this again.*

"There's still time," I say.

"I'll admit, I'm very curious what they might be." His

171

hand on my waist slides up, caressing my body. "I might have some of my own."

"Oh?"

He brushes his lips over my neck. "Yes. You know, to evaluate last night."

I nudge him with my hip and he groans, pulling me tighter into the cradle of his body. "Evaluate?"

"Yes," he says. "I want to know everything you like." His hand cups my breast softly. "We both want to be the best, you know."

"Clear communication," I murmur.

"Exactly. Hard to imagine, though," he says, face in my neck, "how I could possibly enjoy sex with you *more* than I did last night."

The compliment makes me smile. My tears have stopped, the only remnants the tracks on my cheeks. He's still here, and he's still unguarded. The magic spell hasn't broken yet. I hope it never will.

Isaac rises on an elbow behind me. I roll into the cavity he leaves behind, looking up at him. His hair is mussed, and his eyes are warm. He looks glorious like this.

But then his eyes widen in alarm. "Sophia?" He runs a soft hand over my wet cheek. "What's wrong?"

"Nothing."

"You've been crying."

"Yes, but it's nothing."

His jaw tenses. "Please tell me."

"I got emotional, that's all," I say with a smile. "Looking at the sunrise and being here with you."

His thumb rubs slow circles on my cheek. They're soothing, and I lift my leg to hitch it around his waist. "They're good tears. I promise."

"Right," he says it like he doubts that concept. "You're thinking about the past."

"No, I'm not," I say, shaking my head. I lock my hands

around his neck. "No, I want you to ask me an intrusive question."

He raises an eyebrow. "Are you sure?"

"Never been surer about anything," I say and pull him down on top of me. "You got us a late check-out, right?"

And I think he understands, even if he doesn't know why, that it's not something I can explain. It takes us another two hours to make it out of the room. He was cautious after my tears, but with every movement and every word, his hesitation wore down when he saw I wasn't actually sad.

We play tennis, one-on-one, and roast in the spa afterwards. "Excellent choice," he murmurs in the sauna, running a finger beneath the shoulder strap of my emerald bikini top. I kiss him. It's a communal space, and we're both adults, and still, I kiss him like we're teenagers who can't resist.

He shifts me against his hip afterwards, smiling crookedly. His hair is so wet it looks almost black. "I want to see where you live," I say.

He raises an eyebrow. "I think that can be arranged."

"I'm curious, you know, what a hotel emperor's apartment might look like."

"It has a throne, for one."

"Of course, it does. Dungeons, perhaps?"

"No, that would be a bit gauche," he says, eyes sparkling. "And unnecessary. The moat already keeps out all the rabble."

I laugh. "I'm so grateful you're considering lowering the drawbridge for a lowly commoner."

"It'll always be lowered for you," he says. "Let's do an evening this week."

I nod and lean back against the wooden backing. "Isn't this so much better than the sushi lesson you bid on, too?"

He chuckles. "I would have paid more money just to get *out* of that one."

We stay as late as we can that day; until we have to leave the secluded Connecticut getaway. Isaac lifts both of our bags into the trunk of his SUV. In a wool sweater and a down vest, he looks relaxed. At ease. Another version of himself, one that's just as competent in the forested expanse around us as he is in the concrete jungle back home.

"I'm glad we have another full week," I say.

He smiles, and reaches out to brush back a strand of hair from my face. It's still damp from our shower. "Yes," he murmurs. "So am I."

I kiss him, just because I can, and vow to myself that I'll make the next week the best one I've ever had.

20

ISAAC

I lean against the closed door of my apartment and watch Sophia walk down the hall, one foot carefully placed in front of the other, like she's intruding.

"You can snoop," I say with a grin. "Go ahead."

"This place is your *home?* Like, your actual home, home?"

"Yes."

"It looks like a museum!"

"The first couple of rooms definitely do."

She peers into the study off the main hallway. It's a massive space, with three of the four walls clad in built-in bookcases.

"Wow," she breathes and runs a hand over leather-encased books. "Have you read these?"

"No. Most were printed half a century ago." I look at the giant desk with the dark wood and leather inlay in the middle of the room. "My grandfather was the first to live in this apartment."

"This was his study?"

"Yes."

She pauses at three framed portraits. They're ostentatious, commissioned for vanity, and yet, I've never been able to take them down. To change anything in these rooms. My father had felt the same.

Sophia walks past the one of my great-grandfather, coming to a stop at my grandfather's, with the giant moustache and the pronounced frown lines.

"Anthony Winter Senior," she says. "Right?"

"Yes."

"Everything I've read about him says that he was a... demanding man."

I snort. "Well, that's certainly true. Complicated and brilliant."

"Is it true that he had five mistresses?"

I wrap an arm around her waist and meet the gruff eyes of my grandfather over her heat. "Possibly. I don't know the exact number."

"I feel bad for your grandmother."

"Don't," I say. "She was a viper. They were a well-suited pair in many ways."

"You don't think they loved each other?"

"I know they didn't," I say. Their marriage had been forged out of convenience and ambition; my grandmother's was just of a different sort than my grandfather's. They'd succeeded, too. Together they'd made the Winter Corporation what it is today.

I turn us toward the door. "Come on, there are more rooms to explore."

"If every room is like this, we'll be here all night," she says.

"Well, were you planning on going back to yours later?"

Her smile widens. "I might have packed a toothbrush."

"Good," I say, "because I have no intention of letting you go."

Watching her in my space, in the family's space, is a peculiar thing. Like seeing a part of your new self meet with the old. The past with the future. Sophia wanders into the dining room and pauses by the twelve-seater table. The walls are spectacular with wainscoting and custom wallpaper, and from the ceiling, hangs a century-old chandelier.

"Oh," she breathes. "This is… wow."

"I eat in here most nights."

"You do?"

"Absolutely not."

She gives me a playful smile. "I could almost imagine you doing that. Sitting dignified at one end and wishing you could ask someone to pass the salt."

"That's what you think of me?"

"Yes," she says and wraps her arms around my neck. Her body is a sinuous line, lithe beneath the dress and graceful even in stillness. "How often do you entertain in here?"

"Entertain what?" I say. "Indecent thoughts? All the time, lately."

She rolls her eyes. "No, you flatterer. Guests."

"Oh, *guests.*"

"Yes."

I fit my hands to the soft swell of her hips. "Almost never."

"Not even business associates?"

"Sometimes," I say. "These rooms have a certain…"

"Gravitas?" she says. "Pomposity? Legacy?"

"Yes, Miss Thesaurus, I suppose they do."

"But where are the rooms where you *actually* live?"

"They're all here."

She shakes her head. "No, where do you take off your clothes at night, where do you eat your takeout, where do you watch TV?"

I take her hand. "Come on, I'll show you."

We walk through the sitting room and into the butler's corridor. From there, it's a quick step into the kitchen. I point at the kitchen table. "For eating meals."

She lets go of my hand and heads straight for the fridge.

"Hungry?" I ask.

She opens it and then gives a wide smile. "No. Just curious."

I lean against the kitchen counter. "Found anything interesting?"

"No," she says, "nothing at all, which is the funny part. Your fridge looks like mine."

"Empty?"

"Yes."

"I guess we're not chefs."

"No," she says and shakes her head. "I've never liked cooking. Oh, what's in there?"

She walks into the adjoining living room. It's small, but it has a couch, a few bookcases, and a TV. "This is where you relax?"

"Some nights, yes."

She sits down on the couch and rests her hand on a pillow. Having her here feels excitingly exposing. Her beauty and smile fills the well-used space.

"How many people have lived here?"

"On this particular couch? None. I got it when I moved in."

"Good to know," she says and pats the dark blue fabric. "But in the apartment?"

"Three generations, give or take. My great-grandfather died before the building was fully built, and my grandfather took over at nineteen. But I don't have an exact number of all the family members who have passed in and out."

"Don't you want a place that's just yours?"

I sit down next to her. The eyes that gaze back at mine are curious and open, and I don't think anyone has asked me that question in years.

"It works well for now. It keeps me close to the business and to my employees."

Her mouth curves into a smile. "Yes, that would be your answer. But I've heard people say it's important to separate work and personal life. Balance, I think it's called."

Our legs touch, hers bare beneath a knee-length silk skirt. "You saying something over there, workaholic?"

She chuckles. "I know, I know, I shouldn't throw rocks in glass houses."

"A little pebble is okay, I suppose, but no more."

She pretends to lock her mouth shut. "I'm done."

"Good."

"Except I have another question."

I rest my hands behind my head and stretch out my legs so that one is right in front of hers. "Yes, I bought a new bed for the master when I moved in."

Sophia's eyes on mine glitter. "Not what I was going to ask."

"But I'm pretty sure you were thinking it."

She rolls her eyes again. "I wanted to ask how often you, you know. Entertain."

"We spoke about that earlier."

"No, I mean, how often do you *entertain* here?" She nudges my leg with her knee. "Before me, I mean. I know you weren't big on dating, but…"

I run a hand over my jaw, trying to hide my smile. "You're curious about my past, Bishop?"

"Maybe a little bit. You know so much about mine, after all."

I shift closer to her on the couch. "Well, you know what happened to my last relationship."

She nods. "Your engagement."

"Yes."

"Did you date anyone between then and… now?"

"No, not really."

She lifts her eyebrows, and I sigh. The truth wouldn't paint a flattering picture. "I wasn't interested in dating long-term. I work too damn much, and the mess just never seemed worth it."

Sophia nods. "I get that."

"There was someone, though. We didn't date, but we saw each other from time to time."

"You were friends with benefits."

"I guess that's what the kids call it."

She nudges my leg again. "You're not an antique, you know, despite living in one."

"Funny," I say. There's more to say about Beverly, but it's not something I'm proud of. My relationship with her had been based on mutual physical attraction, tolerable conversation, and nothing more. She was stuck, and I was jaded, and it had been pleasurable for us both. No expectations. No future.

But it doesn't belong here with Sophia.

"Did it end naturally?" she asks.

"Yes. I haven't seen her in almost a year," I say. "You know I'm short on time."

She smiles. "Yes, I do know, which is why I couldn't come over until nine p.m. tonight."

"I was in supplier meetings." I reach out and curve my hand over her leg, finding the hem of her skirt. The skin at the back of her knee is tantalizingly soft. "But I cut them short for you."

"Did you? How gallant."

"Mmm."

"What was her name? Your old friend-with-benefit?"

My hand pauses. "Why?"

She shrugs. "In case we go to any more events together and we need to perform for another ex. You know mine, and I know your ex-fiancée. Also, I'm just curious when it comes to you."

I let my thumb sweep higher. Touching her feels like an intoxicating privilege. "Beverly doesn't go to many benefits."

Sophia sighs. "Shoot. Then I guess I won't have to kiss you dramatically in public again."

"Mm-hmm," I say, "but you *can*, if you'd like to."

"You did tell me you'd never object to me kissing you."

"I did, didn't I?"

"It was very comforting at the time."

"It was the truth, too," I say. "I think I still mean it, but maybe you should try, just to be sure."

Sophia shifts closer on the couch. "Should I?"

"Yes." My hand slides beneath the silk of her skirt. "Thanks for coming by at nine p.m. on a Wednesday."

"Thanks for letting me invade your space."

"You're making it much better by being here."

She settles astride of my lap, and I take her in my arms, the weight and feel of her becoming deliciously familiar.

"Let me try, then," she murmurs and rests a hand on my jaw.

I let her kiss me. I even go so far as kissing her back, my hands tightening on her hips, just to show how much I don't object.

She cocks her head, her mahogany hair sliding to one side. "You don't seem offended."

"I don't think I feel it, either."

"Good thing you weren't the first time, or I would have lost you as a client."

I chuckle. "Sweetheart, it would take a great deal more for me to quit the Exciteur deal."

"Oh?"

"Yes. You're far too good at your job." I glance down, at where I'm slowly raising her skirt. Her smooth thighs on either side of me are like an anchor, and yet, it's one that grounds me rather than weighs me down.

I kiss her again. The rhythm of it is becoming familiar, and the familiarity itself is arousing. The knowledge of what she likes, how she moans when I deepen the kiss, how she grips my hair tight at the back of my head. Intimacy grows with repetition, not lessens, and I'm learning the shape of ours.

I shift us, spreading her out beneath me on the couch. A lonely throw pillow tumbles to the ground. Time fades and slips away, reality disappearing around me. She notches a leg at my hip. I look down, watching my own hand push her skirt up past her hips.

"Oh," Sophia says. "I forgot to mention, I have to show you something. I just received prototypes for the Winter coffee-table book I mentioned!"

I rest my head against the pillow next to hers. "Jesus."

She laughs. "Sorry. But I really think you'll like it."

"I'm sure I will," I say, "but if you're thinking about work right now, I'm definitely doing something wrong."

Her laughter is warmer this time, two arms wrapping around my back. "Maybe I just want to impress you."

"You already do," I say, "and besides, there are other ways."

"Mmm."

"You actually requested a prototype of the book?"

She nods, her cheeks flushed. "I couldn't resist. It was supposed to be a surprise at the pitch, something we'd throw in as a gesture of goodwill. It'll only have ten sample pages, of course, but it's a great prototype."

"You're such an overachiever."

"That's why they pay me the big bucks," she says.

A tendril of her hair has fallen over her eyebrow, curling at her cheek. I brush it away. "Sophia."

"Yes?"

"Have dinner with me the night before the pitch."

Her eyes widen. "In the fancy dining room?"

"At a restaurant," I say. "Let me take you out on a proper date before…"

"Before it's too late?" she says, a rueful smile on her lips.

"Yes."

Her hand rests on the side of my neck, and she traces the edge of my jaw with her thumb. "It would help me take my mind off this really important work pitch I have the next day."

I raise an eyebrow. "Oh? A terrible client?"

"The worst," she says. "He's so demanding, and he *never* seems satisfied."

"Sounds like an asshole."

"Yeah, he demands perfection. Even describes himself as someone who won't give less than a hundred and ten percent and probably expects it from everyone else."

"Pretentious bastard," I say and move down her body. The silk of her skirt is now ruched around her waist.

"He can be hard to please," she says and runs her fingers through my hair. "But I think I'm learning how to."

I kiss the inside of her thigh. Warm skin, soft skin, smelling like her. "Well, if he's displeased with you, he's an idiot."

"I'll have to remind him of that," she says, voice breathless, "after the pitch meeting."

"You should." I push my arm beneath one of her thighs, grabbing a hold of it, and open her up for me. Her black panties are edged with lace. "Maybe you should focus on teaching him how to please you instead."

Sophia's breathing picks up, and in my peripheral view I see her arm curving over the back of the couch. "I think I could do that."

I savor the moment I pull her panties to the side. Revealing her to me, to the room, a view I'll never tire of.

"Only way to stop you from thinking about work," I murmur, and lower my mouth. Sophia gives a shaky laugh and threads her fingers through my hair. "Give it a hundred and ten percent," she says, "and I promise I'll forget I'm even employed."

I give it a hundred and twenty.

21

SOPHIA

Isaac's standing by my door. The navy suit looks casual on him tonight, unbuttoned and no tie. It's made more domestic by the cat streaking against his leg.

"Is he always this friendly?" he asks.

I glance over from my spot in front of the mirror. I have an earring in hand, the other already fastened on my left lobe. "I wouldn't really know," I say, "since I don't have guests over a lot. Maybe he was just shy the last time you came over?"

Isaac runs a large hand over Milo's back. I hear him murmur words, his voice deep and soft, but they're too quiet for me to make out. Meant for Milo's soft ears and no one else's.

I watch them for longer than I need to. That cat might not know it, obsessed as he is with long naps on the couch and watching birds from the windowsill, but he had saved my life the past year.

"All right," I finally say. "I'm ready."

Isaac straightens and receives a disgruntled meow from Milo in return, who dramatically flops down by his feet. "You look stunning," he says.

"Thank you," I say. I feel nervous around him again. The formality of this date, the restaurant reservation… we're not going as pretend dates. This isn't an act, or a twisted sort of revenge, or a facade.

This is just us.

One final time before we potentially go into business together. One final time before tomorrow's pitch.

Isaac has a car waiting for us at the door of my building. It takes us uptown, back into familiar territory. Past the marble pristineness of the Winter Hotel and onto streets I recognize well.

He's reserved a table for us at Salt.

I've been there before. It has expensive food by a Michelin Star chef, but it's approachable enough for lunch or a date. I've been with friends, and once with my family when they were in town. And I've been there with Percy.

Often.

The car pulls to a stop outside. "Is this okay?" he asks. Maybe he's noted my silence.

"Yes, yes, absolutely."

"They have a great white wine selection for you," he murmurs. "Several Chardonnay options."

Salt is packed. It always is, even though this is a weekday evening. The nerves in my stomach increase to a fever pitch as we follow a waitress past fully seated tables. I'm pitching tomorrow. It's the biggest day of my career so far, and then, it'll mean an end to this. To him and I.

Isaac lets me pore over the white wine list in silence without as much as a sigh, so unlike Percy, and then we order our drinks.

He knots his hands on the table. "Sophia," he says. "What are you thinking about?"

I sigh. "Sorry. I'm thinking about tomorrow."

"Ah. The pitch."

"Yes. Jenna, Toby, and I ran through it today, but I'll be honest, I'm still a bit nervous about it."

He runs a hand along his jaw. "Because your client is such an asshole."

"Yes, exactly. He also happens to be really good friends with my boss's boss."

"I wouldn't exactly say they're *good* friends," Isaac says. "I mean, not as far as I've heard."

I chuckle. "That's a relief."

"Still, though, I know you've worked incredibly hard on this pitch. Regardless of what my team or I will think about your suggestions for the hotel franchise, nothing can take that away from you."

"No, that's true. But it can make it all a waste of time."

He raises an eyebrow. "A waste of time?"

"Well, not *all* of it, but you know what I mean."

"I do," he says. Then he frowns, those dark eyes intense on mine. "Is it because you know I'll be honest?"

"Maybe that's part of it," I say. "But I appreciate that. I know you'll be fair, too, and I wouldn't want you to lie to protect my feelings."

He nods. "I didn't think you would."

"But I know it's not just me, either. Jenna and Toby have worked really hard on this. All of us want to blow you and your team away tomorrow."

"Of course, you do."

"All projects are important to me, and I love my job. But I'd be lying if I didn't say this one feels even more so because it's you, and it's your company."

"Sophia," he says, and there's a faint smile to his lips. "You've already impressed me."

"Yes, but that's on a personal level."

He shakes his head. "No, not only. I was impressed by your work ethic before... *this* happened. Before we happened."

That makes me smile. "Thanks. You know, when I realized you were the same man I'd met in the hotel lobby that night, it made me want to prove myself."

"You did, not that you had to."

"But I've always had that drive," I say.

"I know," he says, and I know he does because I've seen the same thing in him. I might be an outsider, a foreigner in New York, and I was a novice in my husband's world. I needed to prove myself. Isaac Winter, on the other hand? He had been born the heir to an empire and probably had a monogrammed pacifier. And yet... it hadn't made him entitled.

"It's always been the same for me," he murmurs. Proving that he deserves it all. Proving that he's up to the task.

I reach out across the table, my palm up. He doesn't hesitate in taking it. "How do you think working together will be," I ask, "after *this*?"

"I don't know," he says. "I'm not looking forward to it."

The straightforward admission makes my chest tighten. *Me neither.* I don't want to lose the easy confidences and conversations.

"Not being able to pick your mind will be hard."

His leans forward. "This doesn't have to be an all-or-nothing situation. If you want to talk after tomorrow, I'll always be available."

"I don't think I could resist even if you weren't."

"Good," he says. "Sweetheart, I've been thinking. There's another opt—"

A shadow falls over our table, and Isaac's words come to an abrupt stop. Percy and Scarlett are standing next to us.

In Isaac's grip, my hand goes limp.

"Hello, you two," Percy says. "Sorry to interrupt like this, but—"

"We never got to say a proper goodbye at the tennis tournament!" Scarlett's smile is wide enough to show off her molars. It's a complete one-eighty from when I'd seen her across the room at the benefit a few weeks ago. "Thanks for a great game. You looked like such a great team."

My stomach sinks. Isaac. That's what this is about. She's from this world, her parents are friends with the Brownes, and she went to college with Percy's friend group.

And I'm now, in her view, seriously dating Isaac Winter. That's a brilliant social connection to have, neatly connected through two ex-spouses.

"Thank you," Isaac says. His voice is steady, but there's a hint of hostility beneath the cool surface. "Are you here for dinner?"

"Yes, we're just heading to our table now, but we had to stop and say hello." Percy's eyes shift to mine. There's an emotion in them I can't read.

That surprises me. I used to be able to so easily.

Now I just want them to leave. My last night with Isaac, and here they are? Why had we gone to Salt in the first place? The entirety of New York City is available to us. We could be at a diner in Brooklyn or at my little ramen place, having the time of our lives.

"Soph?" Percy says.

I clear my throat. "Tonight's tasting menu looks stellar," I say. "Especially the chicken."

"Yes, I think that's what I'll have," Scarlett says. Her strawberry-blonde hair is soft around her face, and I suddenly see it spread out on a pillow like it had been when I walked in to see her beneath him. "We actually have some fun news to share, don't we, Perce?"

Percy looks at me with his sheepish smile. It's the one I'd used to find endearing. Now it looks like an act, an attempt at playing Peter Pan. He's the boy who never wanted to grow up.

"We're having a baby," he says.

My mind goes blank. The sound of the restaurant fades away, turns into white noise. Isaac's hand tightens around mine, and I feel it from somewhere far away.

"Congratulations," someone says. Him. He says it.

Percy's watching my reaction. And he sees it when the blow lands. The final insult, the perfectly crafted blade. He knows exactly where it'll slide in between my ribs.

He'd wanted kids. I did too, but not yet. Not while my

career was doing so well. He'd never been okay with that, and my mother-in-law had commented on it all the time, making it clear I was the one in the wrong.

Failure, I think. *This is just one more arena I failed in, and they never let me forget it.*

"Sophia?" Scarlett asks. There's a note of sympathy in her voice, but I can't tell if it's real or fake. "I'm sorry if that's hard to hear. We're really happy for you two, you know, both of us. And we hope that going forward there's a way for—"

"Sorry, will you excuse me?" I say, getting up from my seat.

"Of course," Isaac says. He starts to stand as well, and maybe we could leave, maybe there's a better way out of this, but I can't see it. I turn on my heel and flee both the past and the present, heading toward the safety of the restroom. I barely make it before the first tear falls.

22

ISAAC

Sophia weaves through the tables, her steps a beat too fast to be casual. All three of us watch her flee toward the back of the restaurant.

"Oh," Scarlett. "I really hope we—"

"It's okay," Percy says. His eyes are on Sophia, and he takes a step forward. "I'll go see if she's okay."

I stop him with a hand on his shoulder. "No, you won't."

His eyes narrow. "I was her husband."

"Yes," I say. "*Was.* Now you're just the ex, and I'd suggest you remember that."

I leave the two of them there, standing next to the table that had been ours. *What a small man,* I think. His motives are hidden behind a wafer-thin facade. He still cares for her, in whatever twisted, sick way that might be, and he wants to make her jealous. Wants to test her, again and again, to see if she still cares.

He'd seen us here, and unlike his social climbing girlfriend, he hadn't wanted to mend relationships. He wanted to set them on fire.

The bartender gives me a dirty look when I crack open the door to the women's bathroom, but I ignore him. Sophia's standing by the sinks. Her hands are braced against the marble, back hunched, and she's crying so hard her body is shaking.

I close the door behind me. "Sweetheart, I'm sorry."

She shakes her head. The beautiful face is marked with tears, and all because of the asshole out there. "I'm sorry," she says. "Sorry. I just…"

"Don't apologize." I wrap my arms around her. She resists for a second, but then her chin comes to rest on my shoulders. "That was a shitty thing to tell you like that."

It makes her cry harder, with sobs so strong they rack her body in my arms. I tug us closer to the door and fit my foot against it, keeping it shut for everyone else.

"Sorry," I murmur again. Her hair smells good, and I breathe it in, staring at the lime-washed wall across from us. How could a man behave like he had? Committing the crime, not owning up to it, and then continuing to torture the person he'd already hurt. He'd acted entitled back in school, if I remember correctly. Anthony had been in the same grade as him, and the few things that filtered back to me over the years had never been positive.

I run my hand over Sophia's back, up and down, feeling the curve of her spine and the shaking of her body.

Cordelia cheating on me had stung.

It had disillusioned me, it had been embarrassing, and it had wounded my pride. But it had never hurt quite like this. The betrayal had been one of trust, not of the heart, because I'd never truly given her mine.

I thought I had. But I realize now, in more ways than one, that I'd confused an errant ray of sunshine for the whole sun.

Sophia won't stop shaking. It's half sobbing, and half panic attack, and her hands at my neck are holding on tightly.

"Here," I murmur and shift us to the chair in the corner. She sits down on my lap. "We don't have to go out there again." I run my hand over her back, listen to the muffled sounds of her sadness. She'd cried that morning, too, after we'd spent the night together for the first time.

Someone pulls at the restroom door.

"Occupied!" I bark.

The pulling stops. The crying doesn't, but it turns softer, quieter. And all the tears are for Percy.

"Our dinner date…" she whispers.

"Fuck the dinner," I say. "I'll take you back home, and we can order takeout. Or we cancel the evening entirely if you'd rather be alone," I say, even if the idea of leaving her on her own in this state feels impossible.

"Do you think they're still out there?"

"We'll leave out the back," I say.

"We have to pay our check…"

"I'll handle all of it."

Her hands slide down the front of my chest. She leans back, cheeks flushed and eyes glazed with moisture. But she's not sobbing anymore.

"I'm sorry," she whispers. "I don't know why that affected me so much."

I smile. It's not a happy one. "Don't you?"

"I think I'm ready to leave. If we can."

"We can. Let me leave the restrooms first, all right? I'll pay for the drinks and make sure we can use the back exit."

"Okay," she murmurs and runs her palms over her cheeks, wiping away the tears. "Thanks."

The waiter doesn't miss a beat when I hand her a hundred-dollar bill for our two glasses of wine. "Change of plans," I tell her. "We'll be using the delivery exit."

She only nods. Good old Salt, I think, and the fancy clientele with their odd requests. This isn't the weirdest one she's had today, I'm sure of it.

Sophia and I walk through a kitchen busy with activity. One or two chefs shoot us curious looks, but the seasoned pros don't look up from their work. Yeah, this happens all the time.

We walk for a solid block before either of us speaks.

"Wow," she murmurs. Her voice is still a bit hoarse. "I don't even know what to say about that."

"Want to walk?" I ask. "The hotel is close by."

"Walking is nice, actually, but… I think I need to go home. I have that pitch tomorrow, you know."

"Right, of course."

The air between us feels stiff with anguish. I'd known she wasn't ready to date anyone. That her heart still ached over her divorce, that she was career-focused, that we'd both used one another as mutually beneficial pawns to prove a point.

And yet.

"I'll get us a taxi."

"Thanks," she says. "Want to come on up, too?"

"Yes," I say. "But only if you want me to."

She exhales softly and leans her shoulder against mine. "Yes, please. Let's have at least some fun out of this evening."

Our taxi driver starts off talkative but takes one long look in the rearview mirror and doesn't ask us another question about how our night has been. We must be quite the pair. One somber and the other quiet with red-ringed eyes.

Milo is nowhere to be seen when we arrive to her apartment, and Sophia heads straight to the kitchen. I lean against the doorframe and watch her make a cup of tea.

"Hungry?" I ask.

She shrugs and gives me a tired smile. "Not really. But I think I'll get hungry when there's food on the table, if you know what I mean?"

I open my phone. "Yeah, I do. Anything in particular you're craving?"

"Pasta or pizza. No, actually, I want a burger, a proper one, with fries. Is that okay?"

"Yes, absolutely. Seems like there's a place around the corner that makes truffle burgers."

"That sounds delicious."

I place the order, and then I stand in her kitchen and watch her put the pieces of her injured heart together. She does it gracefully. Minute by minute, the tension starts to leak out of her shoulders.

We sit on her couch, and she props her head up with a hand. "How do you feel?" I ask.

"All right," she says. "I won't fall apart again. I promise."

"It's okay if you do."

She smiles, a little ruefully. "Thanks. But I know that was… a lot back there. I'm sorry about it."

I sigh. "Please don't apologize."

"God, I have to." She puts a hand over her face, eyes closing. "I'm so embarrassed about all of it."

"Don't be."

"I wasn't supposed to react like that. I didn't *want* to react like that."

"That was outside of your control," I say, and feel the sour taste of truth in those words. It's not her fault. Not in the least. And I had always known, deep down, that she was still in love with Percy. Hadn't I?

She sighs. "I guess I ruined our final date, huh?"

"You didn't ruin it," I say. "Your asshole of an ex-husband did."

"Yes, I suppose that's true. Why is New York the smallest town in the world when it's actually one of the biggest?"

"I shouldn't have taken us to Salt," I say. Anywhere else, and this night would have ended differently. Anywhere else, and she wouldn't have broken apart, sobbing in a public restroom.

Sophia shrugs. "They have great food. I understand why you booked it."

"Yeah."

"So, what happens now?" She glances at the clock on her windowsill. "At midnight, when our weeks are officially up. Will I turn back into a pumpkin and you into the untouchable prince?"

"In the analogy you crafted," I say, "I think I was the princess."

A true smile lights her face. "Oh, that's right. How did I forget?"

"Don't worry, I'm not too offended."

"What a relief," she says and pulls her legs up beneath her on the couch. "Tomorrow, I can't do this with you anymore."

"Eating truffle burgers on your couch."

"Exactly," she says. "I'll have to do it alone, and that's just sad."

I run a hand along my jaw. *Still in love with her ex,* I think. The words I'd prepared for tonight don't feel appropriate right now. "We'll see how we feel," I say. "It's not like we've signed a contract."

"No, just a professional one," she says and smiles. It's a soft one. A private one. Different than the sharply tinged professional one she'll wear tomorrow. Hair likely swept back, a pencil skirt on, and delivering the pitch of a lifetime.

I can't wait to see it, and I can't believe I get to see this side of her now, too. The fierce and the soft.

"That's a question for tomorrow," I say. "First you have a terrifying client to pitch to."

She pretends to shudder. "Yes, God help me."

"I doubt he's that scary." I rise from the couch. Stay any longer, and I won't be able to leave. And I should. She has work, and she's sad. It's there in her eyes, even if she tries to hide it.

Sophia rises too. She's standing close to me, body against body, heat against heat. "He's scary sometimes," she murmurs, "but tonight, he was nicer than I could ever have imagined."

"For you," I murmur, "anytime."

She takes my hand and threads her own fingers through it. "Stay the night?" she says. "This isn't technically off-limits until after the pitch tomorrow."

It's late when we finally stretch out in her bed to sleep. It's a queen, smaller than mine, and it smells like her. I pull her close, and she nestles against me, her breathing heavy. I look up at the ceiling and think about Percy's smug face and Sophia's tears.

It's been years since I'd stopped believing that relationships can work, and years since I stopped thinking they were a worthwhile investment in my life. But here I am, starting to believe again, and all thanks to a woman who isn't ready to love someone new.

23

SOPHIA

The next morning, I wake up alone to my alarm. It's early, the rising sun shining through my windows. We'd forgotten the drapes again. I turn over in bed and find the other side, his side, still faintly warm.

In my living room, I find a folded note resting next to my tea mug from last night. The takeout boxes are gone.

I unfold the little note. *Good luck today, sweetheart.*

Short and to the point, like most of Isaac's communication. And then, that endearment again. I don't even think my boyfriends before Percy called me anything like that. Perhaps they used the occasional "baby," casually, like an afterthought. But it was never spoken with warmth or deliberation, not a word offered like a caress.

I set the opened note on my dresser. "Thanks," I say and open the doors to my closet. "I'm going to blow you away today."

Toby is already at the office when I arrive. His hair is styled to perfection, and when Jenna walks in a few minutes later, she's in a canary-yellow shirt, tucked into her cigarette-style pants.

They're both dressed to kill.

"Game day," Jenna says, looking between us both. "Feel like running it through one more time?"

"Let's do it twice," I say, "just to be sure."

I hit all the points as we rehearse. The technology works flawlessly. I don't let myself focus on what happened yesterday. Not on the incident at Salt, not on Percy's declaration, and not the fact that after this pitch, Isaac and I can't continue seeing one another. Not if the pitch goes well, at any rate.

I only let myself focus on the numbers and the words. A pitch is a performance, and I sink deep into the role. We leave Exciteur with plenty of time to spare and arrive at the Winter Hotel early.

The lobby feels familiar now, and so do a few of the receptionists, who give us all cheery hellos. Andrew takes us up to the second floor and the Winter Corporation's official offices.

"Showtime," I murmur to Jenna and Toby. Jenna's tapping left foot tells me she's amped, too. *Nervous*, perhaps, just like I am. But we don't use that word beforehand. I've learned that the line between nerves and excitement is a thin one, and if you tell yourself it's the latter, you can start to believe it.

Andrew shows us into a room. "The executive team will be here in about ten minutes," he says. "Let me know if you need any help in setting up."

Laptops get plugged in and notes pulled up, and I join Toby around the table, distributing the spiral-bound briefs. I breathe in and out—deep, calming breaths—and turn the nerves into excitement.

Just trust me, I think. They need to see the brilliance of this vision. *Trust me.*

They arrive one by one, the entire team. The last one to enter is Isaac. He takes a seat at the head of the table, and the room steadies with him in it. It quiets, too, the audience awaiting a show. Andrew taps his pen against a notepad twice. "We're excited to see what you've put together for us," he says.

Isaac nods. "Please go ahead."

I dive straight in. "We were tasked to deliver a pitch, a vision, for an off-shoot brand from the Winter Corporation. The hotels will be smaller, with a more economically minded price point, and should be easy to franchise across the country in smaller cities. This is already a proven model and has worked brilliantly for other large hotel brands. You've been very generous, all of you, with your time and access. The keywords you gave us were traditional, comfortable, and luxurious.

"But," I say and smile at the group. My stomach is steady now. The nerves have evaporated, replaced with an intense awareness of the moment. "As you may remember, my team and I have also suggested a different direction. Something more modern to set this brand apart from Winter. So, we've decided to do something a bit unorthodox. We'll deliver two pitches."

Isaac's eyebrows rise. "You could do that?" he says. "Without skimping on the quality of either one?"

"Yes," Jenna says. "We took the help of in-house talent at Exciteur to get it done for you in time."

"I see," he says. "Well, this will be interesting."

We start with the traditional pitch. Toby leads it, with Jenna and I assisting. Across the screen graphic projections and calculations flash. The traditional one looks like a less luxurious version of the Winter Hotels in New York and Washington. Fewer columns, perhaps, but with muted gold tones and a logo that strongly resembles the golden W used on the Winter Hotel.

On the last slide, I step up front again. "This is a safe, doable option. It honors the traditional architecture of the Winter and the legacy it represents. It's a smaller, *lesser* version of your flagship hotel."

"But it's not something you'd recommend," Isaac says. His eyes are heavy across the conference room.

"No," I say, "it's not. It might seem like a safe option, but I think it's the opposite. It looks dated, and in locations that aren't historic, it won't attract the clientele you're hoping for. Now, you've told us that the Winter Hotel stands for luxury, for comfort, and for tradition. But it started because its founders were willing to take significant risks. The decor in your lobby, and the art deco styling around your indoor pool, were at the forefront of architecture when they were built. In my opinion, foresight and risk-taking is the true legacy of the Winter Hotels, and I know it'll be better honored by a more modern approach."

There's silence in the room. This is a gamble. With any other client, and any other company, it might not work. Anticipation hangs thick in the air.

"Well, by all means," Isaac says, "show us the version you recommend."

My smile is one of relief. Toby breathes a quiet sigh next to me and moves into position by the laptop, ready to keep the slides moving. I launch into the pitch. This is the one I've slaved over, the one I believe in. But more than that, I try to tell a story of modernity and history meeting.

The logo is a W and H interwoven with a pattern that references the art deco decor in the New York location. The mock-ups of interiors our architecture team had put together are sleek and stunning, and easily replicable across the country.

Andrew clears his throat. "In that mock-up, is the check-in desk a replica of the one in this hotel?"

"Yes," I say. "Just smaller and modernized."

"It's stunning," he says.

We share cost projections, side by side mocks of the websites, the pricing structure, the restaurants we'd recommend in each, along with the keywords we've chosen for this sub-brand. *Upscale. Modern. Sleek. Comfortable.*

Toward the end, we point out which ten cities we'd recommend they start with for the locations, and finally, side by side, we show the results from the focus group tests.

Seventy-five percent preferred the modern look.

"I understand," I say, "that going in a direction different than what you already know, and what's worked for the Winter Corporation in the past, is a gamble. But I would argue that a bit of distance between the two brands is great. Both need to stand on their own. Because at the end of the day, you're catering to two different clienteles with these. Make them too similar, and you're inviting comparison, and the last thing you want is someone checking into a budget hotel and being disappointed because it's nothing like the grandness of the Winter Hotel in New York."

"Fair point," Amanda says. As the head of Winter's global division, she must have had this thought, too, only reversed. Ensuring the international five-star resorts are as similar to the New York location as possible so as to *not* disappoint customers.

The screen behind me goes black.

Pitch over, presentation done.

"All the information has been emailed to you," I say. "Toby has put together USB sticks, too, with the high-definition plans. We're available for any and all questions, whether you have them now or in a month."

The inside of my palms feels sweaty. It's a relief and the sudden return of the nerves. We've done everything we can.

Now it's up to them to judge us.

Jenna starts to gather up our material.

"Thank you," Isaac says. He rises from his seat and buttons his suit jacket. "This was a detailed and well-researched pitch. We'll have to look it through further and deliberate, but we'll get back to you soon. Some of the things you've suggested may require another meeting."

"We're always available," I say.

"Great." He walks around the table and shakes our hands. Toby's, then Jenna's, and finally mine. "Good work," he says. "You've given me a lot to think about."

"That was the goal," I say.

His lips curve again. It's slight, only for me, and then his hand releases mine. "You succeeded. Until next time, Miss Bishop."

"Mr. Winter," I say.

The team files out. Amanda mouths *very impressive* our way, and Jenna gives her a wide smile back.

Afterwards, my team goes out to lunch. "Let's get a glass of wine to celebrate," Toby says. We're sitting at a popular lunch spot, the soft sound of others around us eating and talking.

"What are we celebrating, exactly?" Jenna asks. "Winter Corp hasn't decided if they're going to buy either concept yet, or if they're even going to hire Exciteur to oversee and plan the whole thing."

"No, but we delivered one hell of a pitch," he says, "and whether or not they like it, they can't take that away from us."

"True," I agree. "I'm so proud of what we did in there. What we put together in just a few weeks. They could hate it, and I still know that we over-delivered."

"Hell yeah," Toby says.

Jenna rolls her eyes, but she's smiling. "Fine, let's get wine."

Excitement and exhaustion, and far too many emotions course through my body. It's the familiar feeling that comes after a nerve-racking event is done and dusted.

I make it all the way through lunch before I excuse myself from the table to make a call. I step outside and find his name in my contact list.

Isaac answers on the second signal.

"Sophia?"

"Hello," I say. "Are you in a meeting?"

"No, I'm in my office."

"Great. So, what did you think?"

He sounds amused. "I told you what I thought."

"No, you gave us a few diplomatic sentences. Tell me what you *really* thought."

"You gave me modern," he says, "even though I've told you at every single turn that I don't want it."

"Yes. But I did give you two options, you know, just in case."

"I know, and I appreciate the nominal effort you put into the first pitch."

"It was more than nominal."

"Okay," he says and chuckles. "I believe you. But you still believe most in the second one. Don't you?"

"Yes. We have to move with the times, you know? Especially if this is a chance for an entirely new sub-franchise. It won't have the benefit of legacy, not like the Winter's luxury locations, and trying to artificially cram the same aesthetic into newly built hotels just won't work."

"Mm-hmm," he says. "You're pitching again."

"Force of habit. So, did you hate it?"

He sighs. "I think you're a genius, and that both you and your team are worth every costly cent we're paying you."

"Oh."

"I'll have to look it over more thoroughly. But I see the point you're making. I didn't before, not truly. Now... I'll have to think about it."

"Take your time," I say. "Run it through your own focus groups."

"Yeah, we might do that, too," he says, and then he chuckles again. "It's funny. The first thing I wanted to do after that pitch meeting was discuss it with you."

I lean against the building. The New York air is colder now, the chill of fall here to stay, and it's refreshing against my flushed cheeks. "Funny," I say. "I wanted to talk to you, too."

"Oh, is that why you called me?"

"Funny," I say. "You're just such a comedian."

"It's my true calling."

"So," I say.

"Yes," he says.

I clear my throat. "You know, technically, you haven't made a decision yet, so we're not really in business together."

He laughs. It's warm on the other end, familiar, and a bit private. Not something he shares with just anyone. "That's true," he says. "Technically speaking."

"And I know how much you love technicalities."

"They're my favorite."

I run a hand over a crease in my dress, trying to smooth it out. I'd steamed it just this morning. "Think we can make this two-week thing last a little longer?"

There's silence on the other end. I wish I could see his face, and hear the way the words sounded when he received them. "We could," he says. "I'd like that. But yesterday…"

"I'm sorry about yesterday. That wasn't my best moment."

"Please don't apologize."

"Let's just avoid places where we know a ton of people."

"Okay," he says. "I have a family dinner tonight, but would you let me take you out tomorrow?"

"I have a better idea," I say. "Come to my place. I want to try cooking."

He chuckles. "I'll be of absolutely no help."

"I know," I say, "and we might have to order takeout again, but it'll be an adventure."

"An adventure," he repeats, voice warm. "All right. I'll be there."

24

ISAAC

"For two busy people," Sophia says, "we're surprisingly adept at rearranging our schedules."

I run my hand over her naked back. Up and down, fingers tracing the smooth skin. "Yeah. I'm impressed."

"Me, too," she says and turns her head. Brown hair spreads out on the pillow behind her. "I was particularly impressed by you rescheduling meetings yesterday just so we could play tennis over lunch."

"It's important to get your cardio in."

"Oh, it's vital," she says, her eyes glittering. "Even if I think we're pretty good at prioritizing cardio already."

She's glorious, stretched out beside me on her bed, clad only in the sunshine streaming in through the window and a sheet twisted around her legs. I smile. "You certainly did earlier."

The image of her on top of me, her body moving, is one I'll carry with me to my dying day.

She chuckles. "I had to work off some steam."

"Well, I'm always available," I say. My hand switches direction, changing the patterns I paint across her bare skin. It's been two weeks since the pitch meeting, and over a week since my executive team unanimously recommended we go ahead with the modern pitch.

They're all in favor of hiring Exciteur to execute that vision, too. It'll be a long project. At least a year long, most likely, before our in-house team can take over. Outsourcing the time-consuming start-up phase is a better call for the business. My team knows it.

I know it.

And still, I'm the only person left who hasn't officially signed off on the plan yet. And I'm doing it to keep this.

To keep her.

But it's only a matter of time, and it's better to rip off the bandage. "Sweetheart," I murmur. "I've been thinking."

"Mm-hmm?"

"I can't stall making a decision about your pitch forever."

Her smile widens. "I knew that was what you were doing!"

"Of course, you did."

"My team is very anxious about this, you know."

"Are they?"

"Terribly. You've taken weeks!"

I sweep my hand sideways, over the curve of her hip. "Well, theoretically speaking, we might hire Exciteur."

"Theoretically?"

"Yes."

She starts to smile. "I like the sound of that."

"Me, too. But that doesn't have to be the end of this, you know. I've been thinking about us."

"You have?"

"Yes," I say. *You haven't?* It's been at the forefront of my mind these past weeks as I've turned over solution after solution. I can't jeopardize her career, and I can't ask her to make any decision that might cost her down the line.

I want to add to her life, never detract.

"I'll appoint Andrew as head of the project on the Winter's end. Once the decision is made and the papers have been signed, he'll be Exciteur's main point of contact throughout this."

"You're removing yourself?" There's a faint furrow between her brows.

"Yes. I'll still be briefed, of course, and give my input. But all communication would pass through Andrew."

"So, you and I wouldn't have any contact about work."

"No," I say. "Not through any official channels, anyway."

She frowns. It's the frown of someone deep in thought, and not someone displeased. "You know, when the project is in an operational phase, it will likely be handled by other people at Exciteur. We'll be a much bigger team, and I might not run point by then."

"I figured."

"I could always… excuse myself, too."

"I don't want you to," I say, "unless you want to for other reasons. I trust *you* and your vision for the hotels."

Her frown softens into a smile. "I would really like to see it through."

"Then you should."

"But we'd still be working together, technically, even if we don't interact professionally."

I sigh. It's true, and I have no solution for that. I can't resign my position. *I am* the position. "Yes. I don't know how to change that."

She cocks her head. "It might still work."

"It might," I agree. "We could write up a contingency plan, just in case. I promise I'll always be able to separate the two. You could kick me out of your apartment today, and I'd still want to hire your team for the new hotels."

"A contingency plan sounds good," she says. "And then we just… agree to take it day by day?"

"Yes," I say. "Day by day."

A smile blossoms on her lips. "I think it might be worth the risk."

"Good," I say, "because I'm convinced it is."

She kisses me. It's a soft, warm brush of her lips against mine. "Good," she murmurs, "because I like the hassle of rearranging my schedule to fit more of you into my life."

"Mmm. I agree."

"So, you're going modern, then?"

"Yes. You finally wore me down."

She laughs. "I've been told more than once by my family that I'm pretty persistent, you know, when I'm sure I'm right."

"That doesn't sound like you," I say. "Has to be someone else."

She laughs again. "I'm sorry I was badgering you about it so much."

"Well, I'm glad you did."

She looks at me for a long moment. I look back, brushing the back of my hand over her skin. The ends of her hair tickle my palm. "So, we'll keep doing this," she says.

"Yes," I say, just as quietly. "Although we might need to schedule it out further in advance."

"Yes please. What does your week look like?"

"I'm in Boston Wednesday through Friday on business," I say, "and I have a wedding to attend on Sunday."

"Oh, congrats."

"Thanks," I say, snorting. "I can't wait to agonize through hours of small talk. How about you?"

She reaches past me for her phone. "Let me see…"

Fifteen minutes later and we have coordinated schedules for the coming three weeks. Satisfaction spreads through my chest, along with the knowledge that I will be able to see her several times a week for the foreseeable future.

Sophia's a wonderful thing to have in your calendar.

I put my phone away. "I should have dated a planner a long time ago," I say.

"Oh?" she says, propping her head up on her hand. "Is that what we're doing now?"

"No," I say, raising an eyebrow, "of course not, because you'll only date math teachers."

She purses her lips. "That's right. But let me try something…" Twisting around, she reaches toward her nightstand and rummages around for a bit before returning with a notepad and pen.

"What are you doing?"

"Wait a minute," she says and turns onto her stomach. I watch as she scribbles.

Finally, I'm handed the notepad with a number of mathematical equations on it. "Try to solve these," she says.

"Two plus two. Really?"

"There are harder ones. Keep going."

I work my way down the list of equations. Eighty-five divided by five, and the square root of four. The last equation takes me almost a minute. She's used non-divisible numbers, and when I write the answer, it includes a decimal point.

"There," I say and hand it back to her.

She eyes it over. "A-plus. Congratulations, you could probably work as a math teacher!"

"That counts?"

"It counts," she says and gives me a brilliant smile. "They're my rules, so I'm allowed to bend them."

"Well," I say, and don't know what to say after that. So she's okay with dating me. Victory pulses through me, the feeling heady. I have to remind myself that she'd specified we take it day by day. Her tears in the bathroom after Percy's announcement are hard to forget. They'd been gut-wrenching sobs, the sound of a woman heartbroken.

Day by day.

Sophia rolls closer and rests her head next to mine on the pillow. "We should get takeout again. I have nothing in the fridge."

"That's probably just as well." I brush away a tendril of hair that's fallen over her cheek. It's silky smooth from her frequent blow-dries. I'd seen her hair air dry last weekend, the sleek curls turning into a beautiful wavy mess. It had been just as stunning, a softening feature to her fierceness. "My parents are having a party next week."

"Another one?"

I smile wryly. "The one in August was my brother's."

"Oh, that's right."

"They do this once a year, always in late September. I have to be there."

"Mmm."

"Come with me," I say.

Her eyes shift from mine, down to my jaw. Her fingers trace along it.

"They won't be there," I say. "Asshole one and asshole two."

Her lips tilt upward. "Can you make sure of that?"

"Absolutely."

"Okay," she says. "I'll go with you."

"Thanks. It might be boring, but being somewhere with you is always better than somewhere without."

Her eyes soften, and then she kisses me. I deepen it in return. It's impossible not to with her this close. *Maybe,* I think, *all she needs is time for her heart to heal.* If I wait it out long enough, she'll be ready.

25

SOPHIA

The car moves slowly through the New York traffic. To the left is the darkness of Central Park, and to the right, we pass building after building. I know which one is coming. Isaac is silent beside me, the car soft with the absence of sound. It's not a heavy silence.

Ah. Here it is. Gray stone, silver sign, and the familiar green carpet. I turn my head as we pass to watch the building recede behind us. My old home.

And on the thirteenth floor is the apartment I'd moved into, so terribly in love, years ago. Our place. Except, of course, that it had been owned by Percy's parents. It was never ours, and certainly not mine.

Never was.

I take a deep breath. Isaac has assured me that Percy and Scarlett won't be at his parents' tonight, and I'm not worried. But it will be a similar environment, and with some of the same people, as the parties Percy and I had once attended together.

"You're quiet tonight," Isaac says. His voice is steady. It's an observation and a question, not an admonishment. He's wearing a navy suit tonight, and beneath his dark hair, his eyes meet mine. I focus on them instead of the city passing us by outside.

"I'm just thinking."

"About anything in particular?"

"Well, I told Jenna and Toby today."

He raises an eyebrow. "About us?"

"Yes," I say. *Us.* The word makes me want to smile. "I thought it might have been too early, but with the work we'll be doing, I'd hate for them to accidentally find out."

"Of course," he says. "Better to control the narrative. What did you tell them?"

"That we're attracted to one another and have decided to date, but that the business deal is still our main priority."

His lips tip up in a half smile. "Good."

"Honestly, they were much less surprised than I expected," I say. They'd been stoked. They know about my divorce, and that the circumstances around it hadn't been... ideal. *Get back out there*, Jenna had said. "Apparently Toby's fiancé Quentin was once his superior at Exciteur. I had no idea!"

"Workplace romances," Isaac says, "are much more common than you'd think."

"This is my first one."

His eyes warm. "Yeah, I've never been in one, either."

"Really?"

"No," he says, "unless you count one summer when I worked in the hotel reception after graduating high school."

My eyes widen. "Did you have a torrid affair with your boss?"

"I did not," he says, "but I did have a summer flirt with a receptionist a few years older than me."

"Oh, you're into older women."

He shakes his head, but he's smiling. "Sophia."

"Too bad I'm not much of a cougar."

"Maybe not," he says, "but you have the attitude of one."

"I do?"

"Definitely. It's what attracted me from the get-go."

I chuckle. "Right, when I was running and crying. My fiercest moment, for sure."

"You were beautiful," he says, "even if it didn't feel right to think that at the time, given your emotions."

I roll my eyes. "Now you're just flattering me."

"I did think it." He reaches over and takes my hand, resting it in my lap. My dress is patterned chiffon in burgundy hues, perfect for fall. "It's not every day stunning women run into me headfirst."

"With tears streaming down their face," I say.

"No, that happens even less." His hand tightens around mine. "Once is enough."

The car finally pulls to a stop outside a townhouse on a tree-lined street on the Upper East Side. The house in question is larger than most on the street. It must have been two originally, now converted and integrated, and from the half-open door, I can hear music.

The Winters' annual fall party, apparently, is not so much an intimate gathering as an exclusive catered event.

"They do this every fall?"

"Every last week of September, like clockwork," he murmurs. "It's the end of summer and back to the city party. The fireplaces will probably be lit."

"That sounds cozy."

"It is," he agrees and rests a hand on my lower back. He presses a kiss to my forehead. "Thank you for coming with me."

"Anytime," I murmur and find that I mean it.

An attendant, equipped with an earpiece and a clipboard, opens the door to us with a smile. No names needed.

The inside is a study in old money luxury. The foyer is beautifully decorated and minimalist, from the wooden double staircases to the antique brass chandelier, and infused with understated elegance. It wouldn't surprise me if the stone tiles were sourced from France, the chandelier from Italy, the staircase railings from a crumbling castle in Spain.

"This house," I say, "is stunning."

"It's my mother's pride and joy," Isaac says. "Come, let me introduce you to some people."

"I thought your networking philosophy was to let people come to you?"

He chuckles. "Yes, but I won't be networking so much here as socializing. There's a difference."

"You're on home turf tonight?"

"Exactly. I have the advantage here." He leads us through a large sitting room, past people who nod and watch us politely. Soft music plays throughout the beautiful rooms, and there's a delicious scent of good food mingled with crackling wood and scented candles hanging in the air.

Isaac and I end up in the ivy-covered backyard. Greenery and high walls keep out any curious eyes. Two infrared heaters keep the beautifully landscaped area warm enough for guests, but they don't have to work too hard with the amount of people out here warming it up.

"This is incredible," I say, awe in my voice. "I can't believe places like this exist in the city."

"Say that to my mom later and she'll love you forever."

I chuckle. "Did you grow up in this house?"

"Yes, mostly. We stayed at the hotel sometimes, but it was rare. Summers were—oh."

A couple approaches us. My smile freezes in place, switches from genuine to professional.

"St. Clair," Isaac says with a nod. "And Cecilia, it's always a pleasure to see you."

"But not me?" Victor says. He does it straight-faced, but there's a hint of humor in his eyes. I've never been this close to him before. His leadership at Exciteur is stern but hands-off, and he prefers his orders to come filtered through his COO.

And from what I've heard, that's probably for the best.

He's also the man who assigned Isaac's case to my team with the instructions *special friend of the CEO*.

Around my glass of champagne, my hand turns clammy.

"You remember Sophia?" Isaac says. "You met briefly at Anthony's house out in Montauk in August."

Cecilia's eyes are warm on mine. "Yes, that's right. It's lovely to meet you again."

Victor extends a hand. There's no spark of recognition in his eyes. They're guarded, intelligent. Unreadable. "A pleasure to meet you again," he says. The words are similar to his wife's, but spoken with a lot less feeling.

My stomach sinks. He doesn't recognize me. Not from the brief hello at the party, and not from Exciteur.

"Thank you," I say. "It's Sophia Bishop."

Maybe he knows the name.

But he just nods. Takes a sip of his drink and glances out at the rest of the guests. Cecilia makes a comment about the decorations, and Isaac responds, all while I realize that my boss's boss doesn't know who I am. All he knows is that I'm Isaac Winter's date.

Maybe all he'd done was told the COO to give the Winter project to the best team they had, and she'd chosen mine. Still flattering.

But it's humbling, all the same.

Cecilia takes a step closer to me. "So, I'd love to hear how you and Isaac met," she says.

I chuckle. "Well, that's a funny story. It was about a year ago, but we didn't start dating until recently. I... well, I used to be married."

I tell her the gory parts and leave out the Exciteur ones. The night spins onwards in a tangle of polite conversation and genuine connection. It doesn't take long until we're joined by others, names and faces I recognize from Montauk. Anthony's business partners and their wives are there, too. They talk in comfortable tones about the upcoming holidays, about trips, and companies, and kids.

They're as welcoming as they had been at the last party.

Anthony and Summer sit down beside us in the backyard.

"We finally got away from Aunt Kelly," Anthony says and runs a hand along his jaw. It's a move so similar to Isaac that it makes me smile. "She wanted a beat by beat update about Theo's growth."

"We should invite her and John over for dinner one of these days," Summer says. "Maybe along with your parents. She can inspect him thoroughly herself."

Anthony nods, but he doesn't look thrilled at the prospect. Isaac's lips twitch. From what he's told me, his brother's not exactly the extroverted kind.

"Oh yes, spend time with extended family," Tristan says dryly. "The worst thing in the world."

Anthony shakes his head. "Yeah, it is, when they won't stop asking if and when we'll have another kid."

"They're not that bad," Summer says with a smile. Her blonde hair has a beautiful sheen beneath the string lights threaded over the backyard. "They're just so in love with Theo."

"Well, he's easy to love," Isaac says. Does he want kids of his own? It's not something we've spoken about.

"So, how do you two feel now?" one of the men asks Summer and Anthony. He's auburn-haired, a teasing grin on his face. "Your son might get some competition in inheriting the family business if Isaac's game holds up."

Chuckles erupt around us, some heartier than others. I smile, too. It's expected of me. After all, they're implying that Isaac and I might have kids. *If his game holds up.*

"If it does," Anthony says, "Theo will just have to battle it out the old way with a potential cousin."

"A duel to the death?" Victor says.

"A high-stakes staring contest?" Freddie suggests.

That makes me chuckle. I can see them, Isaac and Anthony, having an argument that involves very few words but a lot of angry looks.

"I think," Audrey says, "it would be better for the two of you to have it out with one another, rather than the kids."

"Oh, Anthony and I never argue," Isaac says.

His brother nods sagely. "We never have."

"Not a single time."

"Never."

"I don't believe that for a second," I say, smiling. "But isn't the traditional way to pitch the current head of the company? Like Isaac did?"

Anthony's eyebrows rise. "Yes, that's true. Our aunt started the tradition."

"Which means you'll have to decide one day," I say to Isaac.

He nods, eyes warm on mine. *You remembered,* they say. The conversation sends a shiver down my spine. The others think we're likely to have kids together?

Audrey sits down beside me, a friendly smile on her face. "It's so nice to see you again," she says, and the conversation draws me away from my thoughts and into topics of print media and working with your partner. It's something she's done, too, apparently. Maybe Isaac had been right, and office romances are much more common than I think.

It doesn't take long for the group to disperse. There are others to talk to, and homes to return to, and kids to look after.

Isaac and I walk back into the house. "He really doesn't recognize me," I say.

"St. Clair?"

I nod.

"No," Isaac says softly. "Do you want him to?"

"Well, I'll admit that it's somewhat of a blow to my ego. You know, I thought he assigned your project to me and my team specifically."

"Oh."

"But it's good that he doesn't, in a way. Postpones the whole 'you're dating your client' conversation..."

Isaac laughs. "Sophia, Victor married his personal assistant."

I pause, right there in the hallway, surrounded by beautifully framed black and white portraits. "He did *what*?"

"Cecilia was his assistant at Exciteur. She was a damn good one, too, from what I've heard. Now she runs her own virtual assistant firm."

"Wow," I say. "That's…"

"Yes," Isaac says, voice quiet. "I know. I think things were rocky in the beginning, but they're a solid couple now. If two people are genuinely meant to be, those logistical problems fall to the wayside."

Yes, I think. *But there might be a lot of carnage along the way.*

We stop to talk to his parents, Amelia and John Winter. Isaac's mother looks dignified, with a dark red lip and her hair swept up in a French twist.

Her eyes crease with a wide smile. "Hello, you two. I'm sorry I haven't said hello to you yet."

"That's all right, Mother," Isaac says and leans in to kiss her on the cheek. "You've been busy."

"Well, that's certainly true. Hosting is never quite as fun as going to a party, is it? Sophia, it's so lovely to see you again. You're always welcome in this house."

I squeeze the hand holding mine. "Thank you," I tell her honestly. "That's very kind of you."

"That's what family does," she says, and her eyes burn a little brighter.

I swallow. "Thank you."

Amelia and her husband are higher on the ladder than the Brownes. They also seem considerably nicer, from the brief interactions I've had with them, but outward politeness is common in these circles. It's a currency, a commodity, and it often masks very different feelings.

I'm not ready for new and demanding in-laws.

"Sophia has put together a brilliant prototype for a coffee table book about the Winter Hotel," Isaac says and puts a hand on my lower back. "It was her idea, too. We could fill it with iconic pictures and stories about guests or parties."

Amelia puts her hands together. "That is a wonderful idea! Oh, I'd love to lend a hand, dear. I don't know if my son has told you, but I've written a little something about the family, and there are a ton of stories about how the hotel was founded."

"He has," I say.

She reaches out and puts a hand on my forearm. "Would you like to come over one day? We can have a drink and talk things over. I can give you material for it."

My smile turns strained. "Thank you for the generous offer, but I'm actually working on it as a project for the Winter Corporation."

"Yes," she says, "I gathered that."

"What she means," Isaac says dryly, "is that it's a job. She's paid for it through Exciteur Consulting."

Amelia drops her hand. "Oh," she says. "Silly of me, of course. That's such a modern way to do it."

I give a dutiful chuckle. "Yes. But I would be happy to meet with you, of course, if Exciteur is hired to put together the official coffee table book. I imagine you have a ton of great stories."

"Yes, I daresay I do. So, tell me more about your job. What do you do?" There's patient politeness on her face, and smile that looks genuine. I don't know if I trust it quite yet. But I do what she asks, telling her about what Isaac and I are working on together.

It's almost an hour later when Isaac and I are back on our own, walking through the main sitting room. It's a beautifully thrown party on all counts: music, decor, food, and ambiance. An invitation to this party must be one of the milestones of having made it in New York society.

Isaac bends closer, his mouth brushing the shell of my ear. "How are you doing?"

"Great. I'd love another glass of wine."

"You sure?"

"Why?" I ask. "Do you think I've had too much to drink?"

He chuckles. "No. But you've been... a bit quiet."

"It's nothing," I say. "There are just a lot of people, and I want to be on my A-game."

"You are," he says. "Mingling is a breeze with you beside me."

"Flatterer."

He smiles and brushes back my hair, notching it behind my ear. "It's the truth."

"You don't often bring dates to parties?"

"Sometimes," he says, "but it's rare. It's usually more work than it's worth."

"That might sound harsh to others, but honestly? I can understand that completely."

"I've been alone for a great many years," he says and gently tips my head back. "It always worked well for me. But I'm starting to think that's just because I hadn't met you yet."

My mouth opens. "Isaac..."

He smiles a little, like he knows he's said too much, and kisses me. Warm lips against mine, right there in his parents' house, surrounded by people who know him well, who all know who he is and what he represents.

He tastes like wine and coming home. I want us to be alone, just him and me, in my apartment or on his couch.

There's a teasing look in his eyes when he finally pulls away. "Feeling ready to leave?"

"I could leave, but I know you have people to talk to."

He shrugs. "That's the good thing about this party. It happens once every year, like clockwork."

"Then let's go, if you're sure."

"I'm sure."

My eye catches sight of a group of people behind him. There's a woman staring at us. Her near-black hair is pulled into a low bun, and she has an impressive necklace around her neck. Even from here, I can see the shine of emeralds.

"Well," I murmur, "I think there are a few more people who want to say hello to you."

He raises an eyebrow. "I don't mind leaving them disappointed."

That makes me laugh. "Yes, but they might not give us a choice. Incoming, behind you."

He turns to see the dark-haired woman striding our way. She's our age, I'd venture, or perhaps a few years younger. Next to her walks a suit-clad man at least thirty years her elder.

"Isaac," the man says and extends a meaty hand. "I haven't had a chance to say hello yet."

"Always a pleasure," Isaac says and shakes the man's hand. "Did the two of you just arrive?"

"No, no, we've been here a while," he says and turns a reedy smile at the woman beside him. He must be in his late sixties. "But you know how Amelia's parties are. Packed with too many brilliant people. Last year, I barely made it out of the dining room!"

The woman is watching me rather than Isaac, and there's a glint of speculation in her eyes. I keep my gaze steady on hers. One of his exes?

"My mother is one hell of a hostess," Isaac agrees. His hand drifts to my lower back, a barely-there touch, but a signal all the same. "I'm afraid we were on our way out."

"Trying to escape?" the woman says with a smile. "Go, then. It was nice to see you both. And I'm sorry, but I'm afraid I didn't catch your name?"

"Sophia," I say and extend a hand.

"Delighted," she says. "I'm Beverly. My husband and I have been to a lot of Winter parties, or so I'd like to think, but I don't think I've seen you before."

"No, you're new," the man says. His eyes have narrowed into slits with the force of his smile, his cheeks red. "I would have remembered you."

"Sophia and I have just recently started dating," Isaac says. His words are matter-of-fact, the way they always are, but there's a faint undercurrent of steel.

"Oh, how lovely!" Beverly says.

"Hope to see you again," her husband says. "Enjoy the rest of your night."

Isaac turns his back on them, steering us toward the foyer, and we finally emerge into the cool New York air.

"Beverly," I say. "That was *Beverly*?"

Isaac's voice is tight. "Yes. I'm sorry, Sophia, I didn't know she'd be there."

"That was your old..." The crassest of terms comes to my tongue, hovering right at the tip, before I remember that there are still guests milling around. Isaac's steps are quick, and I follow him away from the house, beneath the trees that stand like sentinels along the street.

"Yes," he says. "I told you about her."

"She married *that* man?"

"Arthur, yes. He plays golf with my father."

An icy cold hand grips my spine, and I come to an abrupt stop. "When did they get married?"

"Almost a decade ago now, I believe."

My stomach turns. It's the flip you experience on a roller coaster, that shift when gravity drops out beneath you, but you haven't started to fall yet.

But you know it's coming.

"Please tell me it's not what I think it is."

His brow furrows, his face turning tight. "Fuck, I wish I could. Sophia, wait, let me explain—"

"No."

I don't want to hear it. Not while I'm free-falling, imagining Isaac, the Isaac I know, doing *that* with her. Sneaking away in hotel rooms and helping her break her marriage vows. *He had an affair with a married woman.*

They all have affairs here.

Infidelity is like a drug for the incestuous, status-obsessed, insular New York upper class. Is wealth so boring, then, that you take to ending marriages just to keep life interesting?

"Sophia, their situation isn't anything like yours," he says. There's urgency in his deep voice now. "It's not the same."

"Oh, really?" My heels tap sharply with every furious step. "They don't wear wedding bands on their ring fingers?"

"They do," he says. "Sophia, I wanted to tell you."

"But you didn't."

"No, I didn't, and that mistake is on me."

"As is fucking a married woman!" I say. The fury burns through my veins, my atoms, into my very soul. It feels like I've been slapped, a betrayal, yet again.

Cheating is everywhere in this world.

Everywhere.

"Sophia," he says. "I will tell you anything you want to know. Their marriage isn't a true partnership, it's not a—"

"Excuses," I say. "How *could* you?"

He's quiet, and in the charged silence, I hear the sound of us breaking. Fracturing right down the middle, as clearly as if the sidewalk had opened up between us and turned into a gaping chasm.

"It's not something I'm proud of," he says quietly. "Sweetheart, this doesn't change a single thing about us or how I feel about you."

No. I can't handle that endearment, not right now. "There's a reason I didn't want to date Upper East Side men," I say. "There's a reason I was done, and damn you for making me reconsider. Damn you for doing this. Not *you*. It wasn't supposed to be you, too!"

He stands there, gilded beneath the streetlamp. Pain is etched into the planes of his face. "Let me take you home," he says.

"No." This conversation won't get us anywhere. My hands shake, and I don't know if it's the cold or the anger. Both. Neither. Maybe I'm just that close to exploding, to fleeing New York, never to return.

"Sophia, let me drop you off back home."

"I can take a cab."

"It's not as safe—"

"It is safe," I tell him, and yank my arm away. My words feel like they're laced with venom, and I know I need to get away, right now, or I'm going to start crying. "Thousands of people take cabs every damn day. I know how to take care of myself."

"Okay," he says. "Then, at least let me know when you're home."

I shake my head. Everything inside me is vibrating like I'm a bell that's been struck. He slept with a married woman. He goes to parties with her and her husband. He acts like nothing's out of the ordinary.

"I don't think I will," I say.

He drops his hand. "Please let me call you in a few days."

I step off the curb. There's a taxi approaching. They must have been tipped off about the large party here, or they're just constantly in motion, having dropped off guests.

I flag it down.

"Sophia," he says. "Please."

"I thought you were nothing like Percy," I say.

For a long moment, we look at each other. His eyes reflect the way I feel inside, but I'm the one who's furious, I'm the one who's hurt. *And damn him*, I think, *for looking like I'm breaking his heart when he's the one breaking mine.*

"I'm so sorry," he says. "I should've told you."

I slam the cab door behind me.

26

SOPHIA

Milo watches me accusingly from the couch. He's been trying to nap with his head on a pillow next to me, but I keep jostling him.

"Sorry," I tell him when I get up from the couch for the tenth time in an hour. I'm too jittery to stay still.

"For what?" my sister says. Her voice through my headphones makes me feel painfully homesick.

"Sorry, I was talking to the cat."

She laughs. "That's where we're at now?"

"It's your fault," I say. "You're the one who forced him on me."

"There's no forcing a kitten on anyone."

"Yes, there is. You forced me to look at the absolute pinnacle of cuteness, and then I was lost."

"He was the sweetest of the litter."

"Perfect for me, then," I say. "Famously the sweetest of women."

She chuckles. "You are when you want to be, you know. The people who know you know that."

I pour myself a cup of tea. It's my fourth, and I'm not really in the mood for one, but I need to do something, anything, to quell the maelstrom inside me.

"Soph," she says. "I'm sorry."

I sigh. "Yeah, so am I."

"Do you know the circumstances around it? Maybe they had an open marriage, you know. The trophy wife and her husband."

"Maybe," I say, but I sound unconvinced even to my own ears. "But I think he would have told me that right off the bat if it was."

"At least he wasn't the cheater," she says. "I know, I know, but… that's something."

I shrug. Maybe it is, but right now I can't think around it. All of it. Beverly, Isaac, and Percy, the world they all belong to, the world that comes with its own set of twisted rules.

"I shouldn't have gotten involved again," I say. "That's the real mistake, and that's on me."

"Nope. I told you to get out there a month ago, remember? So it's my fault. I take full responsibility."

"Rose, absolutely not."

"Yes, mea culpa. Now stop feeling like you messed up, because you didn't. You were brave! You trusted again! You had a relationship with a man, and you opened yourself up, and that's *fantastic*."

I twirl my spoon round and round in my cup of chamomile. "Feels like a pretty hollow victory."

"Right now, maybe, but not in a few weeks. I promise you that."

"You know, maybe I need to leave New York."

There's a brief pause. "Like leave, leave it?"

"Yes."

"Okay, I'm getting worried now. Should I get in the car and start driving?"

"No, I'm clear-headed. Maybe for the first time in over a year." I lean my head against the kitchen cabinet and look up at the ceiling. "I've tried for a year to make it work. To fit into the Sophia Bishop-shaped hole left behind in the blast zone of my marriage… but I just can't seem to find my place."

"Where would you go?"

"I don't know. Exciteur has a big office in Chicago. Maybe that could work." I take a sip of my too-hot tea. It burns. "New York is the biggest city in the country, but it doesn't seem big enough for both me and my past. I keep running into it."

"Sophia," my sister says. "Do you want to run from him?"

I sigh. "Maybe. I was so sure I'd manage it before, but now... I can't imagine working together with him. I can't even imagine living in the same city as him."

It seems painfully cruel, the idea of living in the same city as him, and working on the same project as him. Just a few blocks away.

"Maybe it's time I stop trying to become a New Yorker. Everyone reaches a point when it's just better to give up, you know? I think mine's come." My eyes burn, and I blink to try to clear them. It doesn't help.

I see his face, the way he'd looked beneath the streetlamp. Like I'd hurt him by getting into that cab. Like he was breaking, too.

"Sophia," my sister says. "You have always loved New York. You had a poster of the city skyline in your bedroom, remember? The one Dad got you when you turned ten? It's where you always dreamed of living. After school, you and I used to lie on the couch and rewatch New York TV shows and talk about whether we're a Miranda or a Samantha, or laugh at Joey and Chandler."

"Every day," I murmur.

"That was just entertainment for me, but you saw it as a manual. You've wanted to become a New Yorker your whole darn life!"

"Maybe that was the wrong dream," I say. "Maybe New York doesn't want me."

She snorts. "Bullshit. You're constantly getting promoted, you earn the big bucks, and you walk really fast now. Look, there's no shame in deciding a dream's no longer for you. But

I refuse to let you run away from it because you're scared or hurt. You have every right to own the city, just like Percy or this new guy."

"Isaac," I whisper.

"Yes, Isaac. So you had a setback in the last year. That doesn't mean this isn't your home. Would it be easier in Chicago? Knowing no one, nor your way around?"

"No, probably not."

"I'm not saying don't do it. Just... know why you're doing it."

I sigh. "Damn it, when did you become the voice of reason?"

She chuckles. "You were that voice when we were teens, so I have to return the favor."

"But it was so much easier when it was underage drinking or bleaching your hair."

"It was, wasn't it?" There's faint wailing in the background. "Shoot, Mia's woken up."

"Give her a kiss from me."

"Will do," she says. "And don't forget what I think about the whole thing."

"And what's that?"

"That you're my badass big sister," Rose says, "and you can do anything you put your mind to, man or no man, New York or no New York."

A tear runs down my cheek. "Thank you."

"Anytime," she says. "Love you."

"Love you, too."

I return to the couch with my big mug of tea. Milo opens one slitted eye, suspicion rife in the look.

"I'll sit for a good long while now," I say and snuggle up beside the pillow he's using as a bed. I run my fingers over his striped fur and listen as his warm body begins to purr. I do have a life in New York. I have a job I love and co-workers that make every day fun. I'll just have to make sure I stay far away from the men who take more than they give.

"Good thing I have you," I murmur to Milo, and rub my thumb over the soft fur between his ears. "You're all the man I need."

***

I ignore Isaac's first call.

It came two days after the fateful party, but I wasn't interested in talking or hearing another excuse. The next call came two days later, accompanied by a text. *Let's clear the air. Please, Sophia.*

That's something I see a begrudging amount of common sense in doing. We will be working together, even if I'll talk to his second-in-command and not him.

Let's go for a walk, I text back. My hands shake as I type the words. In my mind, I see her—I see Beverly—I see her standing next to her husband. And I hear the words Isaac had spoken. *Sophia, I'm sorry.* Because he'd known just how much damage that realization would do.

Maybe that's why he'd kept quiet about it.

A chilling suspicion races down my spine. Isaac had been single for a long time. Before that, he had been engaged to a woman who he, admittedly, had dated partly for strategic reasons.

To further the hotel and to further the family.

So he's already proven he's in the market for a wife. Maybe he wants someone like his mother or his grandmother, who served as the social limb of their husbands. Someone who can help further their place in the social circle and produce the next generation.

Isaac had seen me work first, challenged me on my thoughts about the hotel. He'd introduced me to his family and seen how I acted in society under the guise of our fake dates.

All before anything genuinely happened between us.

The man is a brilliant strategist. He deftly course-corrects, evaluates things five steps ahead, and has used that skill to grow the company to unprecedented heights.

And he's never hidden his single-minded goal of expanding the company. The strength of his family and that of the company are one and the same in his mind.

Maybe I've been evaluated from the start. Evaluated as a potential partner, judged based on my performance and my strengths.

Maybe, I think, *I've been pitching for another project entirely, and I didn't even know it.*

In the end, we meet by the river. There's a great length of sidewalk to pace, and I don't want to walk in Central Park. I don't want to be close to the hotel, or the Upper East Side, or the familiar paths I once walked every day.

Isaac is already there when I arrive. He's standing with his back to the water, his dark hair tousled by the wind. I wrap my own coat tighter around my body. Seeing him is a relief, like a balm to an open wound, and then it hurts. Because there's no more relief to be had with him.

"Sophia," he says, voice cautious. "You came."

I put my hands in my pockets. "Yes."

"Thank you."

I nod again. We start walking north, falling into comfortable step with one another.

"I saw that your company signed the contract," I say. "Winter Corp and Exciteur are officially in business together now."

"Yes," he says. "What I said earlier stands. Andrew will run point on the project from our end, and will be your only source of contract."

"Thanks," I say. Funny how that was meant as a backup plan, but we'd needed it immediately.

"Sophia," he says. "I'm sorry about last weekend."

"Sorry she was there? Or sorry it happened at all?"

"It wasn't something I planned on keeping from you forever," he says. "But I need you to know that I've never been unfaithful to anyone. Not once."

"Congratulations," I say. My tone sounds acidic, and I hate it. I hate this, and I hate the painfully tight knot in my stomach.

"It's not something I'm proud of, and I wasn't even when it was happening."

"Then why did you do it?"

Isaac is quiet for a long time. "It was after Cordelia. She'd cheated, and I was... nihilistic when it came to relationships. It seemed like they didn't work, not for anyone, but least of all for me. Doing something that confirmed my own belief was... comforting, I think."

"It was still wrong."

"Of course, it was," he says. "She's unhappy with her husband, despite the crass agreement they have, you know. He got a younger wife, and she got security and stability, but it's not a good marriage. Beverly and I? We were just amusing one another. At the time, I suppose I thought it was companionship, too."

I cross my arms over my chest. The reasonable words falter against the bulwark of my defences. *Not again. Never again.* "Does her husband know?"

"I don't know," he says. "I never asked. But Sophia, it's in the past. I haven't been with her for almost a year. It's over, and that part of my life is over."

I shake my head. *Just like Percy,* I think. They all are. "Nothing's ever truly in the past."

"No, I suppose not," he says, and there's a rough note in his voice.

"What does that mean?"

He shakes his head. "Nothing. I'll answer any questions you want about it, about myself, about my past relationships."

"No," I say. "There's no need."

"There isn't?"

"This isn't a good idea, anyway. You and me. *This.*"

"And why not?"

"Because you want a wife, a proper wife, and I can't be that."

His voice turns monotone. "What do you mean, a wife?"

"Yes, you want a marriage like... like your parents," I say. "Like your friends, and your family, and your entire social group. A marriage *just* like the one Percy wanted us to have, but I couldn't do it. I've tried that, and I can't do it again. I won't do it again. I won't give up my job and I—"

Isaac stares at me. "When have we spoken about marriage?"

I shake my head again. There's a manic quality to my words, to the unloading of emotions. "I really love my job."

"I know that," he says. "Fuck, don't you think that's—"

"You'd say that, but how would I know if you really mean it? I won't come work for the Winter Corporation. I won't be a trophy wife, I can't, and I won't deal with the pressures of in-laws again and you slowly resenting me because I can't cook you warm meals, and then finding you with *her* again or someone else because you think marriage is just a contract and not a—"

"Sophia," he says. His voice is harsh. "What the hell is all this?"

"It's our future," I say, "and I don't want it. This is for the best."

"That wouldn't be our future."

"Yes, it would. I know it would," I say, but I can see that he doesn't believe me. Why can't he see what I can so clearly?

His mouth tightens. "So you would just give up, then? On us?"

"We were never an us," I tell him, my steps speeding up. We'd started by faking it, and then it had been a day-by-day thing. A go-slow thing, and a test-the-waters thing. Well, the waters have been tested, and they're shark infested.

"Then what were we?" he demands.

"Something fun on the side while we worked together."

"That's not how I saw us," he says. "Not once."

I think of his mother's party, and of the comment about the two of us having kids. I see myself trying to appease his mother and around me, the sound of a cage rattles. "This just isn't a good idea," I say.

His voice turns colder than I've ever heard it. "I see. This is because of Percy."

"What? He has nothing to do with this."

"Oh, but he does, doesn't he? Because you're still in love with him."

I turn to look at Isaac. *What?*

"Your reactions, every single time we've met him, clued me in. But I had hoped…" He shakes his head. "So that's it, then. You're still in love with him, and now you're using my mistake from years ago to run away from a good, new thing."

"You're delusional," I say. "You've lost your mind."

"I don't think I have. I think I'm finally seeing all of it clearly, for the very first time."

"Then you need to get your eyesight checked," I say. Beneath my coat, my blood boils. I want to run away and I want to fight him.

But then Isaac's eyes widen.

Shit. His brother.

"I didn't mean it that way," I say.

"I know," Isaac says, but his voice is harsh. "I wish you could just forget about Percy. I wish you could let him go, finally."

I narrow my eyes at him. "I have. The only thing Percy has to do with this is how much I've realized you're just like him."

"I'm *nothing* like him," Isaac says. "And I'm sick and fucking tired of you comparing me to him."

"I'm not—"

"Yes, you are, and you have been since we met."

"Correctly, then, it seems."

He shakes his head. "I hate that man. I hate that he was ever married to you, and I hate that he hurt you, and I fucking hate that he still shows up in your life."

I turn and walk, my footsteps echoing against the concrete beneath my feet. Faster and faster, I walk as if I can outrun him. Or maybe I'm trying to outrun myself.

He keeps up easily. "Don't you dare use this as an excuse to run from something good."

I shake my head. Words won't form, can't form, or the tears behind my eyes will spill over. It's so easy to see the slow resentment building, the demands, the desires. The gradual need for me to become someone else in order to be the wife he wants.

I won't be able to do it. And I refuse to fail again, refuse to see the love in his eyes dim, and then watch them start to wander.

"Sophia," he says. "Damn it, just stop."

"Don't call me," I say, my footsteps speeding up. "Bye, Isaac."

He stops following me.

27

ISAAC

Andrew rifles through his papers. He's sitting opposite my desk, brisk competence radiating off him. "Let me see..." he mutters and pulls out a binder. "Here. The latest memo from Exciteur just arrived. They've refined the list of cities they suggest we start in with more info on each, and added contact information to reputable brokerages."

I scan the list he hands me. *San Francisco, Portland, Atlanta, Dallas.* "Great. Run a brief in-house analysis on the hotel market in those cities, and then start looking for properties. I want a cost analysis done on each."

"Will do," Andrew says. "Miss Bishop had an additional thought at our meeting earlier today. She suggested we create our own, in-house reward system for customers at the WH hotels. They'll collect points with each stay, contributing to a free night, and it'll also put them in the running to win a weekend stay here. At the Winter New York."

It's a good idea, incentivizing frequent travelers to book with us. "She suggested that, did she?"

"Yes," Andrew says with a chuckle. "Seemed like it was off the top of her head, too. Here, these are the architect firms Exciteur has already contacted on our behalf. They've all worked with hotels before."

"Excellent," I murmur, and skim the list. Andrew is great at his job. This system undoubtedly saves me time.

But it's painful to have him tell me this and not Sophia. That the contingency I've put in place, a fail-safe, is one we've come to actually need. And now I hate Andrew a little, for getting the chance to talk to her on a weekly basis.

After he's finished briefing me, he leaves, shutting the door behind him and closing me in with my thoughts. They turn morose. Maybe this is just how relationships go. They invariably come to this, to a bitter end, to sharp words and even sharper emotions.

What I'd had with Beverly had been empty, occasional companionship. We'd gone through the motions, but it had been hollow, a farce of the real thing. That had been exactly what I'd wanted back then. It had been what I craved after Cordelia when relationships seemed like nothing but pain. Beverly had expected nothing from me, and I expected nothing from her, and there was no pain to be had from that.

That's why I'd ended the occasional trysts about a year ago. The hollowness that had once felt comforting had started to grate, and the immorality of it all weighed heavier by the month. But it had never hurt.

What Sophia and I had? That was the opposite, with potential pain lurking around every goddamn corner, but only because it was *real* in a way I hadn't experienced in years.

And now I've lost it.

The best woman I've ever met, and the best opportunity I'll ever get. Both of them, gone in a moment.

I rest my head in my hands. It's been seven long days since she told me to leave her alone, standing next to the East River. She'd been about to cry. I'd heard it in her voice, but she hadn't wanted me to see it. She ran instead.

Fuck the hotels, fuck the project, and most of all, fuck Percival Browne for winning her affection, and then abusing it rather than honoring it. For making the most incredible woman I've ever met believe relationships aren't for her. But most of all, fuck him for still, after all that, having her affection.

I stare down at the papers spread out on my desk. The plans and names and contracts for the franchise, all drawn up by her and her team. It has her stamp all over it.

You want a wife, and I can't be that, she'd said. Those words had haunted me over the past week. I should have been clearer about what I truly wanted and why. That I care for her because of who she is, and not because of what she can give me down the line.

There's a knock on my door.

"Enter!"

It's Anthony. Walking close by his side is Abel, his guide dog. "Hi," he says. "I'm a few minutes early."

"That's all right. Have a seat," I say. If anything, talking business with my little brother will help take my mind off things.

He narrows his eyes. "Even I can see that you look shot. Have you been sleeping?"

"Not very well."

"No, I can see that." He sinks down into the chair Andrew just left, stretching out his long legs. Abel, seeing that her master is safe and sound, comes around the desk to greet me.

I run my hand over her soft head. "Hi, you."

Abel wags her tail softly and then lies down next to Anthony, ever loyal, ever faithful.

"What's wrong?"

"Sophia and I have called it quits."

He frowns. "Damn. Sorry to hear that."

"Yeah. Thanks."

"How come?"

"Lots of things." I shake my head and push back from my desk, giving my own legs room to stretch. "It's over, and I'd rather it wasn't, but it wasn't my call. She found out about the relationship I had with Beverly and reacted badly."

"Oh," he says. "You know, I heard she's moved on to Paul's younger brother. Can't remember his name right now, but you know, the banker who just moved back from London?"

"Logan," I say dryly. "It wouldn't surprise me. Sleeping with Beverly meant nothing at the time, but Sophia doesn't see it that way. And... I'm pretty sure she's still in love with her ex-husband."

"Well, shit," Anthony says. "That one's hard to overcome."

"Yeah."

"Did she tell you that?"

"No, but I've picked up on the signals."

"Hmm," he says. "Look, I'm not an expert on women."

That makes me laugh. "No, I wouldn't say you are."

My brother pointedly ignores that. "But I do know that nine times out of ten, when you assume what they're thinking or feeling... You assume wrong."

"You get married *once*," I say, "and suddenly you're full of wisdom?"

He lifts a finger. "Being married means you won the dating game, so I'd listen to me if I were you."

I sigh. "Right. Okay. So I shouldn't assume."

"No, you shouldn't. What did she actually say? When she found about Beverly and when she wanted to end things?"

I rest my elbows on the desk. "It's not a conversation I want to relive."

"Come on," Anthony says. "We won't leave to get lunch until you do."

"You're a real menace."

"And you're stalling."

I sigh but give in, giving him a quick rundown of what she'd said. I even repeat those words. *I can't be your wife.*

When I'm done, Anthony looks more thoughtful than I've seen him in months.

"So?" I say. "What do you make of that, oh whisperer of the feminine?"

"Sounds to me like she's afraid of repeating her first marriage. It can't have been a particularly great one," he says and shakes his head. "I remember Percy from school."

"You were in the same year, right?"

"Yeah. I always got the feeling his parents were riding him pretty hard. Can't imagine they stopped just because he grew up. Besides," Anthony says, shrugging, "he always struck me as a man with an appetite for too much fun."

I sigh. "So I made her feel like being with me would be like being with that fucking asshole again."

"Maybe," he says, "but I doubt it's as clear-cut as that. She was hurt very deeply, and now she's afraid of opening herself up to being hurt again. Finding out about your little dalliance with Beverly just dialed that fear up to a ten. Hell, I could probably have figured this out even pre-Summer!"

I raise an eyebrow, remembering the man he'd been before he was open about his diagnosis and before he met his wife. "No, I really don't think you could've."

He waves a hand. "Regardless, the way forward for you is simple, my friend."

"Simple?"

"Yes. You just have to make it crystal clear to her that you're not expecting anything like her old marriage. That you understand her fears and promise to listen to them and take them seriously. And that you're not going to give up just because it gets hard."

"Fuck," I say. "You actually are an expert."

He grins, brief and wide. "Yeah."

"So how do I let her know that?"

"I don't know. What do men usually do when they fuck things up? Pen a heartfelt letter or write her name in the sky with a plane?"

"Two very similar options," I say dryly.

"When I screwed up with Summer, I just went and talked to her. No writing required."

"I've tried that," I say.

"So try again," he says. "You have the look of a man who's pining."

"I'm not pining."

"Yes, you are, because I've seen the same look on my own face in the mirror."

I take a deep breath. He's right on all counts, and maybe a few more that he's too tactful to mention.

"I think I'm going to move out of the hotel," I say.

"What? Seriously?"

"Yes. Showing the place to Sophia made me think… it's not really a home, is it? It's a memorial, a museum, and it's important. But the rooms here are the family's. Not mine. For a long time that didn't matter, but I think it does now. I think I *want* it to matter."

Anthony's mouth widens into a slow smile. "Yeah. That's why I've always wanted to have a life outside of the hotel, too."

"I know," I say. "It's something I've resented you for sometimes. For going down your own path and leaving me alone on the one we were expected to walk."

Anthony's quiet. His hand rests on Abel's fur, moving back and forth in a slow motion. "I knew you did," he says. "Sometimes. But I also know you, and you would have taken my head off if I'd ever tried to challenge you for your position."

I chuckle. "Yeah. Probably."

"If there's one thing you are," he says, "it's painfully, obnoxiously, single-mindedly persistent. Don't stop being that now when you need it the most."

I look down at my hand, resting atop one of the documents from Exciteur. From her.

"You're right."

28

SOPHIA

I turn over in my bed and fluff up the pillow. I fold it over once and then in the opposite direction, trying to get comfortable. It's been an hour since I turned off the lights, and sleep is still nowhere in sight. Funny how that's been a problem since the night of the Winters' fall party.

My body might be tired, but my mind isn't. It spins. The pleasant wine-buzz I'd gotten from drinks earlier with Jenna and Toby has disappeared, leaving me with a painful amount of clear-headedness.

I'd told them I was no longer dating Isaac Winter. *We came to a mutual decision,* I'd said. *It's best to stay professional.*

Jenna had frowned at that. She'd worn a yellow blouse, her lucky color, in preparation for a date she had after our drinks. "Oh," she'd said.

"You don't think we made the right decision?"

"I don't know," she'd said, and looked at Toby beside her. "Maybe you did. But I was rooting for this."

I'd had another sip of my wine and acted casual. "You were?"

"Yes. Well, not really because of him, because I don't know him."

"We know he's deliciously handsome," Toby had said. "So, that's a pretty important point in his favor."

Jenna laughed. "Yes, definitely. He has that aloof hotness, you know?"

"That's exactly what it is," he'd agreed.

Jenna had turned back to me. "But my point was, I was rooting for it because of *you*. I think it's great that you're dating again."

"We're just team Sophia getting some," Toby said with a grin. "He was a means to an end."

I'd rolled my eyes. "Jesus, all right."

"Anyway, if it's over, it's over." Jenna had held up her wineglass to toast. "Here's to moving onwards and upwards. Hey, you can even download the app I'm using. We can become dating buddies!"

I'd wriggled my way out of that one. But their enthusiasm about the whole thing, about something I'd just wanted to breeze past, had gotten beneath my skin.

I turn over in bed again.

Maybe it would be easier to forget if I didn't have to see his name every day. *Winter,* it says in my documents and on my project folders. *Winter, winter, winter.*

It's not even my favorite season.

Damn him. Damn me. Damn all of it for happening and leaving me alone with the memory of it, unable to enjoy its sweetness. Every day something happens that I want to talk to him about. Work, tennis, life, the city.

I'd been doing okay before Isaac.

Not great, maybe, but okay. Life was predictable and monotonous. But now that he's passed like a storm that's breezed through a little town, everything feels out of place. There's an absence now, a lack, where before there was just nothingness.

I turn onto my back and stare up at the ceiling. If only I'd never invited him into my apartment and never let him sleep in this bed. Maybe then I wouldn't feel his absence quite so strongly.

My buzzer rings. The loud, piercing sound jolts me into sitting. Then it comes again, buzzing loudly from my living room.

There's someone calling from downstairs.

Milo gives an offended little meow beside me on the bed. His eyes glitter in the near-darkness as he watches me get up.

"Stay there," I murmur. Unnecessarily, too, because he has no intention of moving. He tucks his face between his front paws and closes his eyes.

I walk to the intercom by my front door and click down the receiver button. "Hello?"

"Soph?" a voice says. "Is that you?"

My anticipation turns to annoyance. "What the hell are you doing here?"

"Soph, please," my ex-husband says. "I just want to talk to you. I *have* to talk to you."

"No, you don't."

"Yes. Please come down," he says, voice too loud in my quiet apartment. "Meet me in the lobby."

"Go away, Percy."

"I won't!" he says. "I'll stay here until morning, until you *have* to leave for work."

Shit. I press down the receiver again. "Fine, but you're not coming in, and you're leaving the second you've said whatever stupid thing you've come here for."

"Good, Soph. That sounds good." His words are fuzzy around the edges.

I march into my bedroom and pull on a pair of sweatpants. Then, I stick my feet in a pair of worn-out loafers and throw over a coat, hiding most of the mismatched outfit. Irritation burns like a flame in my chest.

He's never once come to my new place.

Sure, he must know the address, seeing as the moving company packed up all my stuff from our shared apartment and drove it straight here. But that was almost a year ago now. And while he called, and texted, and emailed nonstop in the beginning, he never came here.

I go downstairs. Percy's standing by the front door of my building. His suit jacket is unbuttoned, and so are the first three buttons of his shirt. His hair looks mussed.

"Soph!" he says.

I open the front door. "What the hell do you think you're doing?"

His smile turns into a frown. "I'm sorry, so sorry. I know you don't… I just needed to see you."

"Well, here I am," I say.

"You look great," he says. "I was out with the boys tonight, but I… I just couldn't stop thinking. I had to know, so I had to come here. Why, Soph?"

"Why what?"

"Why did you have to divorce me?" He puts a hand to his chest like he's injured. "Why did you throw it away, all of it? You, me, our home… our future."

"You can't be serious."

"Soph, I'm always serious."

"You're never serious," I say. "If that was the single, stupid reason you showed up here drunk, then I want you to leave."

"Please, please, just… tell me. Explain it to me. I can't understand it. I've *never* been able to understand it."

"You," I say, enunciating every syllable, "had an affair. For months. With a woman we both knew."

He shakes his head. "I know, and that was my mistake. And I was sorry for it. I told you that, over and over and over again. Why couldn't you just have forgiven me? Please, Soph… I'm not happy."

"That's not my problem anymore."

He sighs like he didn't hear my words. Or maybe he's just ignoring them. He was often good at that. "I'm not happy with Scarlett. She wants and wants and wants, all the damn time. Wants me to take her to places and wants us to get married. I'm not happy… But Soph, I was happy with you. You're so smart, and you're so good at teasing me, and you… God, you're pretty, too. So damn pretty."

"The only thing you've ever chased is happiness," I say, "and only the short-term kind. That's been your whole life!"

"You're right," he says, nodding quickly. "You've always been right."

"Too little too late, though, when it came to you."

"I want you back. I want to be us again."

"You broke us," I say, and I mean it. The words fall like a scythe through the quiet, unassuming lobby of my high-rise.

I want him out of it, and I want him out of my life.

He sighs. "I know, but I'm sorry. Soph, *I'm sorry.* That has to count for something. I'd take it all back if I could."

My voice hardens. "No, it doesn't. It's been a year, and you're having a baby with another woman. And I've already moved on."

He takes a deep breath. And then another one. "Yeah, with *that* man. It hurt me, seeing you with him. Is that what you want me to say? Is that the game we've been playing these weeks?"

The words take the air out of me. Maybe that is what I'd once wanted him to say. But not now. Not when Isaac and I were so much more than petty revenge.

"I don't want you to say anything. What I want is for you to leave."

"Did you just use me?" His eyes have a glazed sheen to them. "Did you just want me to introduce you to society? Fuck, that's it, isn't it. I was a stepping stone. You just wanted bigger and brighter, and you got it. Mom warned me once," he says and points a finger at me, "that you were a gold digger. That she could see it in you."

"Fuck you," I say.

He gives a half laugh. It rings false in the wide space. "That's it. That's why you want him, the almighty, on-his-damn-high-horse Winter, king of the goddamn city."

Anger flares inside of me like fireworks. "The fact that you would say that to me proves you never knew me at all. You know what? It just proves one thing, that marrying you was the biggest mistake of my life."

His face whitens. "You don't mean that."

"Yes, I do. You cheated on me. You constantly degraded my career. You made me feel like a bad wife for wanting my own life, outside of us. You never once defended me against your mother. You didn't want *me* as I actually am," I say. "You wanted me to fit like a puzzle piece into your life instead of building a new one together."

"What," Percy says, voice venomous, "like *he's* so fucking perfect?"

"He's not. But he would never come to my apartment at midnight, drunk out of his mind, and accuse me of being a gold digger."

Percy holds up his hands like this is too much. Like he can't believe what I'm saying. "I gave you a life. I gave you *everything.*"

"Except a loving and faithful husband," I say. "Except support and companionship. You know, I'm glad you found your way into bed with Scarlett, and I'm glad I saw it. Because you and I wouldn't have lasted anyway... and I'm so damn glad I didn't waste more of my life on you."

His chest rises and falls. "Soph," he says. "Fuck, you're right. You're so damn right, and I'm sorry. I'm sorry and I'm miserable."

"I know. But it's not enough. Can you tell me something? Honestly?"

He nods.

"It wasn't just Scarlett, though. Was it?"

Percy turns still, like prey caught in the headlights. There's no reply from his half open lips. But the answer is there in his drunken eyes, betraying him.

There had been others.

"Yeah," I say softly, "I figured. Goodbye, Percy."

"Wait." He reaches out to grip my wrist, but I pull it out of his reach. "Soph, fuck, wait… This went all wrong."

"Yes," I say. "It did. You're going to be a father, Perce. You always said you wanted that. So focus on that, on your kid. Be the best dad you can be to that little baby, and start fresh. And if you ever come to my doorstep drunk like this this again, I'll call the police."

He takes a deep breath, and I can see him try to pull the fragmented, drunk segments of his mind back together. "Yeah. Yeah... You're right."

"Leave now. Please."

He heads to the front door. But he pauses with his hand on it. "I'm sorry," he says.

I know he means it, but not enough for it to matter. "Goodbye," I say.

And I mean that enough for the both of us.

The door locks behind him, and I stay put, watching as he ambles away from my building. He gets in a cab, and it drives off, taking my past away. I had never needed him to fit into this city. It's my home, and I've made it mine all by myself. My relationship with New York is stronger than my marriage ever was.

Isaac had been wrong about one thing. I'm not still in love with Percy. The love had dried up when I saw through the illusion, when that Peter Pan charm of his faded, and I found only immaturity and casual cruelty in its place.

But Isaac had a point, all the same. Because it was Percy's shadow that lurked too large in my mind. It was him, and how he hurt me, and the fear of being hurt once again. And it was myself. I had lost *me* somewhere over the past couple of years, and I've just started finding myself again. And I know now that I'll never give her up.

But Isaac isn't Percy.

Isaac isn't Percy.

And I'm not who I'd been a year ago, either. Like the cab heading up Manhattan, speeding back to a place I'd once called home, it's possible to let go of the past. To let it fade into a memory, nothing more, and be brave enough to create a new future.

29

SOPHIA

The city's a tad too cold for walking with bare legs. The nip in the air is almost painful, but it's energizing too, cooling me down from the tennis lesson I've just had with Marisol. The muscles in my right arm are sore, and the arm hangs heavy at my side.

For a delightful hour and a half, the rest of life had faded away, and it was just me and sweat and the thrill of improvement. I take a few deep breaths, inhaling the fall air. My sweatshirt feels too hot, and my bare legs beneath the tennis skirt feel too cold.

Nerves, unusual and unwelcome, pulse in my stomach. Now that my brain can focus on other things than a ball coming at me in high speed, it's circled back to him.

I've made a decision.

Tonight, after I've showered and had dinner, I'll get in a cab and head to the Winter Hotel to talk. To tell him that I don't know what the way forward might look like... but that I want to try. With him.

By the time I'm back on my block, my legs ache. I can't wait to jump into my shower and have the warm water smooth over sore muscles. I nod hello to the concierge who works in the lobby during the days.

"Miss Bishop," he says. "Just a moment, please. There was a man here earlier who delivered a letter for you."

I pause. "Hand delivered?"

"Yes. Let's see…. Here it is." He hands it over. It's an anonymous white envelope with my name scrawled across it.

"Thanks."

"Anytime," he says. "Hope you played a great game today."

"I sure did. Thank you, Jerry." I barely make it to the elevators before I've torn open the sealed envelope. Inside is a handwritten note.

Sophia,

I'm not done with us. Because there was an us, sweetheart, and it was the best us I've ever been a part of. You told me not to contact you again. If that's still what you want, I'll honor that and won't do it again. But if you're having even a sliver of doubt… let me convince you that our future is unwritten. I will never pressure you in any direction. What we build together is ours, and I think it could be something great.

You once said you wanted us to go places where no one knows who we are and the past doesn't hide around every corner. I wish I'd listened. But I've heard you now, and that's where you'll find me. I'll be at your favorite ramen place every night this week. Come to me if you want to talk.

Isaac

The ramen place.

I'd just walked past it. I walk past it all the time. I have the menu on the inside of my kitchen cabinet and the takeout number saved to my phone.

I spin around in the lobby.

"Everything all right?" Jerry asks.

"Yes, thank you," I say, my steps speeding up. "Just forgot something. I'll see you later!"

The door to my building falls shut behind me, and then I'm half running up the street, back where I came from, still in my sweaty tennis clothes. On my arm, my smartwatch buzzes. *Exercise begun.*

I come to a stop outside the familiar window. Folding chairs fill up the small interior, and there, in the corner, sits a man too tall for the small table. He has a laptop open and his phone tucked beneath his ear.

I can see him talking, steadily, calmly, to the person on the other end. On the foldout chair beside him hangs his suit jacket, neatly draped over the back.

My chest tightens at the sight of him.

He nods, then nods again, at something the person on the other line says. I can see his lips move. And then he looks up and sees me.

I give a tiny wave.

He says a few more words. I can read them through the dirty glass window. *I'll call you later.*

I push open the door, and the tiny bell above rings out, announcing my arrival. "Hello."

"Sophia," he says. "You came."

"I just got your note. I did some errands after work and then I played tennis. Have you been waiting long?"

"Not particularly," he says.

"That's a lie," a voice chimes in. Amy stands behind the counter, wearing a huge grin. "He paid me a stupid amount of money to sit here and work every night this week. He's rented my whole shop!"

My eyebrows rise. "You did?"

"It's only fair she be compensated."

"That's right," Amy says gladly. "Do you want your regular order?"

"No thanks, not… yet, anyway. I'm just here to talk to him."

"Good call," she says. "You've got yourself a handsome one, there."

I chuckle. "Thanks."

She nods again and grabs a rag from the side of the counter. "I'll be in the back. Not listening, I promise."

"Thanks," I say.

Isaac's voice is measured and steady, but I can hear the trace of cautiousness in it. "You look great."

"Thank you, but I've just worked out. I'm a sweaty mess."

"You still look great," he says.

"Did you really… sorry, I can't believe you're here."

His mouth twists into a rueful smile. "Yeah. Sorry if I've overstepped, I just figured meeting on neutral ground might be… anyway. Do you want to stay and talk?"

I pull out the chair opposite him. The air in the small restaurant feels thick with tension. "Yes. Thanks."

"I wondered how to best do this," he says. He's bracing his hands on the table, the wide backs and long fingers stretching out on the vinyl. "I considered writing you a letter or sending an email through the official channels, but that would be violating our agreement. No pleasure mixed in with the business."

"Yes," I murmur. "Winter and Exciteur are separate."

"They are. I considered calling you, or texting. But…" He shakes his head. "Last time, you told me to leave you alone."

"God, I said a lot of things last time. I didn't mean that."

"I hoped you didn't, but I wanted to honor it in case you did."

"So you did this. Ramen," I say, looking around at the framed images on the wall, the neon lighting.

"Yes. Do you remember when we came here together?"

"Of course I do."

"I knew I shouldn't walk you home. Shouldn't follow you inside. Shouldn't think about the way your lips had felt on mine, or how distractingly attractive you were in that skirt, or how well we'd played together."

My cheeks heat up. "I knew I shouldn't have invited you up to my apartment that afternoon, either."

"No," he says quietly, "you shouldn't have. But you did."

"Yes." We'd showered together, his hands on my body, my lips on his... and started something much bigger than just a tennis game.

"Sophia," he says. "It's been a long couple of years before I met you, and during every one, I was alone. Even in my last relationship, when we were engaged, I was on my own. It wasn't a true partnership. And I think I've always preferred that. I think it's always been safer to not let anyone in, not fully. To focus on my work and what everyone else needs me to be.

"That's part of why I spent time with Beverly. It was self-destructive, and easy, and *safe*. Because she never needed me. And I never needed her. I'm sorry I helped her be unfaithful. I'm sorry it hurt you, Sophia, and I'm sorry I didn't tell you about it right away. But most of all, I'm sorry it made you think less of me."

The words wash over me, and through me. They settle something inside that had been nervous from the moment I'd seen him sitting at this plastic table.

"We all do things we're not proud of," I say. "The way I reacted... it was because of my past."

"I know," he says softly. "I should have anticipated that."

I shake my head. "You can't anticipate everything. I reacted more strongly than... I didn't listen to you, Isaac, or to your reasons. You were hurt too, after having been cheated on. I should've listened."

He closes his eyes. Dark eyelashes fan out over his high cheekbones, and stubble traces the sharp line of his jaw. "Meeting you has been the greatest thing that's ever happened to me."

My throat feels tight. "Isaac..."

"I want you to know that I'm willing to work for it. To go as slow as you'd like. To wait. To never ask you to another party or benefit if you feel like you've had enough of them for a lifetime."

I put my hand over his. "I'm not in love with Percy."

There's disbelief in his eyes, plain and simple, and I remember his words from our explosive conversation by the river. "I'm not," I say again.

"But that night, when we were at Salt. When they told us about the pregnancy…"

"I was feeling a lot of things right then, but believe me, it wasn't jealousy. It's more like I saw myself in her, and where I might've been if the divorce never happened. And it's a sore spot, one where I'd always been made to feel like… well, like I'd failed. Percy and his mother loved to hint about kids, but I wasn't ready yet."

The hand beneath mine turns to grip mine. "What do you mean?" he asks flatly.

"I wanted to wait for kids, to focus on my career. Honestly, I'm still… unsure about when I'll feel ready. I'm thirty-three. Shouldn't I be ready?"

"There's no timeline," he says, and there's a fierce undertone to his voice. "You do things at your own pace."

I sigh. "Yes. Well, they made me feel like I *should* want it, like I was a fool for loving my life the way it was, and I was letting them down. Letting Percy down."

"I hate the Brownes."

"They're in the past. And I mean that, you know. The sadness I felt that night… it wasn't because I wanted to be Scarlett. God, do you know how glad I am that I never had a kid with Percy? I'd never have been rid of him!"

Isaac nods. "You dodged one there."

"But that doesn't mean you were completely off base, either," I say. "I have to be honest about that."

His dark eyes sharpen. "Oh?"

"I'm not in love with him," I say, "but I was haunted by

him. By the memories. And I did compare you to him. I'm sorry. That wasn't fair to you."

"I understand it," he says.

"It wasn't right, but I was afraid. More afraid than I realized, more afraid than I could put into words. And my response to that has always been running away."

"What were you afraid of?"

"All of it. Feeling trapped again. Feeling like I… like I love a man who never thinks I'm enough. Feeling like I'm a failure. Most of all, though, I'm afraid of being hurt again. I never want to relive the last year."

"I know," he murmurs and grips my hand with both of his. "You won't."

I smile, shaking my head. Tears feel perilously close. "Neither of us knows that. And maybe that's okay, you know? Maybe that's just part of life."

He looks down at where my hand rests in his. "Yeah," he murmurs. "This might get really hard, and messy, and I've avoided every chance of that since Cordelia. But if it's with you that things are getting messy… I can handle it. I might even want it."

"We're very similar," I say. "Have you thought about that? Because I have."

"Yes," he says quietly. "I have."

"Do you think that's a good thing? Or are we too similar?"

He smiles that lopsided, genuine smile. "I don't know, but sweetheart, it doesn't really matter in my book. I don't think I can be with anyone else. It's you, or it's no one."

My mouth drops open. "Oh."

"I don't want to pressure you," he says, "and I realize that might sound like pressure, but I can go slow. Like I said, we can leave every fucking society thing out of it. If anyone makes an idiotic comment about our kids being heirs when we've never even had the kids conversation ourselves, I'll excommunicate them."

I chuckle. "You can't do that."

"Of course, I can."

"You don't run a church or a cult."

He waves his free hand. "Cut them out of my social circle, then."

"You can't. And we can't avoid society altogether, Isaac. Those are your family, your friends, your business associates."

"I can downsize," he says. "I know you wanted a simpler life. A smaller life. A math teacher."

I shake my head. "I don't."

"Sophia…"

"No, really. I was just afraid, afraid of living the last seven years of my life over again, and instead of facing that, I made up new problems. And I didn't realize that until just this past week. But I'm a problem-solver, Isaac. That's what I do every day at my job. Maybe it's time I started doing that in my own life." I look over my shoulder at the empty counter, unable to stop the smile from spreading across my face. I feel light. "I love this ramen place, but I do live just down the street."

"Do you now?"

"Yes," I say. "Come home with me."

He smiles. "I don't know, I have this place rented out for a few more hours today…"

"Isaac."

"All right, then." He rises from the table, and I walk into his arms. He wraps them around me, and he smells like cologne and soap and him. I breathe it all in.

"Bishop," he murmurs. "If it ever gets too much, any of it —my work, a party, someone's comments… tell me. I'm on your side, you know. Only on yours."

I close my eyes against the burning behind them. "I'm on yours, too," I say. "Okay? We play sets together."

He chuckles. The sound reverberates through the chest I'm pressed against. "We do," he says, "though it's hard to concentrate when you look so hot doing it."

I laugh. "You're laying it on thick."

256

"Just being honest." His free hand curves around my waist, pulling me tighter against his body. "Tell me, does this tennis skirt have those little built-in shorts, too?"

I lean back and meet his brilliant dark brown eyes. "Come home with me," I say, "and I'll let you find out."

30

SOPHIA

A month later

"They're going to open a new Salt," Isaac says. He's leaning against the headboard of my bed, propped up by two pillows, and has the *New York Globe* spread out on his lap. "One that focuses on brunch? Jesus."

I put down my book. "You're not a fan of brunch?"

"No, even if I understand that others are."

"The Ivy's Sunday brunches are legendary," I say.

He gives me a crooked smile. "They are, aren't they?"

"Definitely. So you can profit from it, but not enjoy it?"

Isaac reaches between us to run his hand over Milo's striped back. My cat turns onto his side and stretches in pleasure, his paws kneading the cover.

"Yes," he says. "That's just good business. But it's never appealed to me. It just takes up such a large chunk of the day. It's not breakfast, but it's not lunch, nor is it dinner. It throws off the entire schedule."

"Maybe Sundays are for not having a schedule at all?"

He smiles and lets his warm gaze trace the length of my body. I'm wearing his button-down, thrown on to avoid giving my neighbors an eyeful when I'd made us coffee.

"Well," he says. "Not usually, but if they're like this? I can get on board with that."

I prop my head up on a pillow and watch him in return, bare-chested and tousled-haired and here, in my apartment. He'd flown in from LA late last night and came straight here from the airport. Our schedules aren't the easiest to fit together, but we've managed. The past month has been one of the greatest of my life.

"I told Jenna and Toby on Friday," I say.

He chuckles. "Do they think we're the most indecisive people to ever date?"

"Probably," I say. "But they're happy for me, weirdly enough."

"Weirdly?"

"Maybe it's not weird, but it does feel new, having people so invested in your relationship."

Isaac raises a dark eyebrow. "I know the feeling."

"You're getting comments from people, as well?"

"Yes, including some of my employees."

"Really?"

He nods. "Andrew said he thought I seemed happier."

"Oh my God." I bury my head in the pillow. Andrew had been told a few days ago, and being my contact at Winter Corp, it's weird to talk to him now, knowing that *he* knows about me... dating his boss.

Isaac laughs and shifts on the bed. Milo rises from his sprawl and gives us both the evil eye. He saunters down to the foot of the bed with his tail held high and jumps off, probably to find a spot less human-occupied.

"Uh-oh," Isaac says.

"He'll come around," I say. "He loves chin scratches too much."

Isaac slides his hand beneath my shirt, finding the curve of my bare hip. "You know, when I told Andrew, did you know what he said?"

"What?"

"That he wished me the best, and he wasn't worried at all about it becoming a problem down the line. He said that if he could count on anything, it's me putting the company first."

I chuckle. "He knows his boss."

"Yes. But my first thought was that the same thing is true about you."

I run my hand through the thick, short strands of his hair. "Yeah, I think that's one thing we'll never have to worry about with one another."

"One of many." Isaac leans closer and presses his lips to mine. We kiss for a few long, sweet minutes, my hand running through his hair the whole time.

"Mmm," he says. "I love it when you do that."

I tighten my fingers at his nape. "This?"

"Yes."

I kiss him again, adding my other hand to the mix. His hair feels silky through my fingers. "Look," he murmurs, "how unprofessional we can be."

I chuckle. "It's one of our strengths."

He pulls me on top of him. I settle with a leg on either side and let my hands run over the muscled chest and stomach. He starts undoing the buttons of my shirt, one by one, his eyes dark. "Okay, I'm definitely a fan of unscheduled Sundays."

I look down at his broad hands pushing the white linen of the shirt aside, baring me to him. "I thought we had an appointment at noon."

"We can be late," he murmurs.

"Late? Who are you, and what have you done to my boyfriend?"

A crooked smile spreads across his face. "Boyfriend."

"Isn't that what you are now?"

"Yes," he says, and pushes the shirt off my shoulders. "God, you're gorgeous."

"Thank you. You know, I quite like how you look, too."

"Thank heavens for that." He pulls me down, and I stretch

out on top of him, my bare chest against his. "I haven't been someone's boyfriend in a very long time."

I chuckle. "Well, I haven't had a boyfriend in a very long time, either. It does sound a bit…"

"High school?"

"We could go for 'partner,' I suppose."

His hands slide down my back. "Whatever you want," he says, "as long as I get to call you mine."

I smile against his lips. "That part's a given."

***

The car pulls to a smooth stop outside a high-rise built in the square art deco style so popular a century ago. It's on a tree-lined street just a few blocks away from the Winter Hotel.

There's a woman waiting outside for us. She's dressed in sharp heels, her hair in a low bun, and I recognize a fellow professional in her armor when I see one. It's Isaac's realtor. She shows us into the building, past the grand lobby and the smiling concierge.

"Don't compare it to the Winter Hotel," I whisper to Isaac.

He chuckles and reaches for my hand, threading our fingers together. "I can't, or I'll never move."

The realtor opens the door for us to the empty apartment on the fifteenth floor. "Welcome to what might be your new home!" she says cheerfully.

Dark wood floors stretch out into a beautiful living room, alight with sunshine streaming in through floor-to-ceiling windows. There's a staircase off the hallway leading up to a second floor.

"What do you think?" Isaac asks. "I want your input before I buy it."

"You do?"

"Yes," he says. "I trust your opinion."

And I know he means it, that it's genuine, that this isn't pressure. He isn't asking me to move in. He just wants to share his life decisions with me, the same way I want to with him.

To be partners.

"I love it," I say. "It's walking distance to the hotel for work, so that's convenient."

"Yeah, that was a must."

"Is there space for a home office? I think you need that."

There's a smile in his voice. "Yes, there is."

"How many bedrooms?"

"Four."

"Good, good," I murmur. "I think you should keep your dark blue couches and put them here. They'd fit right in. See, you could have one here, and the other over there. So you can read and still see the view. I think you'd like that. And so would I, you know, when I come to visit."

He wraps his arms around me, hugging me against his front. Out of the corner of my eye I see the realtor step into another room. Smoothly giving us privacy. "Your mind works fast," he says.

I nod. "This could be really good for you. I like this room, and this view. Do you?"

"Yeah."

"Are you sure you want to move out of the hotel? There's no part of you that's second-guessing?" I turn in his arms, wanting to meet his eyes.

"I'm sure," he says. "I've lived for the company, and for the legacy, for most of my life. And it will never… Sophia, it will never stop being important to me."

"I know," I say. "I understand that."

"It will always be part of my life. It will be what I work for, what I want to… well, regardless of who inherits the company, I want to leave it in the best possible shape." Fierceness shines in his eyes, pride in his work, and the drive to do better. To *be* better.

I'm so in love with him, I think.

"But it can't be the only thing I live for. It can't be everything. And I think it's time I had something outside of it that's just mine rather than mine to steward for a time."

"I think that's a great insight."

His mouth tips into a smile. "Besides, real estate is always a good investment."

"Always," I agree and give him a quick kiss. "Want to show me the rest of the place? I'm itching to see what's at the top of those stairs."

"Yes." But he doesn't move, hands still resting around my waist. "Thank you."

"Anytime, but for what?"

"For being here. For being you." His voice drops. "And for being brave enough to try again."

My hands still against his chest. "Isaac..."

"Sweetheart, I love you. I have for weeks and likely long before then. I just hadn't admitted it to myself yet."

"Oh," I breathe.

His hand brushes along my cheek. "I just had to let you know. It's not pressure, and I'm not saying it expecting anything from you. But it's all I could think about on the flight back home yesterday, and I knew I had to tell you."

I lock my hands behind his neck. I feel warm, like I've been hit with a ray of sunshine. "And you only do things a hundred and ten percent."

He gives me a crooked smile. "That's right."

"I love you, too," I say. "I resisted it for a long time... and I was terrified when I first realized I'd fallen. But that didn't make me love you any less. Thank you for being there while I figured it all out."

"My pleasure," he says and brushes his lips over mine. "And I always will be."

EPILOGUE
ISAAC

I drive up the long, gravel driveway to the Marmont Manor Hotel. This trip will be our fifth to the Connecticut spa and resort, beautifully nestled next to a lake, and surrounded by nothing but trees.

"Let the birthday weekend commence!" Sophia announces beside me, shooting me a warm look.

I shake my head. "Right," I say. "Yippie."

She chuckles. "At least it's just the two of us this year."

"Oh, I'm definitely going to enjoy that," I say. Sophia loves to throw a good party, and she'd organized one last year for my fortieth. I'd resisted every step of the way, but in the end, it had turned into one hell of a party. I hadn't minded at all.

Especially not when it gave me an excellent reason to throw her a surprise thirty-fifth birthday party just a few months later.

She leans forward in the car and watches as the beautiful cabin-style hotel appears behind the trees. "Is it crazy that coming here is starting to feel like coming home?"

"No," I say. "Even if our actual home might be offended to hear you say that."

"Considering how much pain it's giving me over the guest bathroom renovation, I don't mind if it does."

"Harsh," I say, but I'm smiling. The apartment we now own together—contract signed with all the i's dotted and t's crossed, lawyers involved on both parties—is a dream. But it's also old and has needed a considerable amount of renovating and touching up.

We'd originally talked about Sophia moving into my place. But at the end of the day, it was important for her that we live together in an apartment that's truly ours. And then, the apartment had just found us. A family friend was selling it, a beautiful duplex with plenty of details left from the late nineteenth century.

The only caveat? The past owners hadn't lifted a finger to renovate it.

In about a century.

"Harsh, but true," Sophia says, unbuckling her seat belt. "If it wasn't for our contractor, we wouldn't have gotten to this point at all."

I put the car in park. "And if it wasn't for you," I say, "we wouldn't be so far along with the renovations. Half the place is already done, and it's thanks to you."

She grins. "I can't help it. Project managing is my job and my passion."

"I love it," I say. "Project manage my whole life, please."

She rubs her hands together. "Oh, I plan to!"

We check in at the front desk and the staff greets us with wide smiles. They recognize us by now. Sophia chats with the attendant leading us to our usual room. He's telling her that the tennis court is free all afternoon, and they've reserved the spa area afterwards for two full hours for us.

I'd suggested we spend this weekend here, but celebrating my birthday had been her priority, not mine... because I have something different planned for us.

In the hotel room, Sophia shrugs out of her jacket and opens her suitcase. I watch as she digs through for her tennis dress. "Are you ready?" she asks, reaching for the zipper of her pants.

I lean back against the closed hotel door. Watching her hasn't gotten old two and a half years later. It's only gotten better. I've never known closeness like this. Each of us knowing how the other thinks, respecting them fully.

It's a true partnership.

"Isaac?" she asks.

"Sorry," I say and push away from the door. "I'll get ready."

Her smile turns soft. "It's been a busy couple of weeks," she says.

"You could say that," I mutter. My niece had arrived early and couldn't leave the hospital for the first week and a half of her life. She'd stayed there with a sleep-deprived Summer and a frazzled Anthony until she was finally given a clear bill of health.

"At least we know she's doing great now," Sophia says. "I still can't get over just how tiny she was when we saw her last week. I mean, I must have *known*, because Mia was that tiny once." She unclips her bra and throws it to the side. I don't take my eyes off her, even as I unbutton my own shirt. "But I think you probably forget. They're just *that* small."

"They are," I agree, pulling out my own workout gear. "Emilia's smaller than Theo was when he was born, though."

Sophia fastens her sports bra. "She'll catch up soon enough. She's home now, and the doctors say everything looks fine. Summer can finally get some sleep. They'll do great." She smiles over at me. "It makes me think how scared I'll be when it's finally our turn."

I take a deep breath. "I thought about that a lot over the past few weeks."

"You did?"

"Yes."

She comes to stand between my legs and rests her hands on my shoulders. "I know we haven't been trying for long," she murmurs. "But even seeing what Summer just went through... holding Emilia afterwards must be worth it. She definitely thinks so!"

I smile at her, this woman I care about more than my own life. "I just don't like the idea of you in any kind of pain," I say. "Worth it or not."

Sophia raises an eyebrow. "Can't say I'm super stoked on the idea either, but you know what I am really excited for?"

"Yes," I say, and pull her closer. "A baby."

She nods, her smile widening. "Just imagine," she whispers.

I kiss her, thoroughly and slowly, and settle my hands around her waist. Imagining it wasn't difficult at all. I'd gone from seeing kids as a distant possibility, to very unlikely, and now something I really want.

And it's all because of her.

We play tennis together for an hour before going to the spa. It's something I never cared for before, never had the time, but swimming in the heated pool is nice on sore muscles. So is using the sauna and steeping in the jacuzzi.

Sophia rests beside me in the hot water, her hair wet against my shoulder. She has her eyes closed, and I look down at her familiar features, her skin still holding a faint tan from our January trip to the Winter Resort in Barbados.

She looks relaxed. Beautiful and familiar and *mine,* I think. And I know that I'd planned on doing this differently. That it was supposed to be over dinner, romantic and special, with the velvet box I'd brought with me pushed over the table.

But sitting here, with the view of the lake and her next to me, I know that's not right. That's the traditional way. That's the way, I think wryly, Percy had proposed. He'd hidden the ring in her dessert in a Manhattan restaurant and gone down on one knee, the entire restaurant clapped, and Sophia had been mortified. That's how I'd proposed to Cordelia, too.

What had I been thinking, planning on doing it in a restaurant, too?

Sophia and I are different. She'd taught me, right from the

beginning, that breaking with tradition could be a beautiful thing.

"I've been thinking about your new hotel in Phoenix," Sophia says. Her voice is soft, a bit dreamy, and it cuts through my plan-making. "You know, with the zoning issue? I think you could—"

"Are you talking about work right now?" I say.

"Yes. Why not?" She looks up at me, arching an eyebrow. Her skin is rosy from the steam, and I have to resist the urge to kiss her. *Marry me*, I think. "It's one of our favorite topics. You helped me on my project last week, and it's only fair I return the favor," she says.

I had, just like she does with mine. We don't work together anymore. Exciteur's project with the Winter ran its course, and it did so beautifully. Four of the ten franchise hotels are now up and running, and one has already broken even.

"It is. But we have the entire spa to ourselves. Look," I murmur, pulling her closer to my side, "at that view. The leaves have just come in."

"It's beautiful."

"It is," I murmur, looking at her. I should have brought the ring down here. I should have put it in the pocket of my bathrobe. But then again, she already knows what it looks like.

I'd asked her about marriage a few months ago. It was to test the waters because I knew she'd been in an unequal relationship before, and I never wanted to put her on the spot again. Never wanted to assume and pressure. We're partners.

The conversation had been raw and honest, and she'd cried before the end. *I want us to get married,* she'd said. *One day.*

I'll still propose, I'd told her. *When you least expect it.*

Over the past couple of months she's suspected it. She's even guessed a few times, especially in Barbados, when we would have beautiful sunset-lit dinners by the beach. But I've kept reminding her that I meant what I said. *When you least expect it.* And now?

I don't think she's expecting it at all.

"Sweetheart," I say.

She looks over at me. "Yes?"

For a moment I can't get my words out. They're stuck in a tight throat, and I stare into her blue eyes, trying to find my composure.

Her smile falters. "Isaac?"

"I'd planned on doing this at dinner," I say.

"Oh," she breathes, her eyes widening. "*Oh.*"

The warm water around us moves with swirling motions, propelled by the jet streams below, and all the words I'd carefully prepared slip away. "You're the funniest, smartest, most brilliant person I've ever met. I didn't know... I didn't know it could be like this, that relationships could be like this."

She gives a tiny nod. *Me too,* it says, and my chest feels painfully tight.

"I'll always listen, I'll always be here... and I promise I'll always be on *your* team. No one else's."

"I know," she whispers. Her eyes look glazed.

"This was supposed to be done over dinner tonight," I say and run a hand through my wet hair. "But I can't help myself. I want to do this too badly. I love you. More every passing week, as unlikely as that seems. You're the best thing that's ever happened to me. I can't get down on one knee here..."

"You don't have to," she whispers.

I smile. I'd suspected as much. She'd told me, months ago, that she'd had a charade of a marriage once. *I want us to be real,* she'd said.

"Sophia," I say. "Sweetheart... I want us to spend the rest of our lives together. Will you marry me?"

She nods, slow at first and then faster, her eyes welling over. But she's not saying a word. I reach out, my hand on her upper arm.

"Yes," she says. "Of course, yes." She locks her arms

around my neck and I tug her onto my lap, our bodies molding together beneath the surface of the warm water. "Thank you," she whispers against my ear. "I love you."

Elation makes me feel lightheaded, pouring through me like beams of golden light. "Thank you?" I say, my hand gripping the mass of wet hair resting against the nape of her neck.

"For doing it here, in our spot. For doing it in private. Thank you for waiting until I was ready… thank you for pre-asking me before you proposed." She leans back in my arms, and her eyes are brilliant diamonds, sparkling with happy tears. "Thank you for being you. I couldn't have dreamed of a better person to go through life with."

I brush my hand over her cheek, emotion making it hard to speak. "The ring is upstairs. I should have brought it with me."

"I'll put it on for dinner," she says. The ring has a family diamond in the center, surrounded by tiny blue sapphires, on a platinum band. She'd come with me when I opened the family safe and had given me her input. *Partners*, I think. I want her to love the ring she'll wear for years to come.

"Wait," she says, "did you do this just to get out of celebrating your birthday tomorrow?"

I chuckle, and she smacks my chest, making me laugh even harder. "No," I say. "It was just to get us here without you being suspicious."

"You succeeded," she says, her smile radiating happiness. It's my favorite expression. "But don't think you're getting out of the waiters singing for you tomorrow."

"Sadist," I say.

Her smile softens. "I can't help myself when it comes to celebrating you. You're the best person I know."

I brush her hair back. *She said yes.* The rush is a heady one, even if I'd suspected, had hoped, had known deep down that she'd accept.

"Come here," I murmur.

We kiss in the empty spa, sitting there intertwined, in

front of the wide expanse of the lake and the sun slowly setting. The path here had been winding, both for her and for me, and so damn long. The best thing would've been to meet over a decade ago. But the second-best thing?

That's this, right here. Building a life together... and savoring every moment along the way.

OTHER BOOKS BY OLIVIA
LISTED IN READING ORDER

New York Billionaires Series

Think Outside the Boss
Tristan and Freddie

Saved by the Boss
Anthony and Summer

Say Yes to the Boss
Victor and Cecilia

A Ticking Time Boss
Carter and Audrey

Suite on the Boss
Isaac and Sophia

Seattle Billionaires Series

Billion Dollar Enemy
Cole and Skye

Billion Dollar Beast
Nick and Blair

Billion Dollar Catch
Ethan and Bella

Billion Dollar Fiancé
Liam and Maddie

Brothers of Paradise Series

Dark Eyed Devil
Lily and Hayden

Ice Cold Boss
Faye and Henry

Red Hot Rebel
Ivy and Rhys

Small Town Hero
Jamie and Parker

Standalones

Arrogant Boss
Julian and Emily

Look But Don't Touch
Grant and Ada

The Billionaire Scrooge Next Door
Adam and Holly

ABOUT OLIVIA

Olivia loves billionaire heroes despite never having met one in person. Taking matters into her own hands, she creates them on the page instead. Stern, charming, cold or brooding, so far she's never met a (fictional) billionaire she didn't like.

Her favorite things include wide-shouldered heroes, late-night conversations, too-expensive wine and romances that lift you up.

Smart and sexy romance—those are her lead themes!

Join her newsletter for updates and bonus content.
www.oliviahayle.com.
Connect with Olivia

facebook.com/authoroliviahayle

instagram.com/oliviahayle

goodreads.com/oliviahayle

amazon.com/author/oliviahayle

bookbub.com/profile/olivia-hayle